SOUL SURRENDER

Immortals of the Apocalypse: Book 3

DANIEL DE LORNE

For Mandy, Fiamma and Laurie

PROLOGUE

On the first night, the thirty-one exiles had been too worried about another sneak assault from Providence to talk or grab much sleep. The next morning, they marched north on Nimue's insistence that an ark she'd scouted, Prosperity, was the humans' best hope for safe haven.

And the Darisami's.

On the second night, their number had reduced to twenty-nine, but not because of anything the three Darisami had done. Fear of never reaching Prosperity or of not being allowed entrance, terror at dying of thirst or starvation on the journey, an agoraphobic response to all that desolate space—or a combination of all three—stopped two exiles from leaving Providence's shadow. They said they'd beg to be permitted back in.

Maybe there was some comfort in starving to death outside the gates of the ark they knew instead of one they didn't.

By the third night, the humans were somber, thinking

about the many miles yet to cross while their feet screamed from walking farther than they'd ever walked after lives spent underground.

Exhaustion attacked them from without while fear assaulted them from within.

The Darisami focused on the humans' wellbeing and did what they could to keep them alive. They dug for water. They foraged for anything remotely edible to supplement their meagre supplies. They scouted for ruins in which to sleep. It kept them occupied.

But on the fourth night, once all the surviving was done and the humans were settled as well as they could be, Galen came in the dead of night. Emrys had been expecting it with a dread that could not be ignored no matter how busy he kept himself.

Galen had been disciplined to wait this long to demand answers.

"Tell me what you did to Ash," Galen said.

Ash…

Nimue swore that Ash lived a good life in Prosperity; not hiding, not trying to pass for human, but out and open as a Darisami whom the Prosperous loved and welcomed. The loving part wasn't hard to imagine; everyone adored Ash. But to be loved *as* a Darisami…

It shouldn't have been possible, but Nimue knew Ash by sight, and she'd read his name in the soul of a human she'd harvested while scouting Prosperity.

Ash…

His heart braced for impact, sending a shockwave vibrating through his arteries and veins. "What do you want to know?"

"Everything. If we're going to have any hope convincing Prosperity to give us a home, I need to be prepared."

Those two sentences were more than Galen had said to him since they'd left Providence. He'd asked for space while he processed what Emrys had done in saving his life and condemning him to a Darisami's existence.

Then there were the humans to fret over. Galen had taken on as much concern for their welfare as Emrys had, conscious of the role he'd played in seeing Emrys elevated to the status of a living god within the underground ark. People had died. He didn't want to be the cause of more loss.

But Emrys felt the distance keenly. Perhaps if he told Galen the truth, there was a chance it would bring the two of them closer again. Emrys didn't doubt he'd been justified in what he'd done to Ash one hundred and fifty years ago, but just because he knew he'd done the right thing didn't mean Ash saw it that way.

Or that Galen would.

Emrys shifted against the hard earth.

"The Darisami who made Ash was a brutal son of a bitch. Magnus considered himself a scientist, and he conducted a lot of experiments, mostly on humans but also on Darisami. A lot of people died, more than was necessary or decent for a Darisami to simply survive. I made it my business to hunt and kill those Darisami who stepped beyond the bounds of what any reasonable person would consider acceptable. Any who—" He swallowed his hypocrisy hard. "Any who flaunted their power to sway humans counter to their own interests. Any who were cruel or wicked or…"

Just pure evil.

"Magnus once made a Darisami only to starve her to death in the name of science."

Even in the dark, he saw Galen's gaze drop to the ground.

"Stopping him was the right thing to do. But Magnus was adept at hiding. I had to be patient. That's when I found Ash. Magnus had made him in the middle of the twentieth century. He'd intended to kill Ash for one of his experiments, but he'd fallen for him instead. Having met Ash back then, I could believe it. Even Satan would have loved Ash."

"And did you?" Galen shifted in his place in the dirt. "Love him?"

He'd first met Ash in San Francisco two decades later and fallen for him. Hard. But he'd chosen his mission and his morals and forced himself to believe that he was only using Ash to get close to Magnus.

But Galen would see right through him if he lied and so he deflected. All that time negotiating with the Five in Providence had taught him that much.

"I befriended him, told him I was a Darisami and sympathetic to Magnus's aims. In the end, Ash led me straight to him and his lab of horrors. One night, I shoved my gold knife into Magnus's eye and deep into his brain. Then, I gave Ash a choice: he could leave, or he could die with Magnus."

Emrys remembered the tears, remembered the wound. He remembered hoping with everything in him that Ash would walk away.

He'd done more than walk. He'd fled, leaving his curses behind.

And if Ash continued to hold a grudge after all this time, it must have grown into something monstrous. Emrys's finger itched to trace the infinity symbol.

"Do you regret it?" Galen asked. "Killing Magnus?"

He looked into Galen's green eyes, relieved that they'd finally lifted from the dirt. "Not for a second. After Magnus disintegrated to join the rest of the dust in his dungeon lab, I found two dozen humans he'd trapped there, barely alive. Then I uncovered *hundreds* of corpses and skeletons. I know we kill often, but what he did was inhumane. It was evil."

"And what of Ash? Why let him go?"

Why? Because maybe Ash's presence had mitigated some of Magnus's worst predilections? Because he didn't hate him enough to kill him? "Because I thought that free of Magnus's influence, Ash might yet become good. I wanted to give him that chance."

He'd forced himself to believe that.

"And did he?"

"I don't know. I never heard rumors of him abusing his power." *Or perhaps I refused to listen to any.* "I saw him once more after that, briefly and from a distance, but otherwise, not for over a century-and-a-half. I'd thought he might have died before the Fall. Or after it. A lot of us did."

Now, Ash was a figure of power in the only place they had left to seek shelter.

"How many of us did you kill?"

Emrys rolled his tongue over his bottom lip. He should have no shame over the scores of out-of-control Darisami he'd put down over the past five hundred years. No one could doubt his motives. No one could condemn his actions.

But Galen's simple questions held the threaten of judgment.

"Forty-nine."

After that, Galen didn't say anything further and the night passed in silence. It took two more nights—just as silent, just as excruciating—before he finished processing all those hard truths.

"Tell me about the very first Darisami you killed."

So Emrys told him about Lysander. Lysander who had made him one dark night in Wales. Lysander who he'd killed so that his daughter might live. Lysander who had died for nothing when villagers had seen Emrys in the moonlight and scorched his world with righteous fire. Sian had died in that fire, and Emrys's heart had incinerated with her. Galen gently took his hand and rested his head on Emrys's shoulder as the awful story fell out of him, but that kindness did not last past dawn.

On the sixth night, a fight broke out between Trellain and Owen who had both been high-ranking officers in Providence's rival cults, the Defenders and the Reformed.

Or, as they were more commonly known, the Golden Goons and the Tornshirts.

Owen blamed Trellain, the Golden Goon, for bringing Emrys into their lives and setting them on a march to death. Trellain answered the Tornshirt with his fists. The Darisami separated them into different camps and watched them like shepherds guarding a flock.

On the seventh, eighth, and ninth nights, Galen grilled him about the other slain Darisami. The more honest Emrys was, the more Galen distanced himself emotionally. He slipped further behind his captain's mask as if he were listening dispassionately to a renegade soldier's report. Being unable to reach Galen deep inside sparked a panic in Emrys, and it swirled and churned and grew to a wild-fire. He became obsessed with pushing the exiles on towards Prosperity.

If only he could get Ash to admit what an evil bastard Magnus was, Galen would understand.

Galen would forgive him.

Then Galen could love him again.

But his manic obsession pushed yet more of the exiles away. By the tenth night, twenty-nine humans had become twenty-six after three humans set off on their own. The idiots thought they'd have a greater chance of surviving alone than following glowing monsters who had lied to ten thousand people, brought turmoil to Providence, and were no doubt leading them to their extinction.

Emrys let them go.

For a moment, it was tempting to chase after them so that he, Galen, and Nimue could harvest their souls and restart their thirty-day cycle. It seemed lunacy to let three perfectly healthy souls go to waste when there was no certainty that they'd be able to eat when they reached the gates of Prosperity. But Emrys wanted to give the humans a chance. He thought it was the decent thing to do.

And he knew Galen was watching.

On the eleventh night, Owen demanded—loudly and publicly—to be made a Darisami.

"We can't make you one of us without someone else dying," Emrys refused calmly. "That's the way it works."

Some exiles shivered, glancing between each other, but Owen wasn't mollified. "As if we can believe anything you say after what you did in Providence. You just want to keep power for yourself. That's all you've ever wanted, from the moment you showed up. We were just too blind to see it."

Juliet, one of the few human allies Emrys had, didn't bother lifting her eyes. "Sit down, Owen. You're not helping."

"I'm the only one who's doing anything here to see that we survive." His voice cracked on his hyperbolic hysteria.

Emrys tried to summon compassion, but the young man had been a thorn for a long time, even before they'd struck out into the wilderness. None of these humans had the slightest idea what it was like to make a Darisami's choices.

"Who would you sacrifice, Owen? Look around and

choose the person that you think should die for you and name them aloud. Because that's the reality of our existence. We could make half of you like us right now, at the expense of the other half. Is that what you want? Who exactly would you kill so you could live?"

Owen glared at him. "You didn't have any qualms in Providence, picking who should live and who should die."

Galen surged to his feet, and his ready defense picked at the scab on Emrys's heart. "That's not true, and you know it. No one's life was taken without good cause."

"But you still made a decision and made it based on lies about Emrys's divinity."

Galen's confidence faltered. "I didn't know it was a lie."

By the twelfth night, Nimue suggested they kill the humans and be done with it. Emrys didn't take it as a serious threat, more an off-handed venting after enduring their bleating for almost two weeks. But Galen cringed at her callousness.

"No, Nimue," Emrys said. "These people are my responsibility and I'm going to ensure they get to Prosperity." He could at least do that for them. Get the humans to safety. Get Galen to safety, maybe even Nimue. As for himself?

Nimue threw up her hands. "Bah! They're humans. They're practically cattle."

It was impossible not to smile. "They deserve a chance at survival as much as we do."

"And what about when we reach Prosperity, and they tell stories about you and what you did in Providence?"

That was the most salient point in their whole discussion. He couldn't deny it. But Prosperity came with a far greater threat than the one posed by the people he led. "We're exiles, just as they are. We're in this together."

She scoffed. "If you'd just listen to me—"

"If I listen to you, we'll be three bloated and blissed-out Darisami arriving at Prosperity's gates. My way, we are a much smaller threat because what Darisami would travel with a group of humans and leave them unharmed?"

She tsked. "I hope for our sakes you're right."

So did he.

On the thirteenth night, Galen came to him alone. "You killed all those Darisami, but you didn't kill Nimue. Why?"

Something in his chest crumbled and caved. Nimue had been responsible for many atrocities—the latest being the death of thousands of people in Endurance—and yet she lived.

Emrys knew the truth was selfish and probably immoral, but he told it anyway. Galen had asked in good faith.

"Because she reminded me of Sian," he sighed. Nimue had a child's body and dark chestnut hair tied back in a ponytail, large moon eyes that could be wielded with devastating effect. She had traveled with Emrys a long time but had been largely indifferent to his slaying of wicked Darisami—except when it suited her plans.

"But she doesn't care about anyone's life but her own."

"That's not true. She came back to Providence for me. She's been there for me throughout this life. She is not a monster. She's…complicated."

"Admit it. You didn't kill her because you loved her," Galen murmured. "I guess I should take some comfort in that."

"What do you mean?"

"You made an exception for Nimue. You made an exception for Ash. Listening to how easy it's been for you to kill—humans and Darisami alike—my head knows that you'd make an exception for me, too, but my heart isn't sure I can trust it. If I can trust you."

Galen's words were talons in Emrys's hollow stomach. Gouging, excruciating, unrelenting stabs. He bore down on it as best he could, but his voice came out ragged. "You have nothing to fear from me."

The death and the killing had *not* been easy and none of it had brought pleasure or happiness. Only justice. But what if he'd become as monstrous as those he'd hunted? What if he just couldn't see it?

"Don't I?" Galen hissed under his breath. "What's to stop you from deciding to end my life?"

The answer came out easily and there was a powerful kind of validation in the immediacy. "Because your life is worth more to me than my own."

The closer they trod to Prosperity, the closer he got to believing that his own death may be the best solution there was. He'd tried to banish the thought, putting it down to the exhaustion or the desolation, but reason had a way of slashing those arguments. If he didn't go to Prosperity, could he guarantee the humans would have a home?

And if he wasn't alive, could he guarantee that Nimue would protect Galen the way she'd always protected him?

"I'd like to believe that, Emrys, but all I have is your word."

"And isn't that enough?" Emrys opened and closed his hand but had nothing to hold.

"Turns out you've been lying to me since the day we met."

"To survive."

It sounded pathetic, even to him.

"And I'm trying to do the same, Emrys. I need to stand on my own for a while. I need to come to terms with what I've become. What you forced on me. I can't do that if I have to depend on you for all my choices. I've spent most of my life accepting the judgment of others, following them when I should have been following my own path. I believed my betters before I believed myself."

Anger made him fierce. "I'm not your better."

"Aren't you? You spent five hundred years acting from the moral high ground, deciding who lived and who died. Even now, you think you know better than all of us."

Emrys opened his mouth to speak but nothing came out. He hadn't meant for his sordid past to convince Galen of a superiority he didn't feel or to suggest that it was a mere whim of conscience deciding who lived and who died.

That wasn't who he was.

Was it?

And if Galen thought so, then what hope did they have of ever being together again?

"Galen, I love you." It was the last, desperate bit of dry ground in his flood of uncertainty, and he clung to it with bleeding fingers.

"But I don't know if I love you. How can I?" Galen got up and walked away.

It would have been easier if Galen said he hated him and wanted nothing to do with him ever again. Then, at least, he'd know. But this…this…*pause* would only drag it out. And when they reached Prosperity, there Ash would be, all primed and ready to fill Galen's head with poisonous revenge.

The following nine nights passed in a blur of pain, past jagged rocks and ruined cities, slowly changing from a dull ache to an agonizing burn as Galen refused to engage with him any further. He tried to continue their discussion, but Galen would not be drawn from his position.

And so it was on the twenty-third night after exile from

Providence, five short days shy of starvation, his soul in the same pained suffering as the bodies of the humans they accompanied, twenty-six humans stumbled out of the moonlit wasteland up to the gates of Prosperity accompanied by three Darisami glowing like warning lights for all of the city—and Ash—to see.

ᛝ   I   ᛥ

If Emrys had any doubts about the kind of reception he'd receive from Prosperity, the look on Ash's face was all the indication he needed. That, and the presence of fifty heavily armed soldiers standing behind him.

"Ash." Emrys nodded at the lithe Darisami standing six feet in front of him. The late morning sun reflected off the soldiers' helmets, caught the radiance of Ash's blond hair, and shaded the unexpected lines around his eyes and mouth. Though it had been a century-and-a-half since he'd seen Ash, the appearance of age, however small, must have been a glamor.

But for what purpose when the humans he stood in front of knew him to be an immortal soul-eater?

"Emrys." Ash's thick, dark mulberry lips thinned as he folded his arms, the fingertips of one hand strumming on his bicep. His ice-blue eyes remained fixed on Emrys, ignoring Nimue and Galen flanking him. They had agreed Emrys should do the talking.

And, if necessary, the begging.

"Thanks for meeting us." Emrys flicked his glance at the soldiers. "We don't mean Prosperity any harm."

"When Darisami show up glowing on our southern border, that's going to prompt an armed response. You must have realized that or else you would have made more of an effort to conceal yourselves."

Nothing glowed quite like a Darisami when the moon hit their bodies. All those souls radiating beneath celestial light provided a warning to those who knew what it meant. By revealing themselves, they'd hoped it gave the Prosperous time to retrieve their people from the structures and fields that abounded outside the ark. Given them time to realize they had nothing to fear.

Ash squinted into the distance behind Emrys, out of firing range. "How many others are with you?"

"Twenty-six."

Ash's eyebrows shot up. "Darisami?"

"Humans."

"You brought them to feed on?"

Emrys forced himself to take a breath. "No. They are exiles like us. From Providence. We seek asylum. *All* of us." He started with everything he wanted, giving room to negotiate down.

Ash studied him for a long time. His eyes were no longer bright and curious, their quality like cut and polished gemstones. Turmoil clouded them, obscuring the person Emrys had once known and hate fought for dominance over his self-control. After all these years, he had Emrys right where he wanted him. What better time to serve his revenge than after a nuclear winter? He ignored Emrys's request and dropped his gaze to Nimue.

"You're Nimue, aren't you? I remember seeing you with Emrys. You help him hunt down our kind."

"That's not true, but I am his companion and his ally."

Ash wrinkled his nose. "I was hoping you two had died long ago." He turned to Galen and cocked his head. "Who are you?" His voice emerged smooth as smoke.

He jutted out his chest and tensed his arms like a soldier but maintained Ash's eye contact like an equal. "My name is Galen Rhodes, and I am a citizen of Providence."

"But you're Darisami?"

"Yes."

"Who made you?" Ash's eyes flicked to Emrys and back to Galen, the muscles tensing and relaxing in his forehead, the actions so fast they were almost invisible.

But Emrys had seen them.

A muscle in Galen's jaw pinged, his nostrils flared. "It's not relevant."

"That's up to me to decide. Who made you?" Ash enunciated the words with as much force as if he beat them on Galen's chest.

Galen frowned then blinked, dialing back the tension that had settled on his face. "Emrys."

Ash's eyebrow flicked up. "I'm surprised." His chilled glare landed on Emrys. "I remember you saying you'd never make another monster."

Galen looked away while Ash's barbed comment hooked into Emrys's heart. He resisted the urge to crumple. He had said that, in those exact words, but the circumstances were different, and he only had to explain himself to Galen, not Ash. "A lot has changed since then."

"I'll be the judge of that."

And going by the derision on Ash's face, he'd be the jury and executioner too. If Ash wanted that chance, then he could do so once everybody was safe.

"Look, Ash," Emrys said, "we've got people who are

tired and hungry. They won't last much longer if Prosperity doesn't show mercy. Will you let us in?"

"And what about you three? Letting wild Darisami loose into our society wouldn't be wise."

"They let you in, didn't they? I'm assuming they know what you are."

"But they don't know what *you* are." Ash narrowed his eyes to arrow slits. This was not the Ash that Emrys had known. Was this bitterness in response to seeing him again or was it the lasting effect of killing Magnus?

"If you two could shelve the hostilities for a moment, we have people here who know what we are," Nimue said. "Talk to them, and they'll tell you we have kept them alive on this journey. We have found a way to live together, but the earth cannot sustain them out there forever. We're asking for a place to stay."

"I invited Emrys into my house once before. I'm not fool enough to do it again." Ash growled the words, and they vibrated through Emrys's ribcage. His lips pulled back slightly to reveal his teeth, bunching up the skin at the bridge of his nose, and his fingers twitched. Everything about Ash said to walk away, that he was in danger.

Had the moment arrived? Emrys had been prepared to walk away if Ash's hate would not grant the exiles sanctuary. But faced with the threat before him and the reality of leaving Galen behind, he struggled to retreat. He opened his mouth, but nothing came out. What was he going to do? He had to leave so the humans could live.

So Nimue could live.

And, above all, so Galen could live.

But what was he going to do?

Nimue raised her hand and clicked her fingers in Ash's face, breaking the tension that had kept Emrys rooted to the ground. "And are you the sole authority over Prosperity? Do you wield total power over who can enter and who can leave?"

Ash folded his arms and over a long, exhaled breath lowered his eyes to Nimue. "No." The word scraped through between his teeth, giving a lift to Emrys's despair. Ash turned to one of the soldiers, and they approached him. Emrys only then noticed they weren't holding a weapon.

They lifted the helmet off their head and revealed a woman with black hair and dark brown skin. "My name is Diwali. I am one of the eleven elected leaders of Prosperity. Welcome."

"We'd feel that welcome was genuine if we hadn't been met with such antagonism," Nimue countered.

Her politician's smile didn't wane. "No doubt you can understand that we must take precautions. We have long trusted Ash's judgment and guidance so to not take his concerns seriously would be unwise."

"Is Ash a councilor?"

"He holds a special status within our society, but he does not sit on our council."

Emrys knit his brows together. "So, you know what he is and accept how dangerous he is, but he doesn't sit on your council?"

"That's correct. Ash assists our people in different ways, and we help him in return."

"By giving him souls?" When Nimue had harvested the soul of one of the Prosperous and discovered Ash in their memories, she hadn't uncovered why they accepted him when it meant death.

Ash spoke before the councilor could. "Diwali and I have been given responsibility to assess the threat you pose to our society. Considering yours and Nimue's history of abject cruelty and wanton murder, I'm disinclined to give you safe harbor."

"But we will *all* starve if we're not given a home," Emrys said.

"Then you should all go back to where you came from."

Galen closed the distance between him and Emrys. It was one step closer to a united front. "We can't."

"Why not?" Diwali's expression was heavy with compassion. "What happened in Providence?"

Galen looked to Emrys for support to proceed. He shrugged. Nothing they said could make this any worse.

"Emrys and Nimue came to Providence about three months back." Galen's voice started steady, reasonable, and official. "At the time, we thought they were human. Factions conspired to force them from Providence as one group who favored the surface's exploration battled another who favored the status quo." Then his voice softened and slowed. "Emrys left, but I retrieved him, and in the process, he…revealed himself to be more than human." His mouth and throat moved like he was trying to pick the words to let out and the ones to swallow, like eating a cherry, pit and all. "We…we interpreted that to mean he was…he was divine."

Ash laughed a cruel laugh. "Him? Divine? He killed our kind for claiming less."

"They deserved it." Emrys regretted speaking the moment the words lunged from his mouth.

Diwali glanced between Emrys and Ash, her dark eyes assessing their interactions before pursing her lips and turning back to Galen. "Please continue."

Galen regained some of his captain's control. "Emrys assumed command of Providence and wanted us to explore the surface outside our ark. Many citizens supported his plan, but there were others who didn't. In the unrest that followed, those who opposed exploration won. They gave people the chance to leave, so some of us did. That is why we are here."

"To rule again?" Ash said.

His glib comment scratched Emrys's gut. "That was not my intention then, and it's damn well not my intention now." He closed his hand into a fist until his knuckles popped.

Nimue squeezed his fist with one hand and clung to him with the other. "You are the only ark we know of that survives." Her voice quavered. "Emrys and I originally came from Endurance, and all the arks between there and Providence have been abandoned. You are our only hope."

Diwali's eyes flicked between Galen and Emrys and into the distance. "Are the humans healthy and strong?"

"They are. They're exhausted, but they've survived. There are soldiers, workers, medics, scientists. They are all willing to do whatever it takes to earn a place in Prosperity."

"And the same goes for you three?" Diwali asked.

Ash spluttered. "You can't be serious about letting them in. Emrys killed many of my kind. And if I'm reading between the lines, he's responsible for the turmoil in not just one ark but two. Where will it end? He could be destroying arks deliberately to wipe out humanity in a suicidal attempt to finish the Darisami once and for all."

Maybe in the past that would have be an idea, but hearing it from Ash's mouth, when everyone had already lost so much, it felt crass and fevered. The councilor looked as if she agreed.

"Is that your goal?" Diwali asked.

Ash rolled his eyes. "As if he'd admit it."

She ignored him and waited for Emrys to answer.

"Of course not. It was never my intention to destabilize Providence or Endurance, and I regret those events deeply. Neither ark knew what I and Nimue really are. Perhaps this time it can be different."

"Fool me once, shame on you. Fool me twice, bring out the gold bullets." Ash faced Diwali. "They are dangerous. They should not be allowed in."

Diwali's expression softened. "But they can be of use, Ash, much as you have been these many years. We knew how dangerous you are, but we gave you a home. We have welcomed you as one of us."

"I'm not like them. They're monsters."

Galen spoke up. "I can assure you we are not. We could have left the exiles to die back in Providence, or killed them along the way, or made them into a Darisami army to attack your people, but we didn't. We found them food and water and shelter, and we have guided them here to submit to *your* mercy. We are good, and they will confirm that."

Ash winced, like his prejudice and anger pained him, but he held onto it, even as he bled.

All because of what I did to him.

"And if you had known what he was before he came to Providence, would you have let him in?" Ash asked.

Galen didn't flinch. "Yes, because we welcomed survivors."

"And look how he repaid your kindness. He brought strife and disharmony. He even turned you into a Darisami."

"He saved my life." Galen stood defiant, more defiant than he'd been the past three weeks.

"Though I'm sure he was the one who put it in danger in the first place." Ash turned to Diwali. "It is my opinion that the humans should be welcomed, but the Darisami should not."

Diwali assessed them, her tongue sticking out between her teeth. "Thank you for your opinion, Ash. I have taken it into consideration, but it is my judgment, that all of the refugees—human and Darisami—should be given the chance to state their case before the council."

Emrys smiled. Nimue squeezed his hand.

"We shall escort you to Prosperity where you will go into isolation for a short period of time until a proper assessment has been completed. Provided the council agrees to let you stay, Ash will teach you what he knows so you can live among us, but you must understand that it is forbidden to take the life of anyone who does not wish it. If you do, it will be your death. Do you agree?" Diwali's eyes landed on each of them in turn.

Had Ash lasted this long by taking the souls of the willing? How could he guarantee that someone would be a willing sacrifice every cycle? And how could the three of them be certain there'd be enough within the next five days?

"This is a mistake." Ash's words rushed out through clenched teeth, and he rounded on Diwali. His fists pumped, and the ropey muscles in his forearms bulged like he was the last soldier holding up the crumbling barricade.

Diwali straightened. "Nevertheless, you will teach them our ways. Do you *all* understand?"

The four Darisami nodded, Ash the last to comply.

Galen returned to the exiles, while the welcoming party, Emrys, and Nimue waited for Galen to give them the news. When the humans reached them, Diwali introduced herself and welcomed them to Prosperity. They set off on the three-mile march to their new home.

Emrys passed Ash, and the Darisami grabbed his arm, bringing him close enough to see the point of his canines.

"Don't even think about causing any trouble. We've got enough gold to kill all of you three times over."

Emrys looked from Ash's white-knuckled fist up to his pale face and saw the fear and the hurt that Emrys had put there long ago. "You won't have any hassles from me, Ash. We just need a place to call home."

※ 2 ※

THE ABSENCE OF PEOPLE MADE FOR AN EERIE PROCESSION
to Prosperity. The citizens had been sequestered inside the
ark, leaving behind empty huts and houses, fallow fields,
and cultivated crops. Knowing they would return, that
hands would again pick up tools from where they'd been
dropped, that feet would again tread through the turned
earth, relieved some of Emrys's unease and allowed him to
marvel at what he observed.

The exiles had passed many ruins on their journey
north. They'd slept in them whenever they could, but they
were dead things. Crumbled, devoid of life, left behind.
But the structures outside Prosperity were complete, sturdy,
and—most importantly—inhabited.

They were simple, built out of scraps, old wooden
planks and corrugated metal sheets, car doors and mud
bricks, and held together with ingenuity or desperation.
Some looked like garden sheds with tools leaning against
their inner walls. Others appeared as small homes. They
were little more than hovels with no running water and no

conveniences, but they were the beginning of the earth's restoration. They were beautiful.

Emrys counted at least fifty on his march. There could have been just one and Emrys would have been happy. Diwali said there were enough above-ground structures to house five hundred people.

"It's more of an experiment than anything else," she said. "Some people can't handle living below ground anymore, so a limited cohort has been granted approval to live on the surface."

"Have they thrived?"

"It is harder than living in the ark because food can't be stored here, and water must be collected from the ark, so we know it's clean. The temperatures can also vary, and the weather events can be hard."

"But they're happier?"

"Oh yes. If it were possible, everyone would live on the surface, but until then, anyone is allowed in or out, day or night. The gates are rarely closed."

As if she'd timed it, they arrived at the gates to Prosperity and entered the tunnel. Emrys's muscles tightened the farther in he went. Another prison, another trap. He was going to die beneath the earth. He fought the thoughts, but each one he ripped out took a bit more of his resolve with him.

He should have been glad they'd reached a new haven, that the humans would be safe, that Nimue and Galen could feed. But after facing Ash, he felt like the journey had only begun.

The only sure thing was death, and even that wasn't straightforward.

The tunnel filled with the sounds of their booted foot-steps marching into Prosperity. The floor was scuffed from the passage of many feet going in and out. The soldiers kept them at a reasonable pace, and they entered the main part of the ark deep into the earth.

Unlike Providence, Prosperity didn't have a central column from which all the levels radiated and paid allegiance. Instead, there were eight levels descending into the earth, one stacked on top of the other, with one open shaft at the far end. It felt more confined than Providence, even more confined than Endurance, but maybe that had pushed the Prosperous harder to emerge.

They reached an elevator, and the soldiers separated into two groups.

Diwali faced them. "You'll be split up here and taken to the cells."

"Split how?" Emrys asked.

"The Darisami will go with Ash. The humans will come with me."

"Why aren't we going together?"

"Until Ash teaches you what is required, it is safer if you are kept separate from the humans."

Emrys blinked his surprise, trying to dispel the sting of an unintended insult. "We brought them here. Why would we harm them now?"

Diwali opened her mouth to speak, but Owen stepped forward. The young man's brown hair was disheveled, the shadows under his eyes were deep, and the bruises on his face were a mix of red, blue, and purple. "I do not want to be housed with them. I have feared for my life ever since we left Providence."

"You little snake," Trellain bit out. His bruises matched Owen's. Juliet hooked her hand around Trellain's bicep. Owen bunched his small fist.

"Perhaps we need to separate the humans as well?" Diwali said. Owen and Trellain stood down as the elevator arrived. "I trust there are no more complaints? Ash will take you first. We will meet again soon."

Ash gestured for the Darisami to enter then stepped in after them, along with eight soldiers. None showed a patch of skin. Not a gun was aimed anywhere but at Emrys, Nimue, and Galen.

Ash kept his eyes on the wall opposite him, the color of his skin flushing up a few shades, skin that was already darker than Emrys remembered. The wrinkles and the skin tone could have been the glamor. Darisami had the ability to make themselves appear older or younger but not change shape. Otherwise, Nimue would have transformed herself into a more identifiably woman-like figure. Yet why would Ash bother with the charade if the Prosperous knew he was immortal?

They reached the ground floor and were marched into Prosperity's prison complex. More soldiers lined their approach, but they were unarmed. Sentinels? Tourists come to gawp? What did they really know of Ash and the Darisami? And why were none of them afraid?

They passed down a short corridor, through a thick door, and into the first cell they reached. More passage-ways proceeded down the walls, but it didn't appear to have Providence's extensive warren-like prison complex where so many traitors of whatever creed had been held.

And where Emrys had killed so many.

More sins to pay for.

Perhaps he should have left everyone behind before they reached Prosperity. Then there'd be no chance of him ruining this ark.

The cell door opened, and they were ordered inside. Soldiers took their packs and frisked them. One of them confiscated the gold weapon Nimue had tied to her belt.

Ash raised an eyebrow. "So much for you not helping Emrys in his mission."

"We didn't know who we'd meet along the way." Her smile was as thick as treacle and just as likely to catch flies.

"How long are we going to be held?" Emrys asked.

"As long as necessary. Why? What does it matter to you? Hungry?" Ash's smile wouldn't melt snow.

He'd be damned if he told Ash how long any of them had to wait until their thirty days were up. There was no sense in giving him even more of an upper hand. He held his expression as hard and as neutral as possible.

Ash laughed, and it almost sounded sincere. "Don't worry, Emrys. I won't let you starve to death."

The door to the glass-fronted cell slid closed and sealed them inside. Ash cast a final glance over Nimue and Galen —a wrinkling of his nose for her, a soft curious frown for him—then left.

The cell had three beds, two chairs, a table, toilet, and a sink. Clearly, prisoners couldn't be trusted with privacy. Nimue climbed onto a bed, kicked off her dusty boots, and pulled her knees up under her chin. Galen took a chair and half-turned his face to the back wall. As much as Emrys wanted to sit opposite him, take his hand, interlock their fingers, and twine their legs together, Galen's body language crushed that fantasy down beneath a hundred-and-fifty tons of steel. He remained standing.

A short while later, the exiles marched past. Owen's expression was one full of triumph as he walked at the head of the pack with Diwali. What invective was he dripping into the councilor's ear?

Owen had gotten increasingly difficult on the march north as the sun burned out the last of his belief that Emrys was anything to be revered. Ironically, the sun's rays never shone on the part he himself had played in their coup. Some things were too blinding to see.

Juliet, Trellain, and a few others cast concerned glances their way then were gone.

Diwali returned a little while later. "Thank you for complying. I know these precautions may seem heavy-handed, but they are for your protection as well as ours. I shall be back as soon as I can."

Emrys struggled to find some subterfuge in Diwali's words and demeanor. She seemed genuine. Then again, Laurence had seemed genuine too but was only one of the Five. Diwali was one of eleven. How many others would be as agreeable as her?

Emrys turned back into the cell. "Can we trust her?"

Galen looked away.

Nimue slid off the bed and went over to the sink. "All I know is that Ash has found some way to live in the open without everyone being scared of him." She turned on the faucet, washed her hands, and scrubbed her face. "Whatever he's done, it's worked, and we need to find out how." She continued scrubbing, her hands moving further up her arms to wash off the dirt and grime, her actions getting more forceful. She was hungry. They had five days left to feed, yet they weren't allowed to kill anyone. How did it work? Emrys didn't think Ash would be forthcoming with that information.

"Did you notice how different he looked?"

"I never got as close to him as you did." She flicked the water off her hands and dried herself with the towel. Her skin had lightened a few shades.

"He looks older. More lined."

She shrugged. "Could be the glamor."

"But why?"

"You're worried about how he looks?" Galen's voice

strained. "He's living here as a Darisami, and you're worried about how he looks?" He let his hand slap on the table's surface.

"I don't mean it like that. He's different from how I remember him."

"All I noticed was how much hate he had in his eyes for you." Nimue slipped back onto the bed and lay down. "He looked like he could happily kill you and make us all watch."

Emrys ground his teeth together to stop himself from shuddering.

"Whatever happens, let's hope he tells us how he's able to live among the humans without spreading fear," Nimue said. "Perhaps it's something we could take to the other arks."

"If any remain," Emrys said. "Considering what we've seen on our travels, Providence and Prosperity could be the last." If he had to leave so Nimue and Galen could stay, was there any hope in finding another ark to take him in?

Or would he perish in the wilderness?

Could he?

"Then we have to make sure we're allowed to stay. Whatever it takes."

"We are extremely concerned that you smuggled a gold weapon into Prosperity." The councilor with graying brown hair, white skin, and long chin addressed Nimue. Emrys thought his name was Finley. Emrys also thought he was an asshole.

Emrys, Nimue, and Galen stood before two long benches of eleven councilors. Spectators could sit in the rows behind the Darisami, but the seats were empty. The session was closed. Ash sat to Emrys's right, between the councilors and the Darisami, where they could scowl at each other.

The three Darisami had spent the night in their cell, watching the exiles file past as they went to deliver their testimonies. They didn't come back, so Emrys assumed they were given new places to sleep. The guards arrived in the middle of the afternoon with a summons for the Darisami to appear before the Eleven.

"Can you explain why you were carrying it?" Finley asked.

"Of course, councilor." Nimue kept her voice light,

child-like, innocent, endearing. Whether they were fooled or not, Emrys couldn't tell. Ash may have explained that Nimue was pushing four hundred and fifty and not to be trusted, but no matter what they were told, people often forgot the truth about Nimue. Often to their detriment. "Unlike Ash or ourselves, many of the Darisami that I have been acquainted with have been brutal, vicious killers who would think nothing of killing us to protect whatever stock of humans they have hoarded. We could not be too careful. Many of them are child-killers."

"From what Ash has told us of your past, neither you nor Emrys could be considered peace-loving. Why should we not think that you came here to kill Ash in an attempt to claim Prosperity for yourselves?"

Nimue grasped her plait and stroked her fingers through its ends. "I can see why you might think that, but we intend no harm to him or any of you. There is history between Ash and us, but there is history between everyone, like there is between old friends. We are merely working with what we have. By all means, if you hadn't taken the gold weapon from me, I would gladly have offered it to you as a sign of faith."

Ash snorted and shook his head.

Perhaps she was laying it on a bit thick, but she didn't let his interruption dislodge her beatific expression.

"I guess we'll never know if that's true or not." Finley looked down his narrow nose at her. "We have spoken to Providence's human exiles." He interlaced his fingers and tapped his thumbs together. "They have told us quite a tale about how you, Emrys, lied to the people about what you are and started a coup that led to great divisions within Providence and the deaths of thousands of people."

The lie stuck needles in his lungs. His crimes laid bare

was one thing, but he wasn't going to take the blame for more than his share. "That's an exaggeration."

"Oh? How so?"

"I'd say only two hundred at most lost their lives, if that, and only fifty or so directly by my hand."

Emrys's admission sparked murmurings along the bench. Diwali shifted in her seat.

Finley frowned. "Why would we allow an admitted mass murderer?"

He gestured to Ash, hoping to point out the obvious to a particularly stupid jury. "You already have one here. Do I need to remind you what Ash is?"

"Ash has learned our ways and found a method that doesn't require killing."

"And we are only too happy to learn." Emrys forced his shoulders to relax. "I understand that my past is unpalatable, but it is better that you know the truth than to rely on rumor. And the actions I took in Providence were not taken lightly."

"And that is meant to give us comfort?"

"Under the circumstances, I did the best I could. In Endurance, Nimue and I and the other Darisami did what most Darisami have done throughout time. We hid what we truly were so we could live among humans."

"And feed off them, is that right?" Finley said.

"We did it to survive. In that way, we are no different from you. We all want to survive, and many of us will go to extraordinary lengths to do so. But the collapse of Endurance was a lesson to us." None of them knew that it was Nimue's meddling with Absolon's mind in pursuit of her revenge that had brought an end to Endurance.

Or that five thousand people had died and one mad Darisami was the jailer of the handful of hundreds who survived.

"Unfortunately, when we got to Providence, we found an ark already in turmoil. Two warring factions with different ideas for the future. We didn't reveal what we were, but that didn't matter as they saw us as figureheads, to either fight for emerging from the ark or stay sealed inside. This only got worse once they discovered my light."

"When you pretended to be an angel." A hook-nosed, toffee-haired matron-like councilor inclined her head and strained her lips into a grudging, indulgent smile.

Finley laughed and leaned back in his chair to share the joke with the councilor. "The people of Providence don't sound too smart to me, wouldn't you agree, Joni?"

"And what did you believe Ash to be the first time he started glowing in the light of the moon?" Galen's voice cut across the titters.

The awkward silence on the bench was enough of an answer.

"In the end," Emrys said, "it was the wrong thing to do, but my intentions were good. I was hoping to do what you have done in bringing people out of the ark and repopulating the surface of the earth. Providence was heading towards a dead end. If they didn't have that push to leave, they would never last."

"But from what the exiles have told us, your mission failed and led to greater collapse," Finley said.

"I accept most of the blame for that but forces within Providence worked against me and the majority will of the people. You must know that your citizens are happier because they are on the surface. I tried to give Providence that and worked with what I had available."

Ash stood. "And now you've come here." His remark lobbed across the room and exploded double meanings all over the council chamber. "What we have in Prosperity has been achieved because we have worked together to build consensus. You were in Providence less than two months, and in those two months, you brought it to its knees. Why? Because you thought you knew best, a trait so ingrained you are incapable of seeing it." Ash turned to the councilors. "Emrys and Nimue are dangerous and must not be allowed to stay. Galen may yet be reformed. I understand that he has only been a Darisami for less than a month. He is practically human."

Emrys's pulse rose. Ash was trying to separate them. Out of spite? Jealousy? But if it meant Galen could stay, he'd go along with it. Still, while Finley's interrogation was uncomfortable, the council had yet to vote.

Finley's eyes hardened at Ash's interruption, and the corner of his mouth twitched. "But Galen, weren't you one of the main proponents behind Emrys's cult? The exiles say you were his high priest and a collaborator on their council. It would be fair to say that Emrys would not have gotten very far without your assistance."

Emrys's chest curled in as if his heart had been sucked out through his back. He'd meant to make himself the focus of their attack, but he couldn't deflect the charge from all quarters.

But while Emrys was momentarily wounded, Galen faced his accusers with his hands clasped behind his back, his chest proud and full. Ever the soldier. "My mistakes are my own, and I bear the responsibility of them. I believed what I thought was the truth about Emrys, and I believed in the mission we had set ourselves."

"And you knew nothing of Emrys's true nature when you decided to support him?"

"Of course not, Councilor."

Finley's eyebrows popped up his lined forehead. "You had no hopes that he would make you into whatever he was?"

"I did not even consider it a possibility."

Finley's disbelief dripped down the line of his long nose. "And what about you, Emrys? Did you think turning Galen into a soul-eater would help your cause?"

Emrys's throat constricted from the memory of trying to staunch the bleeding from the bullet wound in Galen's neck. He swallowed the thick distaste. "Nothing could be further from the truth. I made Galen into a Darisami to save his life. It was the least I could do."

"The least you could have done was not involve yourself in Providence's politics."

"If you knew Providence, you would know such a thing was impossible. I saved Galen's life in the hope that it would make amends for lying to him for the entire time that we had known each other and for not delivering on what I had promised." He hoped Galen took it as the truth in which it was intended.

Finley wiggled in his seat. "Ash has led us to believe that creating another soul-eater is not an easy thing and requires the death of another human for the full effects to take place. It is one of the reasons why he is the only one here. And yet, you quite readily created a soul-eater out of Galen. What do you say to that?"

Emrys knew what he wanted to say. He wanted to say he would have told Galen everything from the start and given him the choice of becoming a Darisami in the hope that he would have said yes.

All because I love Galen. That's what I want to say.

But instead, he stripped the emotion from his voice and words. "I am five hundred years old, and he is the only Darisami I have ever made. That should indicate to you how seriously I take the creation of another."

Joni gave a strangled cough. "Let me get this straight. In five hundred years, you've created no other soul-eater, yet you created one out of this human whom you had known for two months. That hardly seems judicious."

"I did what I thought was right."

"And will you think it right to create another soul-eater while you are here?" Joni asked.

"No."

"Not even to again assuage your own guilt?"

"I promise you, Councilors, you have no need to fear me creating more Darisami. The numbers we have here are quite enough already."

"Perhaps too many." Finley turned to Galen. "Considering you were born in Providence, I'm disinclined to believe that you should share our enthusiasm for repopulating the surface. Providence was ever cautious in that regard."

"On the contrary, Councilor, I have always believed that it is the only possible outcome for the arks, long before Emrys came along. Seeing what you have achieved in Prosperity brings joy to my heart, and I wish to be a part of it."

"And what if only you were permitted to stay? Would you accept that?"

Emrys's heart stopped beating.

Galen looked from one councilor to the other. The tension in the room built. He licked his lips. "I would not. Emrys and Nimue should be given the opportunity to redeem themselves."

Emrys's heart lurched and restarted.

Galen did not look at Emrys, and as much as Emrys wanted to reach over and take his hand, he knew Galen would stiffen. He took comfort in Galen's goodness. He would not let Nimue and Emrys be expelled. Even if it meant they were no longer lovers.

"They cannot be redeemed!" Ash shot to his feet and shouted at the Eleven. "They have lived far too long as wildlings and as masters of their own destinies. They cannot be trusted."

Diwali focused on Ash as ragged breathing billowed out of his chest. She hadn't said much throughout the meeting. "And weren't you like them when you revealed yourself to us? Hadn't you lived with us for fifty-five years before showing us what you were?"

Oh really, Mr. High-and-fucking-mighty? Emrys would find out every last thread of *that* story.

But Ash didn't seem perturbed by the councilor's claim of hypocrisy. "I was different from them. I *am* different from them. I didn't harm anyone while living in Prosperity, even when I was in hiding. It was only because of—" Ash's voice caught in his throat. "I had my reasons, and they were never to take advantage of the citizens of Prosperity."

"That may be the case," Diwali's resonant voice riding over Finley's attempt at regaining control of the discussion, "but the fact is you did not reveal yourself as you truly are until you had won over our trust, love, and friendship. Didn't *you* deceive us much as Emrys did to Providence?"

When it came to Ash, that wouldn't have been a hard thing. Everyone loved Ash.

"And when you did reveal yourself, we were reticent, but we welcomed you because we realized how we could benefit each other." Diwali returned her gaze to Emrys, Nimue, and Galen. "Which brings us to what we expect of you. None of us are at all comforted by the damage you caused in Providence and one can presume in Endurance as well. Most of the exiles talk in fear about you in particular, Emrys, and there is a general unease about how you have come to us. Not to mention Ash's own charges against you. But…" The councilor took a dramatic pause.

Emrys wanted to reach over and throttle her.

"We are not so close-minded to turn away from an

opportunity that can suit us both. We would be lying if we did not say that Ash's presence among us has been a gift." She addressed not only them but the other councilors as well. Finley wrinkled his nose. "It is thanks in large part to him that we were able to emerge from the ark ten years ago. His abilities have made our achievements possible."

"Limited as they are."

All eyes shot to a pale-skinned young male councilor in the back row, but Diwali carried on. "The Darisami have arrived at an auspicious time. We will soon plant a new batch of modified seeds that we are hopeful will provide us with our first crop of food. Such a venture requires the energy which the Darisami can provide. Therefore, Councilors, I propose that the three Darisami and the exiles are permitted to stay in Prosperity and live freely in exchange for providing us with that which Ash has given this past decade. The Darisami are forbidden from killing any human here or the outcome will be death or exile. You should know that that is a punishment we do not hand out lightly."

Galen cleared his throat. "Excuse me, Councilor, but how is it possible for us to survive if we do not take life? We must harvest a soul every thirty days and that requires a human's death."

The councilor shifted her shoulders, uncomfortable with the directness or perhaps uncomfortable with knowing the intricacies of how a killing machine like the Darisami got through life. "That is a question for Ash. He will teach you how to feed safely and without taking life. The only lives Ash has taken were at the request of the person whose life it belonged, and they were terminally ill."

"I find that hard to believe." Emrys looked at Ash to

try to glean some answers of how he had done it, but his expression was as closed as a mausoleum's gate.

"Because restraint is not something you can do, Emrys?" Ash said. "Councilors, I object. Emrys and Nimue cannot live like I do. There is already the matter of an unexplained death of one of our people a little over a month ago." Ash's glare fixed on Emrys, and Emrys fought the urge to pass it onto Nimue. He wouldn't give Ash any more ammunition to blow them apart.

Rumblings on the council, led by Finley and enhanced by Joni, forced Diwali to bang her gavel and demand silence.

"Did you have anything to do with the death of Crawley?"

Emrys wrestled down his annoyance, softening his features into one of sympathy. "I am sorry to hear of this loss. I know as well as anyone that life is precious, but it was impossible for us to have anything to do with their death. We were either in Providence or within its vicinity at the time. Unless Ash or anyone else has proof—and it would be fabricated proof—then I object to the insinuation that we are wanton killers. Especially when it is a charge leveled at us by Ash whose past is not beyond reproach."

Ash sneered at Emrys.

"We cannot do anything except take you at your word. However, there will be no second chances if you step out of line," Diwali said. "Ash *will* teach you and then you *will* aid our people. We *will* work together. Ours will be a symbiotic relationship, not a parasitic one. I will have a show of hands from the council as to agreement."

All raised their hands except for Finley and Joni. They were both trying hard to not look like the results bothered them.

"The majority has spoken." Diwali struck the board

with her gavel. "An armed guard will attend each of you every hour of every day until we are assured of our people's safety. Session dismissed. Welcome to Prosperity."

Some councilors smiled at Nimue, most watched Emrys with a guarded expression, but it was Ash's seething look of scorn that worried Emrys most. Their entire existence within Prosperity depended on him, and that bestowed a power that even the meekest person on Earth would struggle to relinquish.

Emrys might have a home, but for how long?

❄ 4 ❄

THE DARISAMI WERE ESCORTED TO ASH'S APARTMENT ON the fifth level amid fifteen black-clad guards carrying automatic weapons loaded with gold bullets. Though they were sheathed, their bowie knives were also lined with gold along the blade. The warnings were clear, and Emrys tried not to dwell on their silent presence or strategize how he could kill fifteen soldiers without getting killed.

If necessary.

Ash's quarters weren't lavish, but they were more comfortable than those most people were given in Endurance and Providence. Less utilitarian, more user-friendly. Softer furnishings and floor coverings, a warmer white to the walls with a faded and framed art print of a stylized Golden Gate Bridge that had somehow survived the Fall.

Apart from the bed, the only place to sit was on the floor, on pillows and cushions, stuffed with what Emrys couldn't guess. Ash, child of the 1960s and 70s, and still unable to properly use furniture.

Ash invited the Darisami to sit. The guards stationed

themselves behind the Darisami and around the room to ensure they had a clear shot should one be required. Within a minute of taking their seats, two humans walked in, one woman and one man, young, dressed in similar simple clothes to those worn in Providence but in a gentler hue, tan instead of gray.

They smiled at the Darisami, but their eyes were attracted to Ash like iron filings to a magnet. The difference between their adoration of Ash and the wide-eyed zeal Emrys had experienced in Providence was stark. These people were honestly happy and seemed in total control of their senses.

Ash changed as he shifted to welcome the two citizens. The severity of his expression melted as easily as ice becoming water on a summer's evening. "This is Diane and Felipe."

They said hello.

"This is Emrys, Nimue, and Galen. They are from Providence and may be staying with us for some time. They are like me, Darisami."

Diane and Felipe's faces lit up like someone had flicked a switch on a Christmas tree in a town square.

"Welcome!" Diane breathed.

Emrys leaned back from their enthusiasm and shared a frown with Nimue.

"They're here to witness what I do," Ash said. "Do you consent to an exchange?"

"We do," they said in unison.

Nimue tensed. Emrys hadn't heard the word exchange used in this context, and he'd been around a long time. What could the Darisami possibly give a human other than death or immortal life?

"Diane, do you understand what an exchange involves?"

She nodded. "You will take a piece of our soul and energy so you can live, and in exchange, we will experience euphoria and a short-lived increase in strength and vitality."

"Is that your understanding too, Felipe?"

"It is, Ash."

"Hold on," Nimue said. "You go through this every time?"

"We do," Diane said. "Ash insists."

"How many times have you done this?"

She stuck her tongue out between her lips and frowned. "About twenty."

"Fifteen for me," Felipe said.

What was this exchange? How could they have done it so often and not die? Emrys looked to Nimue, but she was fixed on the humans.

"Do you accept that death is a possibility, no matter how small?" Ash said.

"We do, but we trust you to treat us with care," Diane said.

Ash smiled a genuine smile.

Galen raised his hand. "Question. Has anyone ever died while you've done this?"

"No," Ash said. "As Diwali mentioned, the only death I bring is to those who request it. And when I do, it is with mercy. May I proceed?"

Galen nodded.

Emrys had questions, but he kept them stuffed in his throat. They jostled one another, pushed from behind by his increasing heartrate and his eagerness to see what Ash did.

"Are you ready, Diane?" Ash asked.

"I am, Ash. I am ready." Her mouth half-opened into a smile, the skin at her neck growing taut, a slight heaviness to her breathing. She was more than ready. She was primed.

Ash bid the two donors sit on the cushions, one on either side of him. He slunk to the ground, all sinew and sex in his movements. Like lava. Beautiful, hot, and deadly. He flowed to Diane, slipped his arm across the back of her shoulders, and lay her down in his lap. She opened the top of her tunic so Ash could place her hand on her chest above her breasts.

His hand smoothed over her skin. "Are you ready?"

"Yes." She breathed the word out with heavy anticipation.

"Then I'll begin."

Diane closed her eyes. Ash did the same.

For a minute, no one said anything. No one moved. And if Emrys stared any harder, Ash would have combusted. He watched for any sign of a change in either Ash or Diane, but nothing happened.

Then everything happened at once.

Emrys sensed Ash form a symbol, but what symbol it was, he couldn't tell. Either way, his stomach fluttered, anticipating a harvest, stirring his energy in readiness for a fight, recognizing that a Darisami was present and feeding.

But Diane kept breathing.

Ash held onto her, but whereas during a harvest, the symbol would be unleashed and the Darisami could deliver death and be down the hall before the person's heart beat its last beat, Ash tensed and remained still except for the straining of tendons in his neck and throat, the tightening of muscles spreading up his jaw, his cheek, his temple, and veins popping in his forehead.

Then all that tension moved from him into her. She inhaled sharply and arched her back. But as quickly as she raised herself up, she lowered back down in the next breath, easy, calm, quiet. He relaxed with her, the pressure of his hand on her chest slackening, his shoulders slumping, and his head pitching forward. His eyelids fluttered but didn't fully open, then his head circled on his neck, lost in the euphoria that a harvest brought.

A harvest that didn't result in Diane's death.

None of the Darisami moved, staring as if they could penetrate Ash's mind and discover what he had done. *How* he had done it.

Felipe was the only person in the room who wasn't still. He inched forward on the cushions to within a whisker of Ash's back, peering around at Diane and grinning.

What the hell was going on?

Felipe's fingertips caressed up Ash's bicep, and the Darisami turned as if he moved underwater, languid, luxurious, lazy. He slid his arm out from under Diane and lay her to rest on the cushions, then Felipe settled into Ash's arms and gazed up at him with desire and devotion.

"I am ready," Felipe said without being asked.

Ash smiled a big, fat, juicy smile.

Surely, he didn't have enough control in the state he was in. Emrys opened his mouth, but Nimue's hand slammed onto his forearm, and she squeezed with all her might. The words died in his throat.

Ash put his hand on Felipe's bare skin, his eyes already closed, his hand finding its way all on its own. Again, Emrys sensed the formation of a symbol and the long pause that followed before Felipe arched his back and a groan escaped his throat. But this time, Ash wasn't so strained. Apart from a slight tensing at his temple, he was relaxed. Had he lost control?

But as Felipe's body unwound and he breathed, that small bit of tension in Ash's temple also melted. He cradled Felipe, and they breathed in harmony.

Emrys, Nimue, and Galen watched and waited…but for what? Diane and Felipe to die? For Ash to combust? All Emrys knew was that he couldn't move until Ash did.

Moments later, Ash drew himself up, some rigidity returning like scaffolding had been put up around a sinking monument, then opened his eyes. They were misted with a soul-eater's euphoria—but without having taken a soul. Ash floated to his feet like a puppet master had pulled on his strings. As he went, both Felipe and Diane touched him, eager for him to stay, but he bent down and interlaced them with each other. The two willing participants shuffled close together, hugged each other, kissed each other.

"Let's give them privacy." Ash's voice drifted on a cloud.

From the looks of things, they had about five seconds to get out before they'd see more than they bargained for. The Darisami and the soldiers left the room, and Ash closed the door.

"It looks like we've taken you away from something," Nimue said.

"This moment is for them and them alone. We'll go to my sleeping quarters. I'm sure you have questions."

They went to the room next door. The room they left, Emrys figured, was set aside for whatever ritual Ash had performed. The apartment they entered was a single room fitted with a double bed, again with no chairs or couches to sit upon. Plenty of cushions though. The presence of the soldiers made the experience less than comfortable.

The Darisami were forced to sit on the floor at the foot of Ash's bed while he sat cross-legged on top of the mattress. The ecstasy still ran rampant across his face, making it slack and malleable. He was stoned, plain and simple.

"What did you do to them?" Emrys couldn't keep the

annoyance out of his voice. Surely, this was all part of some act. He traced the eternity symbol on his thigh.

"I harvested their souls without killing them."

Nimue's voice snipped the end of Ash's sentence. "But how is that possible? You can't take part of a soul. How would you know if you've taken too much?"

"How much do you actually know about souls? Do you know what they are? Why we need them?"

Emrys held his tongue rather than play into Ash's already low opinion about him. Nimue and Galen remained silent too.

Ash gave an exasperated sigh. "Typical. Roll through the centuries without paying the slightest bit of attention to what you were doing. Still, why should I have been surprised?" He mushed his lips together and bunched them up in one corner.

Smug prick.

Emrys stood. "If you're going to be a self-righteous shit, we can come back when you're done."

Fire flashed in Ash's eyes and evaporated the last of his ecstasy. "Sit down, Emrys. You're not going anywhere." Ash waited until Emrys returned to his seat. "The soul is a human's vital life force, but when it comes down to it, it's energy. And when a Darisami takes a soul, it merely trans-fers that energy into another form that it can use to keep its own cells alive. Every Darisami who ever lived thought they had to take the whole soul. Why?"

"Because that's what the symbol does," Nimue said.

"Yes, but that's what *that* symbol does. Then add another symbol to that, and you get transfiguration, and another to that and you get splitting. But what about the next iteration?"

"There isn't one," Nimue said coldly. "I tried. I searched."

"Not enough. There's a fourth symbol that combines the other three. It's hard, but it's possible, and you don't have to take a life when you use it. But of course, why would a Darisami bother? Plenty of humans around to feed on, right? Take the soul. Move on. Never mind the destruction left behind. Never mind the death and despair."

Emrys was tired of this condescension. "You can't make us feel any guiltier than we already do, Ash. You're not better than us, you're just lucky you found something that meant you didn't have to kill."

"But it wasn't me who found it." He narrowed his eyes at Emrys. "It was Magnus."

Emrys's tongue sat fat, heavy, and useless in his mouth. When he managed to speak, it felt numb. "You can't expect me to believe that that monster discovered how to take souls but not lives? I saw the charnel house you two lived in. I counted every one of those two hundred and eighty-five bodies that I could find, and I'm sure there were many I couldn't."

Ash's gaze flicked to the soldiers standing around the room before coming back to Emrys. "Whatever he did was done for the common good. He regretted every life lost."

"Bullshit. He was a monster." Emrys had known plenty of monsters, and Magnus was way up the list.

"We're all monsters. But can we get back to the matter at hand?" Nimue said with a heavy dose of exasperation. "Magnus discovered the secret of taking the soul but not taking the life. Then what? How does it work? You give the soul back to them? You're revitalized and replenished, but for how long?"

Ash took a long time to swing his gaze from Emrys to Nimue. No way was Emrys going to allow this plaything of a sadistic killer to shirk from the responsibility he bore for the deaths of hundreds, but he would have to take up that fight later. Right now, the most important thing was finding out what he'd done with Diane and Felipe—and if they could do the same.

"I take the soul but not all of it," Ash said. "It's not severed from their body but extended into mine. My body then does what it needs to do to take nourishment, and the soul is returned to the donor. In an exchange, they connect with the euphoria that we are familiar with, the connection to all those other souls we've ever had a connection with. Call it life, call it love, call it universal consciousness, but whatever it is, it works both ways. I get to survive without taking life, and they get strength and ecstasy."

"So you drug them," Emrys said. "No wonder they were eager to participate."

Ash's gaze was as cool as quenched steel fashioned into a sword. "Wouldn't you be? You've seen the world as it is. It's bleak and desolate. Existence is all but futile. Wouldn't you want something to lighten that darkness? Don't you already? Every time you've harvested souls over your long life hasn't it been a moment of bliss and respite from the horror that we are? If you want to cheapen the humans' experience, go right ahead. It makes no difference to them."

"So how much do you have to take? How long does it last?" Nimue had inched toward Ash throughout his telling, a child eager to get close to the teacher as they told a good story.

"I don't know specifically, but I can feel the hunger burning after about twenty days. I haven't been brave enough to go longer to find out. Besides, there have always been willing donors."

"What are the side effects for you?" Galen asked.

"Why do you think there are side effects?"

Galen shared a look with Emrys, uncertain of proceeding. "We've been talking among ourselves. They say you look older than you used to be. Is it a glamor?"

Uncertainty streaked through Ash's eyes, chased by sadness. "No, I gave up the glamor a long time ago. I have aged since you last saw me."

"Aged?" Nimue breathed the word out. "Aged how?"

Her excitement caught Ash's attention, and he considered his words more carefully, curious about Nimue's interest. "I don't know how. It's likely that only taking a portion of the soul means that full immortality can't be maintained. What you see now is only minor but the effects of not taking a complete soul for a long time." He brushed the hair from his forehead and tucked it behind his ear, his fingertips dragging over the lines in his skin. "I haven't aged much, but I have aged."

Nimue stared at him. Emrys caught the flickering of her eyes as they darted over Ash's skin, from wrinkle to wrinkle. This was the miracle she had been praying for.

"Any other side effects? Limits to strength? Healing ability?" Nimue asked.

"None. Same as I ever was."

"What about the humans? After the euphoria and the power wear off, do they get withdrawal symptoms? Weaker than they were before?"

"No, provided they rest, eat, make love, even laugh. All these things replenish their soul and energy. I've not noticed any difference in the souls of people I've already gone through an exchange with."

"Other than turning them into addicts," Emrys said.

Ash glowered. "There are strict rules on how often they can be exchanged. No more than six times in a year and with at least one month in between."

"And this is all endorsed by the council and the citizens?" she asked.

"Gladly."

"But, from what I understand, you've only been out to them for the past ten years. Isn't that right?"

"Correct."

"How did you survive before then?"

Mournful shadows clouded Ash's eyes. "You don't need to know that."

"But—"

Lightning flashed in those clouds, and Ash's voice hardened. "I'm not going to tell you because it's not relevant. All you need to know is that this is the way things are in Prosperity. You don't kill, but you can exchange. Otherwise, you can leave."

"Then teach us," Emrys said.

Ash's lips stretched into a line as thin as piano wire around Emrys's throat. "Not yet."

Iron solidified in Emrys's spine. "What do you mean not yet? The council ordered you—"

"But they didn't say *when* I had to teach you, and as no one else is qualified, it's up to *my* discretion when you learn. And I'm not yet sure you're worthy."

"Worthy?" Galen's voice raised. "Who are you to decide whether or not we're worthy? This is about our survival. Hell, we've only got—"

"Shut up, Galen," Nimue said, but it was too late.

Ash understood, and he smiled. He had them right where he wanted them—on the cusp of starvation, desperate to do anything for him to avoid death.

Ash climbed off the bed in one long molten movement and drifted over to the door. "I'll teach you when you've proved yourselves worthy and not before. Until then, remember the rules. No harvesting. No killing. The soldiers will escort you to your quarters. Goodbye."

Nimue got to her feet first, dropping a ten-ton glare on Galen. She strode to the door with her little head held high. Ash may have thought he had her, but knowing Nimue like Emrys did, she'd find a way to get that secret out of Ash without even trying.

Galen didn't turn to Emrys for solace. Chastened but uncertain, he followed Nimue.

Emrys was the last to leave. Ash tracked his approach. As he reached the door, he closed what little distance remained between them, close enough to see the lines of age on Ash's sun-blemished skin, close enough to see his Adam's apple bounce in his throat and the strain show in the muscles around his eyes.

"We don't need to be enemies, Ash, but if you hold this from us, that's what we'll become."

"You made sure we were enemies long ago. Don't think the apocalypse made one bit of difference."

"But the humans want us to work together. This friction between us will only lead to trouble."

"I agree. So maybe you should consider if it's worth you sticking around."

＊   5   ＊

THE SOLDIERS SHOWED EMRYS, NIMUE, AND GALEN TO quarters not far from Ash's own. Nimue was delivered first and sealed in with soldiers stationed outside her door. She didn't speak to them or to Emrys as she went inside. He missed having access to her mind, as prickly as it was, and felt morose at the likelihood it would never happen again.

That kind of soul-splitting was ten times worse than a simple harvest, and even that was forbidden. Despite her silent treatment, Emrys still bid her a good rest before he and Galen continued to the next room along.

The door opened to a room as large and as pleasant as Ash's. Perhaps they were all the same, every citizen given comfort in an uncomfortable time. Or it was bestowed as a reward for what they would give the Prosperous. Emrys entered.

But Galen didn't follow.

Emrys turned around. "I guess you're not staying." He didn't know why he should have expected anything to be different.

Galen looked at him, sadness weighing on his face but

buttressed with determination. "No. I need my own space for a while."

Ice crystalized in Emrys's stomach. If there was one thing he didn't want, it was his own space. "Can we talk about this? Just for a bit and then you can go. Please?"

Galen chewed on his lip and nodded, but at the soldiers, not at Emrys. He closed the door, leaned against it, and crossed his arms over his chest. The mask of official business slid down his face. Captain Galen was never far away, ready to suffocate all the hurt.

Emrys itched to touch him. Instead, he closed his hands into fists and mirrored Galen's cross-armed stance. "I thought that once we got to Prosperity, things could be different."

"They are different. What Ash has shown us makes them different."

"I would have thought it'd make you happy. You don't have to kill anyone in order to live."

"Yes. That's welcome news. If Ash chooses to teach us."

The way Galen leveled his gaze at Emrys shone with the harsh glare of an exposed fluorescent bulb, burning out all subtlety and shadow. There was only right or wrong, Ash or Emrys. He backed away into the room and sat on the edge of the bed, buying himself some time to grow accustomed to the guilt and discomfort burrowing under his skin.

"He will teach us."

"Why should he? He hates you."

Emrys shook his head, disbelief hooking his mouth up in the corner. "Him not giving us his secret is my fault, is it?"

"It might be."

Emrys flinched, wounded, the angry snake kind of

wounded. "Like everything else? Like saving you from death because *your father shot you.*"

The dam inside of him broke and powered something inside him, like a turbine running at peak capacity. He'd held back on their journey, thinking that time would be all it took for Galen to realize how much Emrys cared for him. But still nothing. He wasn't content with nothing. And the churn and the charge sparked through his body.

"I gave you immortality and *together,* we got out of that prison you used to call home. *Together,* we made it to Prosperity. And now we've got the chance to live open and free as Darisami—something I have never had in five hundred years—and we could do it *together.*"

Galen's face remained like smoothed granite. "None of that would have happened if not for you, but you refuse to take responsibility for it. Just like you refuse to even consider apologizing to Ash for killing his lover."

Emrys rocketed to his feet. "Why would I? I don't think you understand how evil Magnus was. He may have fooled Ash into believing he was working for the common good, but the truth is Magnus liked to torture people. *You* didn't go into his home and find the men and women and *children* screaming to be saved."

Galen looked away, but Emrys wasn't going to let him escape that easily.

"I couldn't ignore it, but Ash did, idiot that he was, believing whatever he had to to justify being nothing more than bait. Everyone loved Ash until they learned he'd trapped them. He did the same to me. Drew me in so Magnus could dissect me for one of his experiments, but he seems to have forgotten that's how we met. That's because it's easier for Ash to hate me than hate himself and what he did."

Galen shook his head, whether at disbelief at Emrys's

words or at his own shame. "But look at what Magnus discovered. Maybe you had it wrong about him. If you hadn't—"

Emrys raised his voice to drown out Galen's conciliatory tone. He felt like he was fighting for his life. "If I hadn't stopped him, he would have gone on killing. Whatever Magnus discovered, he discovered by destroying humans that he considered no better than insects. I feel no guilt for ending his life."

"And if one day you kill me for some infraction?"

Emrys jolted back, the anger shocked out of him. "What are you talking about?"

"What's to stop you from thinking I'm not worthy of being a Darisami any longer?" Fear ripped the mask from Galen's face with a speed and severity that stripped Emrys's heart raw.

"Galen, there's no reason in this world that would lead me to killing you. Nothing. I'd sooner kill myself than even consider it."

"Until one day you change your mind."

Emrys's breath turned to ember-laden smoke and scorched his throat. "How can you believe that?"

"I've believed worse things." Galen turned to leave.

He wasn't going to get out of this argument that easily.

"Would you rather I'd left you to die?"

Galen's hand stopped over the sensor. His shoulders raised, then lowered. He turned his head to the side. "No. I just wish we'd never been put in that position."

"But we were, and I refuse to—" He stopped. Rephrased. "No matter what happens in this life, if I'm given the choice to save you or let you die, I'm going to save you. Again." He blew out a breath. "Even if that means I have to leave."

Galen spun round, but he didn't speak, and that was

worse. He looked defeated, and Emrys doubted he was interested in listening to more of his justifications. Emrys had grown tired of them many moons ago. And out of everything he'd done for Galen—build him up, save him, make him invincible, bring him to a safe haven—some of it should have been enough to prove to Galen how much he meant to him.

Apparently not.

Instead, he was expected to atone for sins committed long before Galen's birth. No one would convince him that Magnus hadn't deserved death, not Galen, not Ash and his stories of Magnus discovering the secret to harvesting souls without killing. Emrys regretted neither his death nor the deaths of the other forty-eight Darisami he'd killed. If Galen didn't understand that, then he didn't know him very well.

And isn't that the truth?

Bitterness dragged its stained fingers down his throat. "Look, I think we're both tired from the long journey. We should get some rest, take some time, and talk about this again later. If you're willing."

Galen didn't say anything, and Emrys had to take some comfort in that, some hope, no matter how miserly.

Galen left the apartment and the guards escorted him away, leaving five soldiers outside Emrys's door. He strode to the touch panel and slapped his hand on it to seal himself away.

Alone in his own space.

Prosperity's citizens left their sequestration and returned to their regular activities. The city hummed, and the Prosperous were welcoming, even if they were a little wary of the fifteen soldiers tailing the Darisami. They seemed more concerned about the guards than the people they guarded.

Ash escorted the Darisami on a tour of the city, from the bottom levels to the top. Prosperity operated on a decentralized system for non-essential services, reducing the chance of creating the silos that had persisted in Providence and made it difficult to change direction in a hurry. It seemed their political system operated in a similar fashion.

"The eleven councilors can only serve for a total of eight years throughout their lives. We used to have no restrictions but found we were getting stagnant," Ash said after they'd visited Diwali, who also worked as a manager in charge of the education system. "It gives most people a chance to own the decisions that keep the ark going, and we find they are more engaged and committed to its overall success."

"How many people live here?" Galen asked.

"About twelve thousand."

"Plenty of souls to feast on," Nimue said by way of a joke that failed to land.

"But I haven't, so make sure you don't get any ideas that it can be done in secret. Once I revealed myself, all deaths were investigated to ensure I didn't have anything to do with them."

"Sounds like they trusted you." Nimue gave Ash a sly look.

Ash looked down his nose at her. "It was my idea. Those procedures remained in place for a few years until they were assured I could be trusted. You killing that human a few weeks back sparked a panic and a lot of unpleasant questions."

Nimue's face didn't so much as flicker. "As Emrys said to the council, that death had nothing to do with us. We were nowhere near at the time."

"Why don't I believe you?"

She shrugged, and her eyes opened wide. She fluttered her eyelids enough to fan the illusion of innocence. "Perhaps you're a naturally mistrustful person. All I can say is I hope no one else dies unexpectedly and we get blamed for it. That wouldn't end well for anyone, including you."

Ash bristled. "If I wanted to get rid of you, I wouldn't need to sacrifice a human to do it." He marched ahead, ending the argument.

Nimue rolled her eyes at Emrys, but while he considered her goading amusing, the humor didn't warm his heart. Galen hadn't looked at him all morning, and he kept himself as far from Emrys as he could.

And Ash sought to turn it to his advantage.

While Ash was all rusty glares for Emrys and Nimue, he was easy charm and affection with Galen.

Ash was trying to make Emrys jealous. He knew that, but knowing it wasn't enough to stop jealousy's pyroclastic flow from scorching and slashing and smoking its way out of his stomach and poisoning his digestive tract. Not after the previous day's conversation. Not with the way Galen seemed to be responding. There was nothing overt between them, just a leveling of status. He kept up with Ash and spoke to him like he was a visiting dignitary. Emrys assumed it was Galen's way of asserting his own authority. Emrys *wanted* to assume that's all it was. Meanwhile, he continued to smell sulfur.

They continued their tour through the ark, asking questions along the way, but it was the journey to the surface that Emrys anticipated the most. When they finally started down the tunnel to the outside, he had to rein in his speed as he kept finding himself four or five steps ahead of the group.

They emerged beneath the mid-afternoon sun. People roamed over the surface of the earth like worker ants picking through the soil. They came in and out of the homes and supply sheds. Children played in the dirt. It reminded Emrys of his village in Wales. It reminded him of his daughter Sian and the destruction he wreaked because of her death. He cut the memory off and focused on what was ahead.

Ash led them farther out from the shelter of the tunnel and into the fields where the soil had been tilled and turned in the hope of building nourishment. Ash let them know that human waste was used to fertilize the soil, but it was a process that required a lot of work. The fields were otherwise plentiful with people working away.

"What are you going to grow?" Emrys asked.

"We're getting this one ready for wheat, but I wanted to show you something else first." Ash pointed into the distance at two farmers. "Recognize them?"

Emrys shielded his eyes and spotted Felipe and Diane, backs bent, tools in their hands, looking like any other farmer, but the speed with which they cultivated the soil and the depths to which they dug were markedly different from the people around them. They looked up and waved in the Darisami's direction, then returned to work.

"They'll have the field finished by the end of tomorrow. We put those who've been through an exchange onto the harder jobs while they've got the strength for it."

"They don't resent it?" Nimue asked.

"Why would they? They're helping everyone out and get to feel more alive by doing it. Come on."

Ash led them past the churned field and farther from the ark, but it didn't take long to see what Ash had brought them to see. Rows upon rows of yellow plants about a foot tall. Emrys stumbled as he looked upon them.

This was the true miracle. Even noticing the burn spots on their leaves and the gaps where plants had shriveled and died, a lot had grown. Prosperity had turned the earth to something useful once more. Emrys crouched in front of one of the plants and held his hand out to it, wonder swirling through him like a flurry of stardust.

"What are you growing?" Galen asked.

"Maize." Ash crouched down beside him. "It's not producing anything edible though. We're growing this to help enrich the soil. It was basically dead when we started working on it, but the scientists have been developing ways to improve it even with the high levels of radiation." Ash's tone with Galen was a lot more conciliatory and a lot warmer than he'd been to either Emrys or Nimue.

"Water must be an issue," Emrys said.

"We've sunk deep wells and drawn from groundwater. We've constructed channels from a nearby river as well. The strength I give them has made it all possible.

Emrys stood. "What about storms? We lost a lot to them at Providence."

"We're fairly safe. Winters can be harsh, but it's a good opportunity for the fields to lay fallow. They're not as bad as they used to be before the Fall, so the heat does help a little. There's no snow to worry about."

"Diwali mentioned you're growing a new crop this season. It seems disheartening that you haven't been able to grow anything to feed yourselves with in the past ten years."

A muscle pinged in Ash's jaw, but he maintained his overall composure. "That's our plan for this year." Ash dusted off his hands. "We've got two other fields that have better soil and have been worked longer. It takes time."

"Time you have, but the humans don't. That must make friction." Emrys pursued Ash's evasiveness.

"They understand what we're trying to do and that we can't snap our fingers and make everything immediately better. Not even the Darisami have that power."

Emrys refused to look at either Nimue or Galen. He wouldn't give away what they'd discovered the night they'd left Providence. When they'd stood over the spot in the ruined city where Emrys had slain Ragnar and Wyatt—slain them to save Nimue and Galen—and seen the freshly grown grass.

The death of a Darisami could turn the earth green.

That knowledge was the one thing they had left to bargain with. Even then they didn't know how useful it would be. If Ash knew the release of the souls held within a Darisami's body could heal the earth, could he be trusted not to denounce them?

Though what would then stop the Prosperous from turning on Ash?

"But now that you're here, I hope you're able to help." Ash said this to Galen and Galen alone.

Perhaps Ash wouldn't denounce all of them.

Breath rasped through Emrys's throat, scouring his esophagus and leaving it raw. *He's trying to come between us.* He swallowed to dull the pain, but it was stuck like a fish bone.

"Is that what you want us to do? Help?" Emrys asked. "I thought you wanted to watch us die."

Ash swung his baleful gaze around to Emrys. "I've told you. I'll teach you the new symbols when I can be certain your intentions are good."

He'd always had good intentions. What had Magnus had? "This is ridiculous. You know we've got nowhere else to go. It would make no sense for us to disrupt Prosperity."

Ash pushed out a frigid smile. "And yet you disrupted Providence. Your track record isn't good, Emrys. You have always thought you were better than the rest of us, always thought the Darisami were living their lives wrong. You thought you knew better than those humans as well, didn't you? The Prosperous may be welcoming, but they're going to be guarded until I tell them otherwise."

Emrys narrowed his eyes. "What do you want, Ash?"

"That should be obvious. I want to protect Prosperity."

Ash's words said one thing but the look in his eye said another. "And what if I tell the Eleven that you're refusing to give us the secret? What if I tell them they're in danger of losing us if you don't share your knowledge?"

"They'll listen to what I have to say, but there's nothing they can do to force me to teach you before I'm ready. If you don't like it, you're welcome to leave."

Emrys and Ash stared at each other, a row of plants

between them, centuries of a grudge bearing fruit. "We both know that the council wouldn't let us leave."

Ash brushed hair blown loose by the breeze behind his ears and closed the gap between them, crushing stalks beneath his boots. "They would. You may think you're important to them, but harmony matters more. And from what the exiles have told them, they're disinclined to think of you as anything other than malignant."

How many had spoken against Emrys? After all he'd done to make sure they stayed alive.

"Where are the exiles?" Nimue asked. "I haven't seen them around."

Ash held Emrys's gaze a moment longer, long enough for the sound of tools striking the earth to rise, long enough for Emrys to feel an itch between his shoulder blades, long enough for Ash to think he was winning. "They're being found homes, jobs. They're being inter-viewed and assessed. We need to find appropriate work for them but that takes time." Ash stepped back, out of the field now he'd won the battle. "We need to be sure they can integrate. You're not the only ones who have to prove their worth and their willingness to work with us, not against us."

"If it would help, I'm happy to speak on their behalf," Galen said. "I've lived in Providence my whole life. I know them and they know me."

"Thank you, Galen. I think that would do a lot of good." Ash put his hand on Galen's arm, and Galen responded with a gentle smile. Not the full-on megawatt radiant one he'd once given Emrys, but it shone bright enough and freely enough that a knife to the eye would have hurt Emrys less. "Unless there's more of the outside you'd like to see, we could go meet with their assessors."

"Let's go," Emrys said.

"Oh, not you, Emrys. Or you, Nimue. Just Galen." Ash gave a grin shot through with the sting of victory. "There's a new warehouse that needs to be built. You two are assigned to help with that. Your strength is invaluable. I'll take you there on our way back."

Ash set off with a guiding hand on Galen's back, leaving Emrys and Nimue to trail behind. Emrys caught snatches of what sounded like comparisons between Prosperity and Providence, but the breeze whipped up every now and then and carried their conversation away.

"I won't starve to death, Emrys." Nimue kept her voice low. "As much as I want to know how Ash does it, I will kill if it means I get to live."

"I know." They had less than three days remaining before they must harvest. "He's trying to make us sweat."

"What if there's more to it than that? What if he's waiting for you and me to die or do something drastic?"

"Prosperity won't be pleased to lose three Darisami."

"Two. It'd only be you and me. You must be blind if you don't see what he's doing by cultivating Galen."

His eyes and his heart saw it as clear as diamond. "What would you have me do? I've got five hundred years of bad decisions to make up for."

"Drop the self-pity. It doesn't help. Besides, you didn't kill me when you thought you had the chance. That was a good decision."

"Do you think I did the wrong thing by killing Magnus?"

"No."

"But what if Ash is telling the truth and it was Magnus who discovered how to exchange?"

"Then that's his legacy, but either way he's dead. You killed him. It's done. What does it matter now?"

"It matters to Ash."

And to Galen.

She sighed. "You did what you thought was right and probably saved a lot of lives because of it. Take comfort in that. But the only thing you can worry about now is the future."

A future that was rapidly fading.

"If Ash doesn't give us the secret in time, I'll leave Prosperity," he said.

"You can't." She hissed and clutched his hand, her tiny fingers locking onto him.

"Why not? I killed Magnus so Ash's problem is with me. If leaving means you and Galen get to live out the rest of eternity here, so be it. That's a sacrifice I'm willing to make."

Nimue didn't speak, but her grip eased without letting go. Whether in gratitude or in fear, he didn't know, but at the very least, he let himself sink into her gentle kindness.

They passed another row of fields thick with crops. A group of humans stood examining stalks and stems, their looks of consternation a bad sign. They crumbled dried leaves in their hands, broke stalks that splintered and caught in the wind. What they had achieved in ten years was impressive to outsiders and recent arrivals, but what did those who had lived with near-success—and constant disappointment—think?

Ash took them to the outer row of houses and stopped them at the construction site. The ground had already been prepared, compacted dirt instead of a concrete slab. The walls had been marked out, but apart from one side of the building, the rest was yet to do.

Ash introduced Emrys and Nimue to the foreman and said they were to follow his instructions. They received a warm welcome, relieved to have the extra pairs of supernatural hands.

"Have fun." Ash turned Galen back towards Prosperity and left behind two-thirds of the soldiers.

Galen didn't say goodbye.

Emrys watched him leave. Conversation resumed between Ash and Galen, their bodies closer than before. Before his view was blocked by a soldier, Galen turned to Ash and laughed. Ash looked back at Emrys and smiled.

Emrys's blood boiled, and for the next three hours, he used that steam to power through the construction of the warehouse. The work was done by mid-afternoon, and the humans thanked him and Nimue, but he barely heard them through the roar in his ears. Because while he could hate Ash for trying to come between him and Galen, it was his own feeling of betrayal that was the hardest thing to bear.

Sacrificing himself by leaving Prosperity to save Nimue and Galen from starvation seemed more attractive by the minute.

$$\text{❧}\quad 7 \quad \text{☙}$$

EMRYS SCRUBBED THE DIRT FROM HIS SKIN BUT COULDN'T get to the anxiety prickling beneath the surface, plucking the strength from his cells, preparing to turn to dust. Two and a half days remaining, and Ash had him tilling fields. He scrubbed harder.

He'd have gotten rid of the filth as soon as the work was over, but he'd gone in search of Galen. The guards might have told him where to find him—*them*—but he didn't want to give Ash warning. He wanted to watch the two of them unobserved, see if Galen was getting any closer to being taught how to exchange.

See if *they* were getting closer.

But all he'd encountered was a lot of the Prosperous eager for him to undertake an exchange. He tried to be polite and good natured about their interruptions, but his impatience and his hunger brought the harvest symbol too readily to the front of his mind.

He isolated himself before he hurt anyone.

The banging at his door stopped him from removing a third layer of skin. He stepped out of the shower, grabbed a towel, and wrapped it around his waist. Sodden, he answered the door, hopeful that it was Galen so he could dispense with the covering.

It was Nimue.

"What?" His voice was as raw as his skin.

She cocked an eyebrow. "Am I interrupting?"

He grunted and invited her in. "Have you discovered anything useful?" He returned to the bathroom to finish drying himself.

"No. Ash is still being stubborn, but that's not why I'm here. There's going to be a party."

He stuck his head out of the bathroom. "A party? For us?" He was not in the mood for festivities, though it might be interesting to have a wake before his funeral.

"It seems we're not that important." She positioned herself on the edge of his bed and smoothed out the top cover. "Three teams of foragers showed up soon after you returned to the ark. It appears they've been out scouring the surrounding countryside for supplies."

He came out of the bathroom, pulling on his trousers. "Did they bring back anything useful?"

"I don't know, but that's not the point. The point is one of them doesn't look very well." A smile dawned across her face, revealing her grotesque yet practical meaning.

He dismissed the idea. "It's too risky."

"Only if you do it without their permission."

"Me? I'm not harvesting. Ash is looking for any excuse to take me down."

"He can't say anything if the forager agrees." She slid off the edge of the bed and walked over to him. "Talk to them, find out how unwell they are, *sympathize* with them. Word has already spread about the arrival of new Darisami. You might be what they want—a merciful death."

"Ash would never allow—"

She gazed up at him and he couldn't look away. "Ash isn't the final authority in this place. You can do this, Emrys." The desperation in her voice dragged its nails down his chest. She should be thinking about saving herself, not him.

"What about you? You should have them. Or Galen." As close to death as he was, he wouldn't put himself above them.

"Of the three of us, you are most vulnerable."

He turned from her, picked up his gray-white shirt, and slipped it on. "There's no guarantee Ash will teach you or Galen. I can't take your only chance or his."

She locked her hand on his forearm. "You must, Emrys. Trust me. This is the best one we have. Ash will have little reason not to teach us if you can outlive us."

He laughed. "Wanna bet? Besides, this dying forager might not want to let me take their soul. Why would they? They don't know me."

"That's why you need to hurry." She shoved him in the chest. She picked up his shoes and thrust them at him. "You have to try, Emrys. For me, if not for yourself." She did a good job of keeping the strong line in her jaw and the resolve in her brow, but the plea in her eyes was what pushed him to take the opportunity she was presenting him with.

Emrys and Nimue stood at Prosperity's exit as people streamed past them. He couldn't tell who had returned from the exploration and who had always been here, but the large presence of people and the growing carnival atmosphere indicated that their arrival brought great joy and expectation.

Twilight had fallen, the village lit up with soft light, the stars twinkled up above… And the first quarter moon waited for them to step forth.

"It'll be all right." Nimue took his hand. "They've seen Ash glowing often enough to not recoil."

"But still, to have another three glowing Darisami… If I were human, I'd be worried. I'd feel under threat."

"If you were human, you'd be dead by now." She tugged at him. "Let's go."

Despite her reassurance, he covered his head with his hood and allowed himself to be led outside in search of the would-be donor. Their guards kept a few feet behind.

Nimue's hair hung loose and obscured much of her bare face from the moon's spotlight, but her hands emitted a glow that combined with his. It drew people's attention along with their smiles and frowns. Some tried to engage him in conversation, but Nimue dragged him into the thickest part of the crowd.

Emrys caught the strong glow of another Darisami up ahead. Whether Ash or Galen, or perhaps both, she was leading them right to it. The crowd swelled, and they struggled to get through. The press of bodies obscured his light.

"Pull back your hood," Nimue shouted through the din.

Reluctantly, he lowered it, raised his face, and moonlight blessed him. The people nearest noticed him—and their armed escort—and stepped back. That gave Nimue the opening she needed to push through. The closer they got, the more the glow ahead settled into two distinct forms, and when the final wall was breached, Emrys saw Ash and Galen standing side by side.

Nimue stopped short and stared at the human standing shaking Ash's hand. Gray hair, wrinkled, but with an energetic and vibrant demeanor, the man basked in Ash's light, a grateful and dreamy smile on his face. Ash shared a similar look, while Galen stared at the two of them with wide eyes and awe like he'd—

Like he'd witnessed a miracle.

Emrys's heart shriveled and shrank into a desiccated husk. He missed being the focus of Galen's adoration.

Nimue swore. Then swore again. And again. "He's healed." She crushed Emrys's hand, and he jumped at her power.

He extracted his hand from her grip and rubbed it. "Him? That's who was dying?" That was the man she'd said would welcome death? He looked like he'd never been sick in his life.

"I don't get it. He was seriously ill when he arrived. Death's door." She stared through the gloom at the man as if his survival was a personal insult.

A woman with pale brown hair turned to the two of them, but the smile on her face was strained as she took in their light and the soldiers. "Ash exchanged with him and healed him. Isn't that what you do too?"

Nimue looked up at Emrys, and her brow flickered. "Yes," she said, half to him, half to the woman. "I just… haven't seen someone so close to death be saved before." Her smile went from pained to pleasant as she conjured the lie. The woman relaxed, reassured. "Does he do this often?"

"Whenever he can. He's saved many people this way, though not everyone survives. Sometimes the body isn't strong enough to go through an exchange."

The man behind her gave a single disgusted laugh. "Or he didn't think they were worth saving."

The woman rounded on him. "That's a filthy lie. Ash treats everyone equally."

"Whatever, demon-lover. Why don't you go over and suck his cock if you love him so much?"

The sudden forcefulness of the man's vitriol brought tears to the woman's eyes, but she kept hold of them, tilted her chin up, and, despite the quiver in her cheeks and lips, managed to sneer at her insulter. "I can tell you've never been through an exchange, so your opinion of it hardly matters."

"Condescending bitch. As if I'd want to end up another brainwashed acolyte of these freaks." The man jerked his thumb at Nimue and Emrys.

"I think we should go," Nimue said.

"Yeah, go back to where you fucking came from." The man pushed Emrys in the back, though Emrys had grounded himself and the shove didn't move him.

Emrys rounded on the man and the harvest symbol erupted in his mind.

"Emrys!" Nimue grabbed his arm, sensing its summoning.

He closed his hand into a fist, quenching the symbol, but as he moved to strike the man, two of their soldiers stepped in and ordered the man to leave. Emrys's attacker shouted at the closed helmets, raising more accusations of favoritism, but the soldiers remained resolute.

"Let's get out of here." Nimue pulled him through the crowd to find a place where they could be alone, the rest of their guard trailing behind.

He slipped his hood back over his head, while her hair hid her face. She brought him to the doorway of a darkened warehouse, out of the uncomfortable light of the moon. She tucked her hands under her armpits.

"What the fuck are we going to do now?" She banged her head back against the wooden door.

But while she was more concerned about the loss of his

meal, he was focused on the hate that had been so easily stirred. Ash wasn't loved by all? Did he pick and choose who he exchanged with? How secure was his position in Prosperity?

"Are you even listening to me?"

Nimue's voice shattered his brooding. He hadn't been listening at all. He was about to ask her to repeat herself, but he was stopped by another sound. An impossible sound, like something heard in a dream. In neither Endurance nor Providence had there been anything like it. As if the Fall had vanquished it or put it to sleep only to be woken again in better times.

But here, in Prosperity, that sound was unmistakable.

Music.

Guitars and drums and flutes. Emrys could make out a fiddle, some pipes. The notes jumped and burst in happy refrain, and Emrys's heart responded in kind. He felt his lips lift into a smile of its own making and draw him in like the Pied Piper. He and Nimue hurried towards it, the melodies getting louder until they were within a bare field lit with bonfires. They stumbled into the center where the musicians had formed their circle.

And Emrys and Nimue weren't the only ones entranced.

Other exiles had been lured, enraptured by the sounds coming from the instruments, at the melodies that tripped from them. Juliet and Trellain had tears in their eyes, and Emrys's burned from holding them back.

He had missed music, but no one in Endurance or Providence had found anything to play about, as if music were too painful a memory to bear. Here, they had cause to celebrate. They had freedom to express themselves and to revel in the joy brought about by the plying of fingers to strings and bows, of hands beating drums, of voices rising in song.

A euphoria different from the feel of souls rushed through him and tingled all the way up to his scalp, forcing his eyes closed.

It was so strong, so strong it could raise him off the ground. Music.

Was there anything more beautiful than music?

He wished Galen was beside him.

The thought slammed him back to the unyielding earth. He opened his eyes and searched for him. Galen was there, on the other side of the field, glowing in the moonlight—beside Ash. Galen was enraptured. At least Emrys could take comfort in having brought him to this wonder.

Emrys lifted his hood and slid to the shadows. He would not succumb to melancholy. Galen needed time, and Emrys needed to feed.

"You should talk to him." Nimue had snuck up beside him. He was far too distracted after weeks and months of vigilance had worn him down.

"He needs space."

"Suit yourself, but Ash is only doing this to get to you."

"I know that. I know Ash is playing games." He hated the bark in his voice.

"And our lives are at stake." Her attention was fixed on Ash.

"What are we going to do?"

In the dancing firelight, her stare was cold. "I don't know. I want to talk to a few of the donors and try to find more like that guy who doesn't like Ash. It might deliver something we can bargain with."

"Good luck."

"Thanks. It would be easier if we didn't have these

soldiers trailing our every move. People seem more put off by them than by us."

He had noticed that. It would also make harvesting a soul a lot easier if they weren't around. But that was the point. "What do you think that's about?"

"I don't know. I'll try to find that out too. You'll be okay here by yourself?"

"I'll be fine."

The cold stare warmed a little, and her face softened before she turned and skipped away. Soldiers trailed her like palace guards following a princess. She let the light glow on her, and as Emrys watched her leave, she drew intrigued eyes after her. When they caught sight of the guards in their black, the intrigue turned to concern.

The music came to a natural end as one song finished and another was yet to start. Juliet and Trellain approached him, almost stumbling as they kept half their attention on the musicians.

"Did you enjoy the music?" Emrys asked.

"I've never heard anything so beautiful in my life." Juliet's face retained its wonder. Even Trellain's depression had lifted. "We never had anything like it in Providence."

"Nor in Endurance."

"What about before?"

"There was always music before the Fall."

"Makes you wonder how there could have been a Fall when there was something so magical." She sighed. "I hope they play again."

"I'm sure they will. How have you been adapting? Are they treating you all right?"

"The interrogations went for a long time," Trellain said.

"Not that they called them interrogations." Juliet roughly dragged her fingers through her auburn hair. It looked like oil in the firelight. "They must have asked us a hundred times about the coup, who was involved, who did what, and of course, what your part was in all of it. You and Nimue and Galen."

"And your part too?" he said.

She wrinkled her nose. "Yes. That as well. We told them everything."

"No matter how uncomfortable." Trellain shifted the weight on his feet. "We were all interviewed individually, then our stories were corroborated. They returned to try to catch us out based on what others had said."

"Other than you, Owen laid most of the blame on Trellain and Galen," Juliet said.

That was predictable. He'd managed to avoid Owen since their first night in the cells, but he would be out there dripping venom.

"But the interrogators seemed doubly surprised at Owen's role in the proceedings." Trellain smiled. "They were left with no doubts as to everything he participated in."

"They let us out eventually," Juliet said. "We must have said the right things to be allowed to stay. I guess they need the extra hands."

"They've put you to work already?"

"Not yet. They're giving us a few days to recuperate after our journey, but they've assigned us to positions. I'm in what passes for their factory, but you won't guess what they have me doing," she said. "Resource recovery."

Emrys laughed. That's where he'd been assigned when he'd arrived at Providence. "I'm sorry. You're wasted there."

She waved away his sympathy. "It doesn't matter. I'm happy to not be in charge."

"You'll be bored in three weeks." Trellain gave her a glowing grin.

She blushed. "For sure. But after everything that's happened, I wouldn't mind some peace and quiet." She hesitated and tucked an invisible strand of hair behind her ears. "Do you think we can stay here for good?"

"I don't see why not. Provided we all follow their rules."

"And you think you can do that?" Trellain asked flatly.

"If I'm given the chance to. Where have they put you? Security?"

He shook his head. "I'm working with Juliet." He came closer, lowering his voice, showing his back to the guards. "Security wasn't an option. Their security forces aren't large. I don't know if you've noticed, but the people seem really perturbed by the presence of your guards. It's not what they're used to."

Emrys looked over Trellain's shoulders. The black-garbed soldiers were as mute as ever. Shadows were more active. He nodded.

"Over the past ten years, the size of their military has decreased," Trellain said. "They decided that more effort should be put into returning to the surface and letting a more harmonious citizenry flourish. That's part of the reason for cutting off communication with Providence. They feared attack, so it was better to let them believe they were dead."

"But it's worked," Juliet said. "The Prosperous aren't like us. They're genuinely dedicated to working together. The sight of security makes them uncomfortable."

"They're a city of twelve thousand," Emrys said. "They must get some unrest."

She spread her hands. "If there is, it doesn't need a lot

of force to subdue. From the people we've spoken to, it all works well."

"If you don't include the dissenters," Trellain said.

Emrys thought of the argument he'd witnessed. "I met one tonight. Are there many?"

"There are enough for the citizens to mention them. They mostly grumble about the lack of progress while enjoying the benefits of free movement on the surface, but talk to them long enough, and it's clear their biggest complaint is Ash."

"They think he's evil," Juliet said. "They don't trust him. They believe that anyone who goes through a…a… what do they call it?…an exchange. Yeah, when they go through an exchange they lose part of themselves and are worse than when they started. There are a few who are fanatical about it."

"And you can guess who's fallen in with them."

Emrys straightened. "Owen? Already?" Perhaps giving the exiles time to recover wasn't a smart idea after all. Idle hands did the devil's work. Or the devil's former disciple.

Trellain nodded. "And a few of the former Tornshirts. Not Leya, though. That was a surprise."

"But a couple of the Golden Goons too," Juliet said.

Trellain grimaced. "Tala and Port were always easily swayed."

Emrys decided not to point out how quickly Trellain had fallen to his knees when Emrys showed his light. He was glad the former Golden Goon was comfortable enough to stay in his presence after that experience.

"About Ash," Juliet said. "The Prosperous say that he takes their souls but doesn't kill them. Can you do that?"

"I can take souls, but I don't know how to do it without killing. And that's the truth. If I'd ever known it, I'd never have taken a life."

"But you didn't have to take a life at all, did you?"

Her interrogation poked and prodded the soft parts of his conscience, but no matter how deep they penetrated his core was solid. "Only if I didn't want to go on living. You can hate me for it, Heaven knows enough people already do, and you'd be right to, but I'm a living being as much as anyone. I wanted to survive. But you have my word that I won't harm anyone here. Either Ash teaches me how to do it, or I'm leaving."

She flinched. "You'd leave? What if it meant you'd die?"

"Then so be it. I've accepted the rules of this place, and I won't destroy another ark for my own selfish needs."

"I suppose it's good that you learned that lesson eventually," Trellain said.

But Juliet didn't follow Trellain's low blow with an uppercut. "The citizens are genuinely excited you're here. From the sounds of it, this exchange thing they go through with Ash is something almost everyone wants. Though after hearing that music, I don't know how anything could compare."

"Gee, thanks." Trellain laughed.

Juliet blushed. "You know what I mean. There's a real push for you to be integrated as soon as possible. They say you're able to give them strength as well as euphoria. Part of the complaints have come about because Ash has his favorites."

"Or perceived favorites," Trellain said. "I'm not sure some people aren't just greedy and think others are getting preferential treatment when they're not."

"Whatever the reason, there's friction. Not a lot, but enough that it has to be managed."

"And their mission on the surface?" Emrys asked.

"Very popular. They rotate people as much as they can,

so everyone gets the opportunity to work out here. Not everyone goes for it, but they try to be fair. The only negative has been the lack of edible crops."

"And it's a big negative," Trellain said. "They plow a lot of fields and plant a lot of seeds." He said the words as if they were new. "But not much grows, at least not much they can use. The foraging is a big deal."

"Because it provides a distraction?" Emrys asked.

"Exactly, but it's been ten years, and they're still eating the same gruel we had in Providence. They're wondering if it's been worth it."

"And some wonder it aloud."

The music started again, and Juliet and Trellain turned their heads towards the sound. Emrys wanted to know more, but he wouldn't deprive them of this moment.

"You should go enjoy the music," he said. "I'll catch up with you another time."

"That means you're staying, right?" Juliet was already distracted.

"For now. Have fun." It was an unusual thing to say, so unfitting with his experience of the past sixty-five years since the Fall, but he enjoyed the tingling sensation that came from saying it and having it be a real possibility.

Juliet said goodbye and took Trellain's hand. They walked off, but they'd only gone a few yards before Trellain stopped and returned to Emrys. He looked at the ground and paused like he was summoning the words to say something important.

Bands wrapped around Emrys's chest, squeezing him of free breath. Was this the moment Trellain too blamed him for all that had brought them there? Owen had raged at him plenty on the journey. Was it Trellain's turn?

Trellain lifted his head, straightened his spine, and squared his shoulders. "Thank you for bringing us here,

Emrys." He stuck out his hand. "Thank you for keeping us alive." He didn't smile but neither did he wear an expression of defiance or grudging gratitude. It was freely given, confident, and right.

The bands loosened and let Emrys breathe, let him smile. He took Trellain's hand and shook it firmly. "You're welcome, Trellain."

The former soldier nodded and returned to Juliet, slipping his arm around her waist. At least there was some good to come from this. Trellain was a decent man, far better than Juliet's former lover, Brink. He was happy for the both of them and let that happiness have free rein through his body.

But as the music rose in volume and picked up in tempo, he was drawn to Galen, shining in the night beside Ash. Galen was looking at him, but as their eyes met, eyes half-hooded by a frown, Galen turned away, and it was as if that action ripped the heart from Emrys's chest.

At least he got to hear music again before he died. If only he could have danced to it with Galen.

8

Emrys and Nimue were back in the fields the next day, pouring their supernatural energy into plowing fields that refused to yield much of value. His fellow farmers tried to engage him in conversation, but his responses were as barren as the dirt he attacked. Nimue gave them what they wanted or tried to.

The humans were eager to know whether Emrys and Nimue would soon be giving out the same benefits that Ash delivered. Their bright, eager faces shone with the expectation of an upcoming exchange. Nimue had to give them an answer that was more diplomatic but equally as empty as the ones Emrys gave.

It wasn't like Emrys and Nimue didn't want to go through with it. It would have made the day's work easier if the twenty or so humans they toiled beside were full of Darisami dynamism.

Their disappointment was stark, and they had to accept that they wouldn't get a good reason as to why they were denied. Emrys was tempted to explain in full so they could take their complaints directly to Ash—or the council

—but Emrys was trying not to give him any more reasons to let them starve to death.

The workers left them alone.

Emrys got closer to Nimue and rested on the handle of his hoe. "At least we know none of these people have a problem with Ash."

"Don't be so sure. That one over there hasn't come near us the whole morning." She nodded in the direction of a middle-aged, dark-skinned man three-quarters of the way down the field. "And two of the ones who just asked are not Ash fans."

"How do you know?"

"I found out last night. It was hard to get much out of the Prosperous without the soldiers' presence stifling their willingness to speak, but there's definite tension between those who welcome Ash and those who don't. Four of the eleven councilors are committed to the anti-Ash camp."

He ground the hoe into the dirt. "But only two voted against us."

"In public." She wiped her hand across her forehead. "The other two vote whichever way is going to be most popular while secretly indicating to their supporters where their sympathies truly lie."

"Still not a majority."

"But impossible to ignore. I think most of it is born out of jealousy for what Ash can do and how much praise he gets, but he's also selective of his donors."

"With good reason, I'm sure."

"Better to give it to those who are grateful than to those who want to bring him down. Or the violent ones. None of our guards have been given his strength in the past four months. They'd be easy to subdue."

"If it came to that."

And only if they could disarm them of their gold weapons.

"I guess that would be one way to have a quick death," she said.

"It's not going to come to that."

"No? We have two days left. Ash still refuses to teach us —even Galen. And if we do feed, we're likely to get shot. This is not how I expected my world to end."

"We'll find a way. Even if we have to leave and take a few souls with us."

She sagged, turning her pick on its point. "The problem is, I actually want to stay. I want to know how he does it. I want… I want…"

Her words unpicked the seams in his heart. "You want to age."

The full misery of her unfulfilled potential washed through her dark eyes. She'd seen more, done more, experienced more than almost anyone who'd ever lived. But she'd always been the child, the girl, the cherub, and never the adult, the woman, the archangel. He could sympathize, but he could never understand completely how it felt to be trapped in a body that didn't quite fit with her reality.

He had to do something to give her that gift.

"Help!"

Emrys's head snapped up at the cry of alarm. A worker lay writhing on the ground, another by their side, a woman, calling out and waving for them.

"Help him!" Desperation cut a jagged line through her voice.

Workers ran into the field as the woman's pitch dialed to shrieking. Emrys and Nimue sprinted to the fallen man. He was the one Nimue had pointed out, the one who'd kept his distance from the Darisami. He was holding his neck, blood slicking his hands and his face. His eyes were wide, and his expression strained. His chest billowed as he tried to breathe while shock took hold.

"It was an accident. He got too close. I didn't see him." The woman fired her panicked excuses until someone took her away.

The soldiers gathered, and the bleeding man's eyes locked onto Emrys's. He shuffled closer and replaced the man's hands with his own. Blood pumped up to douse them. However it had happened, she'd nicked his artery. Emrys applied pressure.

"Get a medic out here fast!" Emrys shouted.

He heard the squawk of radio orders, but he feared they wouldn't arrive in time to save the man's life.

"Heal him, Emrys," a man said. "Why can't you heal him?"

What could he say? That this man was going to die because Ash hated him? But maybe he could still save a life while this man's slipped through his fingers.

"Nimue, help me stem the bleeding."

She dropped to the dirt opposite him. She replaced his hands with her own, while Emrys gripped the man's free and blood-soaked hand. Emrys looked into Nimue's eyes and wished she could still read his mind. He poured as much pleading into his expression as he could without raising anyone else's suspicion. She scrunched up her face and gave a little nod. She understood that this life was hers for the taking.

The workers begged for him to save the man's life. His name was Jonas. They demanded to know why Emrys couldn't heal him as Ash had healed the forager the day before and countless others in the past ten years, but it was all so much background noise as he sensed Nimue form a symbol.

"Stay with us, Jonas. You'll be okay," Emrys said.

He and Nimue waited until it was almost too late. They needed his breathing to slow. They needed death to rattle in his throat. They needed it to look like he died from blood loss. Jonas had no idea how much gratitude Emrys had for him and for his dumb luck.

"Stand back!" Ash's voice fired through the crowd.

A woman burst into tears.

Nimue snarled.

"Step back now!" Ash pushed Emrys aside and shoved Nimue in the chest, knocking the homicidal look from her young face as she scudded into the dirt.

They'd been so close.

Ash formed the symbol, the strain showing in his face and neck, then it was out. Jonas tensed, then he was healing.

The people applauded.

Emrys got to his feet, not wanting to grovel in the dirt for his life. Ash wouldn't get that from him. They'd been so close. Nimue could have fed, and Emrys could have left, confident that she would survive another thirty days. Galen would learn the secret of how to exchange, and Emrys…

Well, he could have taken a soul and slipped into the night to starve as far from human eyes as possible.

That was still very much an option.

Nimue stood beside him, rigid in her fury, her hands dripping blood. Galen joined him on his other side, lines etched into his forehead. Emrys caught his eye but the worry only deepened. In the distance, Galen's soldiers were running to follow their charge. He and Ash must have sprinted to reach them in time.

Jonas was breathing easier, and Ash lifted his hand off the closed wound. They remained in their dreamy state, recovering from the euphoria, from the brush with death and the reaffirmation of life. No one said a thing, and the only thing that moved was the wind.

Slowly, Jonas sat up. Workers rushed forward, cheering and sobbing, to hug Jonas and thank Ash.

Emrys, Nimue, and Galen retreated. Did they realize Jonas had been within a second of death? Emrys didn't want to stay around for the recriminations. He nudged Nimue and jerked his head towards Prosperity. They had to wash the blood off their hands.

To Emrys's surprise, Galen came with them. They walked in silence, meeting Galen's soldiers, and continued on to the ark.

"Would you have really done it?" Galen whispered.

"We didn't do anything except keep him alive until Ash got there. Understand?" Nimue's words dripped acid and acrimony.

"I don't believe that, and neither will Ash or the council."

Nimue spun and rushed Galen, forcing him to stagger back. "Whose side are you on?"

"I'm not on anyone's side."

"That's the problem."

Emrys tried to get in between them. "Come on, Nimue. We shouldn't fight among ourselves."

"Stop defending him, Emrys! He's doing nothing to stop you or me dying."

"That's not true." Galen glowered down at her. "I'm trying to win Ash over by talking to him while all you two can do is glare at him. I'm trying to form a relationship with him."

She barked a laugh. "Emrys not enough for you, is that it?"

Galen's anger slipped and revealed his shame and his wounds.

Emrys had his suspicions but hearing them out loud brought his heart misery. "That's enough, Nimue."

She glared at him and blew out a long breath. "Fine. I apologize for being indiscrete. I'm just...I'm just FUCKING HUNGRY." She flicked out her hands like it would dispel the clawing in her veins. "I need to get this blood off me, and then the three of us must come up with a plan." She turned for Prosperity. "Fucking hell, what now?"

Emrys tore his eyes from Galen but his heart remained nailed to him. He followed Nimue's gaze. Diwali and four councilors were marching across the field towards them.

"Bad news travels fast," Nimue groaned.

The Darisami waited for the councilors to reach them, the sight of the dried blood on Nimue and Emrys startling two of them.

"Councilors." Emrys nodded his hello.

"Can you explain what happened out there?" Diwali's expression was as ungiving as her tone.

Emrys looked to Nimue. What had Diwali been told? Could Ash have already accused them of preparing to harvest Jonas's soul? But even if he had, there were always two sides to every story.

"Jonas had a life-threatening injury," he said. "We called for assistance and staunched the bleeding until help arrived. Ash came in time to exchange with him and saved his life."

Diwali frowned. "Why didn't you heal him?"

"Because we don't know how." Emrys tried to keep the snark out of his voice but failed. "Ash refuses to teach us."

The lines on her forehead deepened further. "Is that so?" Her eye was drawn over Emrys's shoulder as Ash arrived. If Emrys didn't know otherwise, he would say he looked puffed. "Ash, explanation. Now!"

Ash stopped beside Galen, the four Darisami lined up like naughty school children trying to pass the blame. "What happened? I stopped these two from taking Jonas's life."

"Councilor, that's a lie!" Nimue's voice cracked. It verged on a wail. "We were trying to save his life. If anyone should take the blame for Jonas almost dying, it's Ash."

"What?!" He rounded on Nimue, his blond hair flicking like a whip.

"It's true." She stamped her foot on the ground and let her bottom lip quiver. "If Ash had taught us how to exchange when we arrived, we wouldn't have had to risk precious seconds waiting for help."

"She has a point." Emrys's smile broke free, but though he enjoyed the glower on Ash's face, the disappointment on Galen's scrubbed it away.

"Councilors, the only reason I haven't taught them yet is because I don't trust them, and today's incident proves that they are a danger to our people."

Diwali considered each Darisami in turn, and Emrys understood what it was to be at the whim of this council. When he'd been just another Darisami pretending to be human was only subject to human laws. He could hide his nature and his crimes behind the humans' lack of knowledge of the Darisami's existence. After all, people died of natural causes all the time.

But in Prosperity he'd been exposed as what he truly was. There was nowhere to hide. They knew exactly what he was and what that meant, and as such, he was subject to their laws, their strictures, and their goodwill. He wasn't used to such vulnerability.

Diwali looked at Ash. "The way I see it, your actions have put our people—and the peace of Prosperity—at risk."

"But Councilor—"

"But nothing, Ash. The council made the decision to welcome these Darisami into Prosperity, so you *will* teach them what you know, and you *will* do it now. If you do not, we will consider it insubordination, and the consequences for you will be dire. Is that clear?"

The spectacle of watching a forty-something-year-old human dressing down an almost two-hundred-year-old Darisami amused Emrys, but it was knowing Ash had finally been cornered that truly lifted his spirits. He refrained from hollering and slipping into childish taunting. Ash seemed crestfallen enough as it was.

"Well?" Diwali said.

"I shall do as the council has decreed. I'll teach you in two hours. Meet me in my room." Ash stalked off, cutting through the councilors. They turned to watch him leave. Galen followed, leaving Emrys with a worried glance.

"Thank you, Diwali," Nimue said.

"Make sure I don't regret it." Diwali nodded at Emrys and led the councilors into the field, presumably to check on their human citizen.

Nimue waited until they were left alone with their soldiers before speaking softly. "Well, we got what we wanted with two days to spare." But the way Nimue said it reflected Emrys's gloom.

Ash had agreed to teach them, but there was still the chance he could double-cross them. And then where would that leave them?

❀   9   ❀

EMRYS and NIMUE had enough time to shower and change before arriving at Ash's quarters. Galen's soldiers were already outside. After making them wait five minutes, Ash answered the door and invited them in. He ordered the guards to remain in the corridor.

Galen stood from where he'd been sitting on the edge of Ash's bed. He straightened his tunic and met Emrys's gaze but gave away nothing. He was composed like a safe, of hard and difficult-to-pry-open edges. How disappointed in Emrys was he? How angry? How indifferent?

"Take a seat." Ash gestured to the cushions while he took the bed. "This requires some explanation." His damp hair was tied back into one long ponytail. He was dressed in pale brown kaftan and trousers, looking as close to relaxed as he could, but his tongue worried at his back teeth, making his cheek bulge.

Emrys took the middle. Galen sat on his left, close enough to touch but far enough away that it couldn't be an accident. Nimue sat on Emrys's right.

"Do you all know the three main symbols?" Ash said.

92

Nimue and Emrys nodded.

"I only know the one for harvesting," Galen said.

Ash smirked. "Looks like you've been lax in your duties, Emrys. Some maker you are."

"We can discuss the qualities of a good maker until the sun explodes. Get on with it." No way was he going to be lectured to by the creation of a psychopath.

Ash shifted his shoulders like he was settling his feathers.

Nimue leaned forward and spoke around Emrys. "Galen, they come to you naturally. The first is the harvest symbol, the most important one. Then you add the second for making, then the third to the first and the second for splitting."

"And you add the fourth to the previous three and you get the exchange but," Ash raised a finger, "it's more complex than any of the other workings."

"Is this dangerous?" Emrys asked.

"A bit. There is a risk of losing control of the symbols and the whole thing unravelling. Then you will kill the volunteer."

"Is it important that they volunteer for this?"

"It makes it easier." Ash looked uneasy. "But it's not essential."

How many 'volunteers' had he and Magnus murdered to discover this secret? It had probably been an accident while Magnus was searching for a way to increase how much torment he could cause. He'd been perverted that way. Which was why it was such a shock to learn that Ash was his consort. No matter how hard Emrys searched for Magnus's evil in Ash, he hadn't found it. Then again, standing by while others committed atrocities was its own form of evil.

"The difference with an exchange is that there are

connector symbols. For your information, Galen, normally you can do one symbol after another, laying them one on top of the other without anything to join them, but with an exchange, you need to push the power of one symbol into the next then collectively into the one after that. You do that through a conduit symbol, much like cursive writing, connecting one letter to the other."

"Surely that shouldn't be so hard," Nimue said.

He huffed. "Wait until you try it. The symbols don't want to be connected. They like their independence, and they're more stable that way. When you run them together, their definition blurs."

"This sounds too fraught," Emrys said.

"But what choice do we have?" Nimue scratched the back of her hand.

Emrys was more worried about Galen, whose grasp of the symbols was new and largely untested.

"Quite," Ash said. "You start with one, push the energy into the second, push the energy of the first and second into the third, and push the energy of the first, second, and third into the fourth. Understand?"

They nodded.

"Good. You then have the added problem of the fourth symbol, which requires a level of concentration all of its own. It's a construct that we're not used to, even me, and I've been using it a long time."

"Why do you think it's so difficult?" Nimue asked. "Is it unnatural?"

"I don't think so. We had a theory that the first Darisami knew how to do this easily, but they lost the ability over time. Because it was more complex, they got lazy, and then there weren't so many Darisami left to teach the next generation and so on. We thought there might be some sort of shared consciousness that existed between all things, but as the symbol fell out of use, we forgot it. When we learned it again, it was rusty."

"Sounds like something you'd believe."

Ash scowled. "Scoff all you want, Emrys, but I prefer to believe that there is some connection between all living things. It makes the world a far less hostile place."

"What's happening to the soul during this?" Galen asked.

"Nothing happens until you release the fourth symbol. Release too early, and you'll kill them."

No doubt learned through sweet experience.

"When you do release the symbol, something like a small incision is made where the soul connects to the body. That's the harvest symbol. The transfiguration symbol takes it into you and leaves a part of their soul behind. The third symbol, for bonding, splices part of your soul and takes it with them. And the fourth symbol returns their soul and heals the wound."

"And that's it?" Emrys said.

"That's it. You both get the vigor and the euphoria. It's not as strong as when you do a complete harvest, but it's enough for a Darisami to survive on, and in some ways more rewarding."

"So now you'll teach us." Emrys didn't mean it as a question.

"I'll teach you one by one. It'll be easier that way."

"I'll go first." Nimue made to stand, but Emrys grabbed her arm.

"No. If anyone's going to risk themselves learning how to do this, it's going to be me. If anything goes wrong, then it's me who'll take the blame. I'm the oldest."

"Fine," she said. "But be quick."

"You can all watch anyway," Ash said. "But I admire Emrys's selflessness."

Sure he did. Emrys sneered at him. "Get on with it, Ash."

He smiled with all the sweetness of barbed wire. He went over to the table and picked up a silver pot before sliding in between Emrys and Galen. He took the lid off the pot and dipped his fingertip into the black pigment inside.

"Right, you know the first three symbols. The connector is fairly simple, but it takes effort to lock it in place. Symbol one." Ash put his finger on the smooth floor and drew the symbol.

"Then from the bottom of the end of it you draw upwards in a wide half circle to connect to the top of the second with a small loop. You'll get a sense of it, and it'll fight you if you go too close or too far. Trust it, but don't let it dissipate."

Ash drew the second symbol next to the first. "Then the same connector again."

And the third symbol and the connector before leading into a complicated set of lines and loops that formed the fourth symbol.

"Draw it again," Emrys said.

Ash wiped the floor clean with a rag and repeated the symbol while Emrys traced it in his mind. It felt uncomfortable to draw and unnatural but that could have been because of its novelty. A feeling came with it, but it didn't come easily. It made him a little nauseous, but that could have been nerves.

"Got it?"

"I think so."

"Connect it all together in your mind."

Emrys closed his eyes and ran through the symbols.

"Don't forget to pull the energy from one into another."

He lost control of the symbols more than once, his concentration slipping, his grip loosening. Sweat sprang up on the back of his neck before he could make it to the fourth. This was impossible. How were they going to learn it in time?

"Relax, Emrys," Nimue said. "You're trying too hard."

"Yes," Ash said. "You can't be all brute strength. You have to encourage it to go where you want it to go. Be forceful but not violent."

Emrys breathed into it, lit up the first symbol, connected it to the second, which he connected to the third. He vacillated on the cusp of the fourth, lost it, and it unraveled in his grasp. But he knew he could do it. He was on the verge of success.

He settled his thrashing heart and went through the process again. He felt the energy connect and pull through, then with a firm and steady mindset, he launched into the fourth symbol. It felt strange, but it felt complete. Would it work when he had a live body beneath him? There was still a sense of something peculiar about it, but maybe Ash was right. That the lack of use meant they were unpracticed. In time, it might become easier. Though Ash hadn't looked any more at ease when he'd put it into play.

Emrys held onto the symbol, the energy quivering through his body, but with nowhere to send it, he was forced to let it go. The symbol shattered, and he released an explosion of breath.

"How does it feel?" Nimue asked.

"Like hard work."

"But worth it?"

"We'll see."

"Do you have it under control?" Ash asked. "Or do you need to practice some more?"

"No, I think I've got it."

"All right. Let's bring in a volunteer." Ash went to the door and spoke to a guard in the hallway.

Nimue leant over and lowered her voice. "Are you sure you want to do this, Emrys?"

He wasn't sure about anything when it came to Ash, but none of them had time to be timid. At least if it went wrong, they would be saved.

"Yes, I'm sure, but it wouldn't hurt to think of a plan B if this doesn't work."

A volunteer arrived looking more uneasy than Emrys thought he should. He was about mid-twenties, olive skin, light brown hair, medium height and build, with a strong jaw and a large forehead.

"Emrys, this is Boston." Ash's hands were on Boston's shoulders, guiding him towards Emrys. "Your volunteer."

Emrys stood and held out his hand. "Hello, Boston. Thank you for doing this."

Boston stared at Emrys's open palm then at Ash. "Is it going to hurt?" His voice was small.

Emrys frowned. "You've never done this before?"

"No, I—"

Ash interjected. "But Boston has always wanted to. Haven't you, Boston?"

He swallowed and quickly nodded.

Emrys's heartbeat raised, preparing for an attack that he couldn't see coming. Something was off. Perhaps Boston was nervous. Perhaps it was Emrys's hunger. "You can say no, Boston. This is purely voluntary."

"I know," he said with a small voice. "I'm not afraid."

"Of course, you're not. There's nothing to be afraid of." Ash pushed Boston into the room, and the door closed behind him. "I find it easier to do this lying down, as you saw the other day. It helps you maintain control."

Emrys suggested a spot for Boston, and they got into

position. "I promise you this won't hurt." Emrys looked down into eyes that were too terrified to trust. Why would Ash give him someone so new to this? Surely that would make it harder. But then again, everyone had to have a first time.

"Undo your shirt, Boston," Ash said. "Emrys needs to touch your bare skin."

"Or I can hold your hand if you prefer?" Emrys rushed to give him an alternative.

"No, no, it's fine." Boston did as instructed and exposed the top of his chest, dark curls over his pecs.

Emrys placed his hand onto his skin. "Are you ready?"

Am I?

Boston nodded and screwed his eyes shut. His body tensed in Emrys's arms.

Now or never.

Emrys took a deep breath and formed the first symbol.

10

"Stop!"

Emrys's eyes fired open and lasered onto Galen. The symbols shattered.

"Boston, come here." The command in Galen's voice was unshakeable, but Emrys had to continue. He had the experience; Galen was a novice.

"I'm going first," Emrys said.

"No, you're not. Boston, lie here please." Though his order was for Boston, Galen's focus was fixed on Ash.

"But you haven't had enough practice," Emrys said. Galen couldn't do this. He was going to get it wrong, and Boston would die and so would Galen. "Why don't we give it some time, and once I've confirmed it works—"

"No, Emrys. I was watching. I know what to do." His tone was sure, hard, accusatory. There was no defensiveness in him. This was assertive, dominant, and hot as hell. But no matter what it was, Galen couldn't go first.

"Ash, say something," Emrys pleaded. "You know how hard this is. Tell him."

"Emrys is right." Ash rubbed and squeezed his hands.

"Be sensible, Galen. He has more experience with the symbols. Come on. You're unsettling Boston."

"Why should that matter? We've all got to go through this at some point." Galen turned down to Boston whose body was even more tense and rigid. "Are you ready?"

He looked too scared to say no, too scared to say anything. He nodded.

"Good." Galen looked up, a quick glance at Emrys before he locked eyes with Ash. "Let's do this." He closed his eyes.

Emrys sensed the formation of a symbol.

"Stop!" Ash shouted. "You're not going to do it right."

Galen halted and opened his eyes, but instead of being curious to Ash's intervention, he looked like he had Ash right where he wanted him. "Why's that, Ash? Why won't I do it right?"

Emrys understood then and that understanding rose on a swift swell of rage. "Boston, get out," he growled, and Boston fled the room. The door closed, sealing them in. Emrys rolled onto his hands and knees, ready to pounce at Ash. "Why did you make him stop, Ash?"

"Yes, why?" Nimue's voice rumbled.

Ash swallowed and tried to maintain some dignity, but it was like it had already been dragged down by lions and torn to shreds. Which is what Emrys was about to do to him. He hadn't torn a Darisami apart before, but with the three of them present he was happy to try.

"I don't know what you mean. Galen is too—"

Galen launched at him, grabbed his wrists and pinned him to the ground. He bore down with all his weight. Ash struggled beneath him, but Galen's face got lower and lower, nearing Ash's until he must have felt his breath on his skin. "You taught Emrys the wrong symbol."

Ash's skin paled three shades lighter than normal. "What? No, I didn't. How would you know?"

"Because you hate Boston. No way would you want him to be exchanged."

"I love everyone." He shoved some fortitude into his voice, but it withered under the blaze of Galen's inquisition.

"No, you don't. I've been with you enough and heard enough to know you have your favorites and your enemies, one of which is Boston. That's why he looked so surprised to be here."

"It's a lie. You've got no proof."

"Oh, really? Then why did you stop me?"

Ash scrambled for an excuse. "For your own safety. I know how much you hate harvesting. I didn't want you to be in danger of killing anyone because you're unskilled."

Galen was still as he faced Ash, an immovable bulk that the Darisami's excuses could not deflect. "Thanks for your concern, but I can take care of myself."

"I didn't do anything wrong."

"If that's so, then I'll choose the volunteer. How about Kaia?"

Ash's eyes rounded, and Galen smiled.

"Thought so." Galen let go of Ash's wrists and climbed off him. He turned to Emrys. "If you use that last symbol, you're going to kill someone. I'm sure of it."

Emrys barely heard him as fired fury blasted his ears with white noise. Ash had nearly forced Galen to commit murder. If he had his gold knife, he would have killed Ash without hesitation. He'd have to do the next best thing. Emrys advanced on Ash and smashed his fist into the lying bastard's face, knocking the Darisami across the room.

Ash lay where he was thrown. He was breathing. A

punch in the face wasn't enough to kill him. And the moment of disorientation was only going to give him time to come up with another plan.

"What do we do now?" Nimue said. "If he refuses to teach us, we're done for. We may as well take a soul and run."

"If we take souls on the surface, we might have a chance to get away," Emrys said.

"Provided the guards don't gun us down first," Galen said.

He laughed. "If they do then——"

Gunned down? Dying in the dirt? Of course! Emrys grinned. They still had one thing left to bargain with. He approached Ash and crouched in front of him. The Darisami refused to look at him, but he didn't have to see his eyes. He only had to listen.

"Do you know what happens when a Darisami dies, Ash?"

He kept his lips shut and sucked on his cheeks.

"Answer him!" Nimue warned.

He lobbed his disgust at her then swung his disdain to Emrys. "All the souls get released, and you turn to dust."

"But that's not all," Emrys said.

Ash sensed hidden knowledge. He furrowed his brow but didn't lose all his contempt. "What do you mean? That is literally all. That's the end of it."

Emrys's smile softened. "It looks like we discovered something that Magnus didn't. When a Darisami dies and all the souls come out, they make things grow."

Fear shimmered through Ash's eyes. "What do you mean?"

Nimue stood at Emrys's shoulder. "He means that the release of energy is beneficial to the earth. Emrys killed two Darisami outside Providence, and where they died, green grass grew out of the dust and dirt."

"I don't believe you." Ash looked to Galen.

"It's true, Ash."

"But don't take my word for it." Emrys put his hand to Ash's chin and turned his head to face him. "In two days, when our time is up, Nimue and Galen will be long gone but I'll still be here, standing in the middle of a field to show them all one last miracle. Because when I did, you and all of Prosperity will know how true it is."

Ash tutted and folded his arms. "You won't do it. You won't sacrifice yourself."

He would. He knew that deep in his soul. Nimue and Galen might argue but he'd force them to seek a new home. They might die on the way, but it was better than starving to death in Prosperity.

"What other choice do I have? You'll have forced my hand. And when it's done, I'll have given Prosperity the one thing you have been unable to provide—a fertile earth. We know that there are rumblings about your effectiveness. We know there are factions that don't agree with exchanging. And we know that people are wondering if they'll ever grow anything useful in those fields. With my death, I can show them just how useful the Darisami can be. Just how useful *your death* can be."

Ash's jaw hinged. "But the Prosperous won't harm me. They lo—" He stopped himself. "They need me."

"And they need us too. The councilors have even decreed it, so what will they think of you when they see me die? When they know you *let* me die in contravention of their wishes? Teach us, and we can live together in harmony. Deny us, and we'll die together in discord."

"Please, Ash. I know you want to do the right thing."

Galen's voice was the softest and gentlest thing in the room.

Ash looked up to him, flickers passing over his face, defeat chipping away at his defiance. He'd worn the same expression the night Magnus died. "Fine. I'll teach you properly."

"How can we trust you?" Nimue asked.

"Because I'll teach Galen first, and he can use Kaia."

Emrys turned to Galen. "Do you trust him enough to go through with it?"

"I do."

As it was, the difference between the fake symbol and the real one was minimal. This immediately primed Emrys to suspect another double cross, but something in the way he taught Galen, the way in which his body and head curved towards him, the conciliatory tone of his voice, the careful way he instructed him, reassured him. Ash's hand lingered over Galen's a moment longer than Emrys considered necessary but there was gentleness in his touch.

For all that Ash had tried to come between him and Galen, Emrys didn't doubt Ash held some small kindness and regard for him. It was hard not to when it came to Galen.

"I think I've got it now," Galen said.

Ash retreated and called for Kaia. She was a striking woman with jet black curly hair and funeral white skin. She was much calmer than Boston had been and caressed Ash's arm in greeting, confident in her special place in Ash's heart. When he asked if she would exchange with Galen, she readily agreed.

She lay down without needing to be instructed,

prepared herself for Galen's touch, and smiled up at him with naive trust. How many times had she gone through this with Ash? How much of herself had she given to him? And how much had Ash given in return?

Galen's forehead was damp with his prior concentration, but he seemed excited to start the process. Emrys scooted closer to him, trying not to crowd but wanting to be near to witness this experience and to sense the formation of the symbols in his mind.

"Are you ready?" Galen asked.

Kaia nodded.

He went through the series of questions confirming her consent, which she didn't hesitate to give. He blew out a long breath. He was ready. He closed his eyes, and Emrys sensed a symbol come into being. As seconds passed, Galen's face gathered more tension, his skin darkened, his veins popped. He paused, held, dominated.

"Easy, Galen," Emrys murmured. "Be careful."

He gave no indication he'd heard Emrys, but a moment later he let go and released the symbol into Kaia's body. She arched her back. Galen maintained his focus and his hold. She screwed up her face, looking as if she were in pain.

Was she dying? Had he got it wrong? He looked at Ash.

The Darisami's attention was on Kaia, worry deep on his forehead. And those lines were a lit fuse to Emrys's panic.

How did they stop this without her dying? Emrys wanted to intercede but didn't know how. He fidgeted, gouging the figure eight into his thigh, the two loops getting bigger. Perhaps if they stopped now, it wouldn't be too late.

But as he reached forward, Kaia and Galen relaxed.

She sank into his arms, and he bowed his head, his body relaxing and curling. She breathed.

Emrys remembered to do the same.

He and Nimue and Ash waited while the euphoria swept through Galen and Kaia. An ease swept into Galen's muscles, an ease Emrys hadn't seen in the whole time they'd known each other, as he was granted a reprieve from stress and strife. He was loose, floating like a leaf down a gentle brook on a warm pre-Fall Sunday summer evening.

Kaia's hand drifted up and blindly yet assuredly sought Galen's chin. She turned his face towards her and raised herself so her lips met his. She planted a gentle, fond, and grateful kiss on his mouth. He returned the beautiful bene-diction.

Ash came forward and scooped Kaia into his arms. He turned to the three of them. "Now that you know how's it done, you're on your own. There are volunteers waiting, or you can find anyone you choose who's willing to partici-pate. But I want you to leave." He didn't wait for them to comply. He placed Kaia on the bed and lay down facing her and brushing her hair with his fingertips.

Nimue fled the room, startling the guards as she exited. They hurried to keep up with her. Emrys picked Galen up and carried him in his arms. He resisted at first, muttered that he could stand and walk, but Emrys shushed him. He wanted him to bathe in bliss as long as possible. Galen slipped his arms around Emrys's neck as surely as if he'd placed a chain around Emrys's weary heart.

He had hope again.

He looked over at Ash and the way he focused on Kaia, how he kept her company, and touched her. One of her hands was linked in his, and he cradled her in his arms like a father rocking his child. His fingers caressed her hair, and he smiled down upon her. For all that Ash and Magnus had done, Ash had created something beautiful.

"Thank you, Ash," he said softly.

But Ash didn't acknowledge him. Emrys left the room with Galen in his arms and the taste of dried leaves and regret in his mouth.

11

Emrys carried Galen to his room and lay him on the bed. He wanted to curl up next to him, but what if Galen roused to find himself where he didn't want to be? In Emrys's arms.

Emrys retreated, picked up a chair, and set it beside Galen's bed. A dreamy smile strayed onto Galen's lips. The ecstasy undulated through him, the caress of only the second soul he'd ever taken.

What a gift that Galen hadn't had to kill to get it.

Emrys wished it was something he could have given Galen before now, something he could have given that would have swept away the mistrust and rancor that had festered over the past few weeks.

But he couldn't dwell in the past. It was filled with too many sins.

Galen stirred and stretched, arching his back like a cat waking from a seven-hour nap. His eyes opened halfway, and a sigh murmured in his throat.

"How do you feel?" Emrys said.

Galen's head pivoted to Emrys, and he responded with

a broader, thicker smile. "Amazing." He breathed out the word. "How's Kaia?"

"She's fine. Ash has her."

"That's good. I'll thank her later."

"I think she'll be the one thanking you," Emrys laughed, "if that kiss was anything to go by."

Galen blinked rapidly and propped himself up on his elbows. "We kissed?"

Emrys chuckled. "Just a small one. I think she was pleased with how things went."

"Oh." Galen frowned then shrugged. "Well, I guess that's all right then." He curled onto his side and extended his hand for Emrys. "Lie with me for a while."

"Are you sure?" How much was Galen's genuine emotion and how much was the euphoria?

"Yes." He patted the bed.

Emrys didn't want to lose his chance so he climbed next to Galen, his scent of sandalwood, sun-warmed leather, and summer evenings brushing Emrys's nose and burrowing into his stomach like a pang of hunger.

Galen draped his arm over Emrys's body from behind, cuddling close. The weight of his arm welcome yet worrying. How long would this last?

Emrys cleared his throat. Maybe Galen needed something to hold on to. He'd distract him as long as he could. "I'm impressed with how well you coped with the symbols. It didn't look easy."

"It wasn't." Hot breath against Emrys's back. "They're all pretty new, and I strained to keep them together, but… well…it's like they were there already, and I just had to fumble my way to them."

Heat from without met heat from within. "Did you ever think you might lose control?"

"Yes. But Kaia's life was at stake, so I had no choice but to hold on. Life is still precious."

"Life is precious to me too." The words leaped from his mouth. He regretted the hard edge to his voice.

"I didn't mean it to sound like that. I know how you feel, but even the thought of taking a life is difficult for me at the moment."

Emrys decided not to argue. This was not about him. He settled back into Galen's hold. "Do you think you can do it again?"

"Absolutely. Now that I know I can take a soul without killing, I'm more willing to do it again. I'm surprised Ash doesn't do it all day."

"Maybe he's worried about getting addicted." He'd known Darisami like that. He'd almost become one of them.

"I can understand how it's a possibility."

Galen stopped speaking. The rush of words that they shared must have dispelled the remains of his rhapsody. Emrys felt it too, the room's energy flattened. Did he regret finding his arms around Emrys? Did he regret how they'd forced Ash into giving up his secret? Emrys hurried to fill the silence.

"How did you know Ash had double-crossed me?"

Galen's arm slid from around Emrys's body, and he rolled onto his back. "He smiled when you said you'd go first."

Emrys turned. "That's it?"

"That was enough to make me suspicious. He knew enough about you to know you'd want to be the hero. It's what you do. But when he brought in Boston, I knew something was up. He's one of the agitators who doesn't like Ash and the way he selects his donors. Offering him to you would have solved two problems at once."

"That was a big risk to take. You put yourself in a lot of danger. What if he hadn't stopped you?"

Galen's lips disappeared into a sad smile. "He wouldn't let me do it. I know how he feels about me, so I was confident of the outcome. As much as Ash wants to play hard, he isn't cruel."

"And yet he was happy to sacrifice me."

"Can you really blame him? You killed Magnus."

"But—"

"Emrys, admit it." Galen sat up and the volume of his voice rose with him. "You did it, and you hurt Ash, and not only *that* you did it but also *how* you did it. Admitting the truth doesn't take anything away from you. If anything, it'd give you something."

Emrys swung his legs over the edge of the bed and gripped the sides of the mattress. A rough wave crashed through him, and he had to breath a few times before it settled. It gave him time to soften his tone but not by much. "So you think killing Magnus was the wrong thing to do?"

"I didn't say that. From what you've said and from what Ash has told me, he wasn't someone I'd ever want to meet. But what's important is that what you did to get to Magnus hurt Ash. That doesn't go away because you say Magnus deserved to die."

"Did he tell you what happened?"

"He did. His version anyway."

"And I bet he has no remorse over any of his actions."

"Don't be so sure." Galen rested his chin on Emrys's shoulder and wrapped his arms around his chest. "If you spoke to him, *actually* spoke to him, instead of berating him, you might learn more than you think."

"He won't listen to me."

"It depends on what you have to say."

"And what do you suggest?"

"Did you ever feel remorse?"

He paused. He'd denied feeling anything for Ash for so long that it was easy to believe nothing existed beneath his anger. But he'd never settled for easy. He knew how he felt about Ash then and what he'd done. Accepting it was another thing entirely. But if he couldn't tell Galen, they couldn't heal.

"Yes." His throat went dry. "I didn't like the way I treated Ash. I thought I was doing the right thing, but it didn't feel like it in the end. And if Magnus found out how to exchange… Who knows what else he could have discovered to benefit us and humanity?"

"Don't let that bother you."

"Why not?"

Secrets crammed into Galen's smile. "Magnus had started the experiments, but Ash perfected the exchange symbol. And even then, it was only after you killed Magnus that he discovered how to make it work."

Emrys's hand closed into a fist. He wished he'd punched Ash more than once.

Galen nudged him. "Don't let self-righteousness get to you. He's dealing with his own demons and that doesn't always mean we act in the best manner." He touched Emrys's chin and turned his face towards him. "I know I didn't."

Emrys stayed very still. He didn't want to prejudice anything Galen said, but staying silent was like tightrope-walking barefoot along a razor thin piece of wire. He had to hold himself still no matter the damage.

"I thought I wanted to do this on my own, but I've learned I don't. And I can't. I thought I could make a better job of it than you, that I could be the hero for a change."

"You're my hero, Galen." Emrys kissed his fingertips.

Galen smiled indulgently and even Emrys heard the corniness of it. "Nice of you to say, but it's not the same. I wanted to see if I could get the secret out of Ash. I thought I knew a better way of doing it. I was going to save us all, but in the end, I fell under Ash's spell as easily as everyone else. And I hated how he was using me to torture you."

"But you did save us. And you saved me. That only happened because you got close to Ash. And only because Ash got close enough to see your goodness."

"I'm not sure he's very happy with me now."

"I wouldn't be so sure. He stopped you from killing Boston. You must mean something to him."

Galen ducked his eyes, and Emrys's heart dropped.

"Do you want him to mean something to you too?"

Galen looked up, a quick flash of wariness before it fizzled and confidence burned bright. "I'd be lying if I said I didn't warm to his affections, but I didn't act on my feelings because of you. I don't know what that means for all of us going forward."

Emrys's chest felt hollow, but when he probed he found everything still where it was meant to be. His love, his respect, his center. Galen was in there as strong as ever, but did that mean Galen felt the same? He couldn't let his fear decide their fate.

"I know I have a lot to atone for to make this up to you, and to the exiles, and yes, even to Ash, but it's my wish that we're able to work together. Perhaps you can find a way to love me, the *real* me, as much as I love the real you."

Galen's smile was pale, like one painted in watercolors. "It's not been easy keeping away from you. As much as I don't like everything you've done and all the lies, there's still this damn feeling that I can't shake, that I want to be with you."

His declaration resonated in Emrys's heart, a sonorous sound that brought his walls tumbling down. Hope swept through him. He placed his hand over Galen's and squeezed. "I want that too. More than anything."

Something shuttered across Galen's face. "But I'm scared, Emrys. I trusted that feeling before, but it was built on so many lies. I'm not sure I can trust it again. Or that I'm willing to." The power faded from his voice.

But Emrys could be strong enough for the two of them until Galen was ready. "But things are different now. There is no need for any secrets between us. We're the same now, you and I."

"That's the scariest thing of all." Trepidation glimmered in his eyes. "Now the barriers have been removed, now we can live honestly and openly with each other, what if it doesn't work out? What if we're not what the other needs?"

"That's a risk I'm willing to take. Are you?"

Galen's tongue licked his bottom lip, and he breathed out and turned his head away. Emrys guessed he had his answer. But as he prepared to get up off the edge of the bed, as he opened his mouth to speak unwanted words, Galen's head whipped round and he mashed his lips against Emrys's, stopping all action, all thought, all heartbreak.

Yes, he had his answer.

Emrys's love for Galen burned through him, made him raw, made him tremble. He blazed with the need for this man, and as the fire erupted in his breast, he groaned, a pent-up guttural sound that revealed the desperate longing he'd tried to deny for nearly a month. Tentative, teasing, testing, their lips parted and tongues stroked. The last time they'd kissed had been back in Providence when Galen trusted him, back when Galen thought better of him. He dashed the thought from his mind and lost himself in Galen's mouth.

When they broke apart, he was panting, a heavy breath galloping out of his mouth, oxygen livening his body and his need. He pressed his forehead against Galen's, hungry again, desperate to taste him.

"Are you sure you want this?" Emrys panted out his words.

Galen's mouth curved like it had horns. "This, and so much more."

Desire rippled through Emrys's body, electrifying his skin, waking all his muscles and pumping blood into his cock. He grabbed Galen with a growl and threw him back onto the bed.

Galen peeled off his tunic, exposing his hard muscled body, the light brown hair on his chest, the dark areolae around aroused nipples, built chest and ridged abs with the dusting of hair from his navel and beneath his waistband. Muscle that was indestructible and as close to eternal as he could ever want.

But Galen didn't let him linger, didn't let him devour his body with his eyes. He slipped down Emrys's body, fingers exploring and delving to grip the waist of his trousers and pull down. Emrys raised his hips, and Galen stripped him naked. He removed his tunic himself while Galen lifted off his shirt. Both of them were hard, but it was Galen's stiff cock that he was more concerned about. Rigid, veined, ready, Emrys shuffled to the edge of the bed and took it deep in his mouth.

"Fuck, Emrys." Galen barked out the words, then twined his fingers into Emrys's hair as he built up his rhythm, his cock sliding in and out of Emrys's throat.

He took him as far as he could, his free hand fondling Galen's balls, before using two fingers to stroke his perineum and inch closer to his hole. Galen's thrusts took on force and he held Emrys's head by his hair and fucked his face, spreading his legs wider so Emrys could push against the puckered skin of his hole. Emrys gave over control to Galen, relaxed his jaw, his throat, his restraint. Galen rewarded him with strangled cries and curses.

All of a sudden Galen froze, then ripped his cock out of Emrys's mouth. "Fuck." His grip tightened on Emrys's hair, making his scalp scream, but he didn't mind. He wanted it more. Galen tensed, backed away so Emrys couldn't touch him, and his cock twitched like it was ready to blow.

Galen breathed out hard. "That was close."

"You can come if you like. I definitely won't mind." The thought of swallowing brought him close too.

"No way." Galen flashed a greedy grin. "I'm going to get what I came for." He pushed Emrys back onto the bed, then leaned over and sucked his cock, getting it good and wet with his saliva. Emrys spat on his fingers and pressed them to Galen's hole, the muscles around it relaxing and tensing like he was kissing Emrys's fingers. Emrys had to concentrate as Galen went deeper and deeper, driving him to the edge when he pushed back onto Emrys's fingers and the first began to slip in. Galen moaned.

"Do you like that?"

"Mmmmmm." Galen couldn't say anything else with his mouth full.

With care and determination, Emrys pressed forward and into Galen, and his back rippled with pleasure. He moaned against Emrys's cock and went slack for a moment while Emrys probed him deeper, gradually stretching him wider. Galen sucked him again. Emrys slipped in another finger, and Galen groaned deep.

He broke, arching his back. "You'd better fuck me soon, or I won't be able to hold on much longer."

Emrys finger fucked him again for good measure, enjoying the effect he had on Galen as he shuffled back further, a sexy curve to his spine and the prominent bulging of his ass cheeks. He wanted to be inside Galen.

Deep inside.

Galen kissed him, his saliva thick and salty, and shifted. Emrys slipped out of him. He straddled Emrys's body and used his hand to guide Emrys's cock to where it craved to be. Galen stilled, his lips held against Emrys's, and he gave a sharp intake of breath as Emrys pushed into him. Emrys didn't move and let Galen control how quick or how slow Emrys entered him.

Inch by breath-taking inch he slipped in, the muscles inside Galen tensing and releasing to allow him to fully immerse himself, the ring of muscle locking over the base of Emrys's cock. He gripped Galen's hips, crunched up as the sensation rode through him, and tensed his thighs to stop himself from shooting up into Galen's ass before he'd had his fill. Even when Galen began to move, it took every ounce of willpower to not plow him like a fertile field.

The slow burn was ecstasy. The two of them moved in sync, and the intensity of Galen's gaze consumed him. With eyes locked, the pleasure coursing through his body was secondary to this moment of connection. The two of them were naked in all senses. There was no longer any need to hide what Emrys was, no longer any need for them to be secret in what they were doing, no council to control them or tear them apart, just the two of them.

Immortal, invincible, eternal and together.

Galen pitched down and kissed him, a long lingering

kiss, that stopped everything else, that stopped Emrys's heart. They had already survived so much; they could survive whatever came next.

"Fuck me, Emrys, and fuck me hard."

Emrys laughed, finding the juxtaposition funny, but wasn't game enough to argue or play for more time. He thrust into Galen harder than ever and watched him writhe, knowing he could not break Galen no matter how hard he tried.

And he was going to try very hard.

❧ 12 ☙

EMRYS KNOCKED ON NIMUE'S DOOR THE NEXT MORNING. Guards accompanied him from the walk from his quarters to hers. Galen's soldiers remained outside his door. There was something comforting about that, something to find hope in.

He'd left Galen to rest, but it wouldn't be long before he was up and they would be put to work. Emrys wanted to stay with him, wanted to make love to him again, but he had to check on Nimue.

Then he'd find a volunteer and go through with an exchange.

The seconds stretched while Nimue kept him waiting. Or at least he hoped she kept him waiting. If she were still alive. Piles of dust could do nothing but keep people waiting. Had she miscalculated how many days she had left? Had something gone wrong? Dread stopped the blood in his veins and snap-froze it into tungsten.

Ten…

Nine…

Eight…

Seven…

He turned to the guards. "Can you—"

Nimue opened the door. Breath exploded out of his mouth, and his blood started flowing again.

"What took—" But he couldn't finish.

She sagged against the doorframe. Dark circles rouged her eyes.

"Nimue, what's wrong?"

She didn't speak but shuffled aside to let him in. He marched into her apartment, the body of a woman on the bed. Metal shards peppered his heart. He slapped his hand over the door sensor, and it slid shut. "What happened?" He hurried over to the woman.

"Don't worry. She's alive."

Her chest rose and fell. He felt for her pulse and found it strong. His touch disturbed the woman into rolling over and waking. Lips smacking, she smiled at him. She was in her early fifties, with a streak of gray hair in an otherwise black mane.

"Good morning, Emrys." The woman stretched.

"Uhhh, good morning…"

"Samantha." She smiled. "Sorry, I didn't mean to stay the night. I hope you didn't mind, Nimue. I'll be on my way." She climbed off the bed and walked over to Nimue, reaching down to take her hand. "Thank you. That was wonderful. I hope I was able to give you everything you needed. And I hope we can exchange again."

Nimue forced a smile. "Yes, thank you, Samantha."

The donor left happy.

"She seems nice."

Nimue grimaced. "She lost a child. I saw it all, felt all that pain. It was…hard to not take it away." She shivered like she could dispel the memories of Samantha's grief.

Had he ever wanted anyone to take away the pain of

losing Sian and Myfanwy? It was excruciating, but it had defined him. "You gave her respite."

"I suppose." She winced.

"What's wrong? Did you not take enough?"

"I took everything I could." She walked away from the door, stumbled a few steps, and sank onto the edge of the bed. She looked hungover.

"Then why do you look so…so…"

"Shit? I've been thinking about that all night."

"Any clues?"

"I think it's growing pains."

He laughed. "What?"

"I'm serious. Exchanging allows Ash to age. Not a lot, but enough to be noticeable over time."

Emrys sat on a chair. "Then why doesn't he hurt when he does it? Or Galen?" He hadn't expressed any pain during the night.

"Ash has been doing this a long time. He's probably used to it. And Galen is only a new Darisami. Growing is natural for them, whereas for me…well, I haven't done it in over four centuries. It's bound to hurt a little. I'm not sure I like it."

"It's better than the alternative."

She looked at him. "Is it? We're giving up immortality and independence."

"I thought you would welcome that. You get to grow, Nimue. You finally get to become the woman you always wanted to be." Excitement bubbled in his chest on her behalf. She could reach her full potential, live the life she always wanted. What was the loss of eternity for the attainment of that goal?

She stared forward into nothing.

"Nimue? What's wrong?"

She looked down at her hands in her lap. "I'm scared,

Emrys. I'm scared of dying."

He knelt in front of her. "You've got a long way to go before then. Ash has barely aged in all this time. You've got many years ahead of you, way more than me."

She jutted her chin forward and scrunched up her nose. "I can see the reason of it; I'm not a child. I'm just not used to being afraid."

"I know, but I think that's part of growing old."

She scoffed and rolled her eyes. "I'm four hundred and forty-one years old."

"Then you should know all about it." He sat next to her and placed his arm around her shoulder. To his relief and delight, she cuddled into him, and he pressed his lips to her head, breathing in the familiar woody spice of her hair. "Does it hurt a lot?"

"It's bearable. It's just unusual. I freaked out at first. I thought I was dying, that I was too late, but it's morning, and I'm still here. I'll feed again today and that might ease some of it. Or it might make it worse. Who knows?"

"Something for you to look forward to."

She looked up at him. "Oh, I think you have to go through it too. You were only twenty-nine when you were made Darisami. There's bound to be some changes."

He wrinkled his nose. Perhaps harvesting was preferable after all.

"Unless you've fed already and I'm the only one blessed with this affliction?"

He chuckled. "No, I haven't."

"Don't leave it too long, Emrys. If we have to make a quick getaway—"

"Why would we have to leave?"

"We should always be ready to leave. Things change. I know that better now than I did before."

Who would he exchange with? Prosperity had no end

of willing donors to choose from. He would find someone soon.

"Do you think we can trust Ash now?" he asked.

"Hard to tell. He was a lot more devious than I gave him credit for, but he has nothing left to bargain. We know how to exchange, he's been backed into a corner and lost all bargaining, but that might be when he fights hardest."

"I'm sick of fighting." The words were out of his mouth so fast he hadn't had time to think them, and they extracted the strength from his body. He truly was sick of fighting. He'd been sick of it ever since Endurance, probably before. He wanted peace, and Prosperity could provide him with that. But it came with a price. And in the grand scheme of things, it should have been easy to pay.

"Then we stop fighting. We trust Ash as much as we want him to trust us."

"Will he believe it?" *Not after the way I've treated him.*

She shrugged. "The mercenary part of me says he's got little choice. The post-euphoria-connected-to-all-humanity part of me says he wanted Galen enough to let you die, so I think he's craving some deeper connection than the one he gets from humans. We forget—because you and I have had each other for so long—that there's some benefit in being with other Darisami. And Ash was always a little codependent on Magnus. As much as Endurance was stifling, I am thankful that I had you throughout those years."

"And Absolon?"

Absolon may have been Ragnar's lover for five centuries, but he'd also meant something to Nimue. He'd meant enough that when he withdrew his love, she'd destroyed Endurance.

She screwed up her eyes, and while she could have easily told him that it was the growing pains, he wouldn't have believed her. She got off the bed and straightened her clothes. "We should go. No doubt they have some work for us to do." She splashed water on her face, and he followed her to the door.

Ash and Galen were waiting.

Ash pulled his hand back from knocking. "Good. You're alive. The council want to meet with us."

"What about?" Emrys didn't have time for this. He needed to find someone to exchange with.

"I don't know, and that worries me." Ash turned and headed down the corridor. Nimue fell in behind him, while Emrys took the back. Galen slipped next to him, and his hand slid against Emrys's. Warmth spread up his arm and enveloped his heart.

Whatever happened next, Galen would be by his side.

"We have received concerning reports about conflict between the four of you. Far be it from us to manage your relationships, but when they put the lives of our people at risk, we must do due diligence and ensure their safety." Diwali spoke from the central seat on the bench. Her countenance brooked no fuckery.

The eleven members of the council were present, as well as the Darisami's guards, but otherwise the chamber was empty. And instead of Ash occupying a separate seat, he stood with Nimue, Emrys and Galen.

Co-accused.

"Who's raised a complaint this time?" Annoyance turned Ash's voice to gravel. His tone wasn't that of an arrogant Darisami who could have killed everyone in this room without a second thought, rather it was the exasperated plea of someone who'd fended off many vexatious complaints.

What trials had Ash been through prior to their arrival? And were any pending that could spell trouble for them?

"Did you or did you not put Boston in harm's way?"

Ash closed his mouth and considered his response. "What did he say?"

"Answer the question, Ash."

"I really don't have to defend myself against claims from jealous people. My record speaks for itself. I have given plenty of aid to Prosperity—"

Finley slapped his palm on the bench. "In exchange for us keeping you alive. Let's not delude ourselves that this is a mutually beneficial relationship, not one that you do out of the goodness of your own heart."

Ash chewed on his cheek. "Be that as it may, I have always worked in the best interests of the people of Prosperity. I have never done anything that would harm them."

Diwali regained control of the meeting. "And yet we have this report that you put Boston in danger after you were specifically ordered to teach the others how to exchange safely. I don't mind admitting to you how disappointed this makes me. I have always been one of your fiercest supporters, but I am also a guardian of Prosperity, and in order for our relationship to continue, we must have faith that it is safe. Your actions, if true, have jeopardized that, and no matter how much strength you give people, it must be built on trust."

"And some would argue that what you have given us has not been beneficial," Finley said.

Galen cleared his throat. "If I may interject, Councilors. From the little I have seen, and from my own experience in Providence, where exploration of the surface was harshly discouraged, I can tell you that Ash has brought you nothing *but* benefits."

Finley swung his hunter's sights to Galen. "But the earth still does not produce."

"That is not Ash's fault." Galen reigned in the emotion that hedged his voice. "That is not even Prosperity's fault but merely the sum of the actions taken before the Fall in damaging the earth, seemingly beyond repair."

"If that is so, then spending all this time on the surface gives little reward, and the terror that Ash's condition—and yours, I hasten to add—engenders within our community is not to our advantage but to our detriment."

"And if the four of you cannot co-habitat peacefully, what chance does the rest of Prosperity have in living with you either?" Joni added from her position at the far right of the lower bench.

"I assure the council that Boston was never in any danger," Ash said.

"How can we be sure of that?" Finley took the lead once more. "Boston said he feared for his life. You may not think that any of our lives are worth much, but they are."

Which lives exactly, Finley did not elaborate. Emrys was certain he did not include Diwali in his sphere of concern. Much like evangelical ministers had never worried about fetuses once they became newborns.

"I take offence at that. All life is precious!" Ash's control slipped, and he lunged forward at the barrier that kept him from the bench and the councilors' throats.

"Only because you need it to feed on," Joni spat.

Diwali banged her gavel. "Councilor, please. We must keep this civil."

Joni leaned forward in her chair to stare down the line at Diwali. "I'll keep it civil when he starts telling the truth. This is deliberate obfuscation."

"We haven't heard anything from that one." A bald male councilor in the back row pointed at Emrys. "Boston told us a great deal about your argument. He said you were the one who was meant to exchange from him, but Galen interceded."

Galen and Ash looked at Emrys. He traced the eternity symbol on his thigh. He could tell them everything. He could tell them how Ash had tricked him into learning the wrong symbols that would have murdered Boston. But if he told them all that, they'd want to know why. Or maybe they wouldn't, and they'd just order all four of them to leave.

Emrys wanted to stay.

And as he'd already told Nimue, he had lost his lust for the fight.

His finger stopped tracing, and he looked the councilor in the eye. "At no point was Boston in any danger. I admit he may have felt that way at times, but Ash treated us fairly and strove to ensure we were working with him, rather than against him. He was testing our commitment to the ideals of Prosperity and did his utmost to ensure that *every* citizen was safe. After all, he is a citizen of Prosperity too, is he not?"

The us-and-them rhetoric had gotten stronger throughout the meeting. Emrys got the impression that many did not accept Ash as one of them but merely a presence to be tolerated.

And dismissed when it pleased them.

Humans were as parasitic as Darisami.

"So you're saying there is no quarrel between you?" Joni leaned back. "I find that hard to believe. You have had many disagreements in the short space of time you have been living here."

"I thought our guards were there for protection, not

surveillance," Emrys said. "I thought I was free to speak my mind with a fellow citizen, no matter how much we disagree. I shall choose my words more carefully in future so your spies don't report incorrect information."

Joni's eyes bugged. "We do not spy on our citizens!"

"I am sure. I only hope that I can count myself lucky to be considered one of them. Or does that right only extend to current humans?"

A few on the council shifted in their seats, glances passing between them. He liked that they were uncomfortable. It was easier to shift their focus from him and Ash.

"No one in Prosperity has any reason to be frightened of us," Emrys said. "We do not want strife. All we want is a home and to make a contribution."

Finley leaned forward and locked his hands together. "Like the contribution you made to Providence? Many of the exiles have raised concerns at your continued presence here."

"And I will strive to make it up to them, but I can only do that if I can stay. I reiterate—thanks to what Ash has taught us—that no human need fear us. We have nothing to gain and everything to lose by going against the wishes of the Eleven. We are sorry that Boston felt unsafe, and we hope we can regain his trust, but Kaia and Samantha have already gone through an exchange with Galen and Nimue respectively, and they are unharmed, healthy, and happy. It is what we would like to give all willing citizens."

"And the quarrels between you?"

"Disagreements that might occur between anyone, human or Darisami, but you have my word that they will not affect Prosperity's equilibrium."

"How can we trust you?"

"How can we trust *you*?" Emrys replied. "I don't know how to impress upon you how much we want to stay. Only you can decide whether to trust us. But you might want to start by removing the guards."

Finley laughed. "You're joking."

Joni showed much less humor. "They're the only thing that's keeping us safe."

Emrys leaned forward and pressed his fists into the bannister. "Our *agreement* is what keeps you safe. I don't say this to frighten you, but your guards can't stop us if we decide to attack. One of us *may* die during an altercation with them, but we are faster, stronger, and deadlier than all of them combined." More than one guard shifted in their stance. Emrys pulled back. "But we don't want to fight. We want to live where we do not have to hide and we do not have to fear. We want to help the Prosperous. Not rule them, not destroy them, but be part of them, because it is in our best interest to do so. Do we have concord?"

"But what about—" Joni started.

"Enough," Diwali bellowed. "We have heard their defense. They conflict with the reports, but the truth is that no one has died, and we have two more people who've been blessed with the Darisami's strength than we had yesterday. That is useful to us. That is useful to Prosperity." She nodded at Emrys. "Let us vote. All those in favor of allowing the Darisami to stay and for the guards to stand down, raise your hands."

Six of the eleven voted with Diwali. Emrys noted the five who did not. They had grown bolder in their dissent. A marked raising of tensions. Was it an indication of tougher times ahead?

"The majority has spoken." Diwali struck the block. "The guards are to stand down and return to their regular duties. We are planning a new mission to the ruins and the Darisami's gifts are required to enhance the foragers' strength. They will attend you tomorrow. Meeting adjourned."

Emrys waited and watched the councilors stand and gather. Two of the five dissenters left the chamber immediately, but the remaining three huddled together with two who had voted to allow the Darisami to stay. They talked, but none raised their voices or shouted accusations. One of them looked at Emrys.

Ash followed Emrys's line of sight, sneered, and turned back to Emrys with the sneer intact. "If you think I'm going to thank you, think again."

"I wouldn't dream of it, Ash." Emrys licked his bottom lip and turned to the Darisami. Ash's defiance remained, probably expecting another argument. "On the other hand, I thank you for giving us—for giving *me*—the gift of the fourth symbol." He moved closer to Ash and felt a frisson through his chest as Ash bit his lip and looked with guarded eyes at Emrys. He sensed all that potential from centuries ago and how he had used it against him. Shame sluiced through his veins, but though it swamped him, his hope for a better future with Ash didn't drown. "Can we talk about this in private? All of us. Away from *them*." He nodded in the direction of the councilors.

Ash frowned, but he nodded and the Darisami left the humans to their plotting.

"THAT WAS CLOSE," NIMUE SAID.

The four of them were alone in Ash's apartments. The guards had been dismissed the moment they left the council chamber and had drifted off to wherever they had come from.

"Closer than it should have been." Galen glowered at Ash.

The Darisami looked away.

"The fault was mine," Emrys said.

Ash flinched at Emrys's gentle tone and admission. His frown softened but his wariness remained. Would what he said next wipe it away, or cement it further? Despite the quiet beating of his heart, the thickening in his muscles, and the drying in his throat, Emrys had to speak.

"I broke your confidence all those years ago. I tricked you into giving me your trust, and I manipulated you into betraying Magnus's location. I lied to you, and whatever justification I felt I had, it doesn't justify how much I hurt you." And Emrys felt that pain clawing at his own chest. "I am sorry for that and for the suffering that you have carried all these years. I understand that seeing me again has reopened a wound that you wanted to keep closed." The clawing stopped and sank its nails into his flesh. The sting gave him something to brace against. "For my heavy-handed nature, for my own failings, and for the wrongs I did you, I'm sorry."

Ash blinked at him. "You think that's enough for me to forgive you?" His voice shook, but Emrys couldn't tell what from. Incredulity? Hate? Did he dare to think it could be anything more?

"I don't expect forgiveness. I haven't earned it. Not even with today's events. But know that I feel it, and it is my hope that in some small way, I have been able to make it up to you so we may at least work together moving forward."

"I…I don't know what to say. I don't know if I can get past it, but…" He looked at his hands in his lap, his fingers wound painfully together. He forced them to separate. They shook, even as he smoothed the pad of his middle finger. He looked up at Emrys. A flash of something dispelled the wariness, something that Emrys had thought lost to the past, but then it was gone, replaced with Ash's resolve.

"I'm willing to try, for the sake of us all and for Prosperity. I know you think I want to keep Prosperity for myself and that I don't want to share the home I've got, but the truth is it has been lonely having no other Darisami around to confide in. The humans can only understand so much." Ash sighed. "But I am sorry I allowed my fear and hunger for vengeance to put us all in danger, particularly you, Galen. I want you to know that I did not lie when I said I'm glad you are here."

"Well, isn't that lovely?" Nimue clapped her hands together. She'd brightened considerably since the morning despite the trial. "I think we can all agree not to try to destroy each other for at least the next few days, can't we? Because there are factions in Prosperity who would rather do it for us, and it would be better if we worked together to neutralize them."

"Neutralize them how?" Ash narrowed his eyes at Nimue.

She held up her hands in surrender. "All within the rules, of course. Our arrival could not help but precipitate a reexamination of the relationship you have with the humans, and the integration of our exiles may have strained that further or given dissenters a banner behind which they could rally."

Ash frowned at her. "I think you'd do well on the council."

She gave him an imperious look. "Only if I can rule in my own right. Now, tell us what you know."

Ash flopped onto his body and lounged back as if the discussion bored him. But boredom often hid discomfort.

"You've seen it all, though today's vote surprised me. I knew three of the councilors were against me, but two of them left the room at the end of the meeting. That gaggle of five is altogether new."

"Then it's intriguing that they should be so frank in their objection to you."

"My gut tells me they are signaling to their supporters that they're ready to be outspoken about the Darisami, considering our increased numbers."

"Are there likely to be demonstrations?"

He shrugged. "Who knows? There were when I first outed myself, but they were largely peaceful rallies, and most of them were swayed to follow the majority who saw the benefits I provided."

"But you've been out for about ten years now, and progress has been slow," Emrys said. "It's unfair to pin the failure of the surface development on you, but for many, it seems that the two are linked."

"And if they knew that a dead Darisami could make the earth green, they'd be pushing for a different approach." Galen's words hung in the air like the dust of slain Darisami. It tickled the back of Emrys's brain and left a chalky taste on his tongue.

Ash studied the three Darisami. Did he think he'd been hoodwinked? "Do you really believe it's possible? I've never heard of anything like it. Nor had Magnus. And if he'd had suspicions, he would have investigated."

Emrys knew that with the certainty of stainless steel. "That's the hypothesis we're working with. The only thing that could have brought the grass to life was the death of Ragnar and Wyatt."

"The release of souls did that," Galen said.

"Same thing."

"But what if they're not?" Galen asked. "If we can

take the soul without killing the human, surely there must be a way of removing harvested souls without killing the Darisami."

"If there is, I haven't any suggestions of how to do it," Ash said. "But that doesn't mean we shouldn't try to find one."

"Perhaps we need to experiment on the plants instead," Galen said.

"I don't think I've ever tried to harvest a plant, let alone complete an exchange." And Ash had experimented on a lot of things.

"It should stand to reason that there's some life force there worth investigating." Possibilities bubbled in Galen's voice.

"It would help prove to the people that we're a force for good," Nimue said. "And it would silence the dissenters once and for all. Should we do this?"

"What do you say, Ash? I'm willing to work together if you are." Emrys held out his hand.

He hesitated, looking from Nimue to Galen to Emrys. He shook his head. "I don't know how you do it, Emrys, but you've managed again to assume control."

Emrys stilled, cooled, and closed his open palm into a fist, but Ash got off the bed and met his hand with his own.

"At least we can all blame you if it goes ass-up." Ash smiled, and that one unguarded, welcome smile melted the ice that had snapped Emrys's heart frozen.

※ 13 ※

The sun was well past its peak, but a cool breeze blew across the land, and Emrys stopped to welcome it. So did Galen and Nimue.

"What's wrong?" Ash asked.

"Nothing. Absolutely nothing." Emrys smiled as the gentle air eddied around him and rustled over the plants in the field. It reminded him that the Earth still turned, that the seasons still came and went, that there was life in the old thing yet.

The wind gamboled as they strolled to the edge of the field with trowels in hand. Workers noted their presence, and a few came to say hello to Ash. They commented on the lack of guards. They seemed pleased, relaxed, and expectant.

Would they feel the same if they knew the Darisami were about to experiment with their crops?

"What do we do?" Ash asked when they were alone.

Emrys spread his palms. "I guess we should pick a plant each, the healthiest we can find, and...test the symbols as they are."

Nimue shrugged. "As good a plan as any."

They spread out and knelt in the dirt. In front of them grew pale green plants with long stems and narrow leaves. Behind them grew nothing. He stuck the trowel into the dirt, giving only the barest pretense of digging the soil, then extended his hand to the leaves of the plant in front of him. He let it hang a few inches away, closed his eyes, and breathed deep.

He summoned the harvest symbol, trying to sense something, *anything*, but all that happened was the wind buffeting against his palm like a cat demanding attention.

He waited, but the longer he stayed in the dark, feeling the prickling of awareness, of human eyes and their curiosity, the more distracted he became. He shook his head to dispel the thought. Let them think what they want. He huffed a sigh, opened his eyes, and placed his hands on his thighs. He stared at the plant. The breeze had gone. Sweat settled along Emrys's neck. He had to try again.

He centered himself, extended his hand, closed his eyes, and formed the harvest symbol in his head.

Nothing.

No response.

Nimue gasped beside him.

Emrys's eyes shot open. "What's wrong?"

She scooted back from the plant but her focus remained fixed and aggressive. "I felt something. Something alive."

"How?" Ash said from her left. "I didn't feel anything."

"Neither did I." Galen peered around Emrys.

"I touched it, and it responded." She shuffled forward again and examined it.

"What are you looking for?" Emrys asked.

"I'm checking I haven't killed it." She turned the leaf

over. "Nothing. It was just a sensation. Or a trick of the mind. Try touching the plant while you make the symbol."

"I was. It didn't do anything," Galen said. "Did you make the symbol, then touch it, or touch the plant, then make it?"

Nimue opened her mouth, stopped, frowned, squinted. "Touched the plant then made it."

They turned back to the plants. Emrys touched one of the rough leaves gently, closed his eyes, and formed the symbol.

He made it just over halfway when something flickered against his fingertips. The symbol brightened. Breath hitched high in his throat then the sensation vanished before he finished the rest of the symbol. He let out a strangled groan, opened his eyes, and frowned at the plant.

What was that?

And could he repeat it?

He pulled his hand back and rubbed his fingertips, then placed them on the leaf. He kept his eyes open. Forming the lines and curves of the symbol, the sensation returned, but it stopped before he could finish, leaving behind a fluttering in the pit of his stomach.

He turned to the others. They all stared transfixed at the plants.

"You all felt it that time, didn't you?" Nimue asked.

"Yes, but it stops." Emrys pressed his palm against his belly to smother his disquiet. "At least it stopped for me before I could finish the symbol."

"Same," Ash said. "It's like it's responding to part of it, but once it reaches a certain point, it shuts off. I was worried I'd killed the plant, but it's still alive."

Galen scratched his chin. "I felt the same thing. But it definitely stopped responding at a certain point."

Nimue stood and dusted the dirt from her knees. "So

what do we think? Plants respond similarly to humans, but the symbols are not right to continue?"

Ash brushed his hair out of his eyes. "Potentially. But the problem then is what is the rest of the symbol?"

"And what does it do?" Emrys had a thought, and it chilled his body. "Can we take the plant's life force, or does it take ours?"

Ash withdrew from the plant.

"What if it works on a similar basis to the other symbols? Maybe there are four that work in a similar fashion to the ones we already have?" Galen looked between Emrys and Ash.

Ash frowned. "Or maybe they work completely differently."

All they knew with any certainty was that the death of a Darisami made grass grow. And the depth of what they didn't know was a bottomless trench on the ocean's floor, a void where light couldn't reach. Darkness and danger dwelled within.

"If we investigate, it could kill us." Emrys got to his feet. "If Ragnar and Wyatt's demise is anything to go by, the earth isn't picky about how it gets the soul-energy."

"What's for certain is we shouldn't be messing about with it all at once. We could have all died," Nimue said.

Ash rose and faced her. "That's a little dramatic, don't you think?"

"Better to be a little dramatic than dead." She tucked her hands into her pockets.

"But considering what we know, that souls can replenish the earth, don't you think we have a duty to investigate?" Galen remained on the ground, staring at the plants as if that alone would force them to reveal their secrets.

"The humans get enough out of this deal already

without us having to put our lives in greater danger." Nimue backed away from the plants but kept her voice to a harsh whisper. "And what if we make things worse? We have the potential to kill whole fields if we go blindly into it."

"But we're not blind, are we?" Galen spoke in a rush. "We can see the potential. Emrys, what do you think?"

He looked between Galen and Nimue. "I don't want you to get hurt."

Galen groaned. "This was your idea."

"I know, but I hadn't fully thought through the implications."

"So it was all right when you were going to sacrifice yourself to get the exchange symbol, but now that I want to do this, you're opposed?" Galen rose to his feet, his hand clutched defensively around the handle of the trowel.

Emrys showed his palms. "They're different. The risks are different. Look, let's take a moment and think about it some more. We've only just learned how to exchange, and I haven't even gone through with it yet. Let's get accustomed to that before running off and changing things."

"I thought you would be the keenest out of all of us."

Not if it meant Galen's death. Emrys closed his hand into a fist then forced it open again. "I can see you're excited about the potential, but all I'm asking for is for us to go slowly."

"What if we don't have the time? Factions are already speaking up against us."

He stepped closer to Galen, conscious of how much his voice had risen. "Then let's not make their job any easier. I'm not saying no, I'm just advising caution."

"Which sounds a lot like you're saying no. What about you, Ash?"

Ash opened his mouth.

"I can guess what you're going to say." Emrys wouldn't be surprised if Ash disagreed with him out of spite.

Ash paused and lifted an eyebrow. "I didn't realize you were clairvoyant as well as presumptuous, Emrys. I was going to say I agree with you."

Emrys almost choked. "You were?"

"Yes. I know how long it took to work out the fourth symbol and the casualties involved. I wouldn't want a repeat of that, so I think we should take things slow. But —" he held up a hand to Galen to stop his interjection— "it does need investigation."

"Agreed. We can't let this go." Galen's eyes were defiant as he looked at Emrys.

"I've got no intention of letting it go." How could he impress upon Galen that he was only looking out for his welfare? But considering their history and how much Emrys had done to ensure Galen was safe—ruled Providence, turned him into a Darisami—perhaps making him aware of that was the problem.

"Ugh. What now?" Nimue said with a roll of her eyes.

Emrys followed her line of sight. A large group of people was making its way towards them from Prosperity. Owen marched at their lead. He looked older than his years, his once-cherubic face lined and creased into one of pent-up rage. The others with him looked no better. Including Boston.

Owen halted in front of the four Darisami, well out of arm's reach. Emrys got flashbacks of angry villagers, the same ones who'd burned down his house with his daughter inside.

"What do you want, Owen?" Emrys asked.

"We heard about what you did to Boston."

"We didn't do anything to him. He's all right. Aren't you, Boston?"

"You almost killed me!" The man showed more gumption in that moment than he had before. It was easier to feel secure when your species was in the majority.

"You weren't in any danger. But we're sorry if that's how you felt." Emrys layered soothing concern over the tight annoyance in his throat.

Owen sneered. "You're a liar, Emrys. All of you. You're trying to assume control of another ark."

"I assure you none of us has any desire to rule." He was mad to have thought it possible before and even madder to have wanted it. "We're just as peace-loving as Ash."

"Him?" Owen's lips unbuckled. "He's drugged more than half the population and turned them into his mindless fanatics."

"You'd know all about that, wouldn't you?" Galen said.

Owen narrowed his eyes. "As would you. Only I was able to escape with my life intact."

Ash stepped closer to Owen, and he flinched. Despite the insults, Ash spoke calmly. "I haven't drugged anybody. I don't force anyone to participate in an exchange who doesn't want it. And it's incredibly safe."

"Oh yeah? What about Larissa?" Boston said from behind Owen's shoulder.

Ash raised his hand to his forehead and traced his middle finger up and down the center of his brow. "Not this again. I've told you. She died of natural causes weeks after the exchange."

"And Hank? And Uma?"

"Yeah, and what about Tyrell?" another member of the mob cried.

Tension returned to Ash's forehead and it brought his shoulders closer to his ears too. "All. Natural. Causes. They've been investigated over and over again."

"People who go through an exchange die quicker than those who don't," Boston said.

Ash sighed and turned to Emrys. "Did you have people this stupid in Providence too?"

"Stupid, are we?" Owen's volume and pitch skyrocketed. "We know the truth, and you and the council are trying to cover it up."

"How many times do I have to tell you this?" Ash sounded like an astronomy professor reasoning with Flat-earthers. "The scientists have run all the tests, they've looked at all the data. Those who've exchanged die no sooner than those who haven't. They do, however, report donors as being happier, stronger, and fitter than those who don't. You just refuse to accept it."

"You mean we refuse to accept your lies."

"I think we're done here." Ash threw up his hands. As far as they were concerned, the Earth was still flat, and as far as Ash was concerned, they were still idiots. "Let's go."

"Not so fast," Owen said. "I stood by and watched while atrocities were committed in Providence—"

"Stood by?" Galen choked on his words. "You committed half of them."

Owen ignored him. "And I'm not going to stand by and let you commit more."

"People are free to make their own choices, Owen," Emrys said. "If they wish to go through an exchange, they can. If they don't, we don't force them."

"But they don't know the side effects. They can't make an informed choice because you drug them."

Ash smiled. "Do we drug them in order to exchange with them, or do they become drugged *because* we exchange with them?"

"Stop twisting my words!" Owen was getting more

agitated. The relative calm of his fanaticism in Providence had given way to rabid denialism.

And Emrys had played a big part in that.

Emrys stepped forward and reached out to put his hand on Owen. "Look, Owen, we're not—"

"Keep away from me!" Owen ducked from him and crowed to his cronies. "Did you see that? He tried to take my soul to keep me quiet!" He whipped around and stabbed his finger at Emrys. "You are evil, and you must be stopped."

If Owen knew how close to harvest Emrys was, he wouldn't test his patience or his control. But Emrys swallowed down his hunger and doused any flicker of the harvest symbol. "Owen, we have the council's backing to remain. We don't hurt anyone. If you'd let me show you, you'd understand that it's perfectly safe. You'll even enjoy it."

He laughed. "As if I'd trust you again. You'd take my soul and kill me and claim it was an accident. You won't get it. It's mine."

Emrys put up his hands and stepped back. "Fair enough, Owen. The offer's there whenever you wish it, but we're done here." He signaled for the others to follow, but Owen kept up and the mob trailed behind.

"That's it. Run away! We're onto you, Emrys. All of you, and this evil will be stopped. You can't just take people's souls and expect us to do nothing to stop you. Everyone will know what you really do, and I won't rest until all of you are banished from Prosperity."

Owen and his gang pursued them inside, taunts and jeers and conspiracy theories and twisted logic twisting Emrys's gut into knots. He forged ahead even as they dogged his heels. When the elevator arrived, the Darisami entered. Emrys faced Owen.

The mob stayed back, though Emrys could have snatched one of them and dragged them inside before the doors closed. He could easily have taken Owen. He could have easily taken Owen's soul.

"Going down?" Emrys asked.

"We are while you're still alive," Owen said.

The mob stayed put, too afraid to be in a confined space with four Darisami. The doors closed, affording them a moment of silence.

"He's a problem," Nimue said.

"Agreed," Emrys said. "Does everyone in Prosperity know we're vulnerable to gold?"

"Yes," Ash said. "It was part of the deal when I came out. I told them what could kill me, so they had some protection."

"Unfortunate."

"Do you think we're in danger?" Ash said.

Emrys shared a concerned look with Galen. "I think Owen will get worse, and if what we saw at the council meeting is any indication, we should be wary."

"I guess it was only a matter of time before they spoke out."

"Speaking out isn't the problem. It's when they start brandishing gold weapons that we really need to worry."

$\mathcal{H}$ 14 $\mathcal{H}$

THE FOUR DARISAMI SEQUESTERED THEMSELVES IN ASH'S exchange room, hopeful that being out of sight would put them out of the mob's fevered mind. But as the discussions revolved around their predicament and what to do about the plants and unlocking their souls, the walls started to close in.

The repetitive summoning of symbols, if only in name, scratched Emrys's skin, hunger's talons digging deeper to scrape his nerves. He stopped speaking then he stopped thinking about anything other than a harvest.

"Emrys?" Nimue shook him.

He pried his eyes open. He hadn't realized he'd closed them or how tightly.

"Emrys, you don't look well. You…" She flinched. "You haven't fed yet!" Panic sharpened her voice to a needlepoint that pierced his chest.

"No, not yet. I've got time. But perhaps—"

She scowled. "Perhaps nothing. You go feed right now. Ash, get him a volunteer."

Worry etched Galen's face, and he leaned over to

squeeze Emrys's hand. "Go on, Emrys. It's time. You won't miss anything."

Ash frowned at him. "You're no good to us dead, Emrys." He gave the name and location of an exchange volunteer, and the three Darisami pushed him out the door.

Why had he left it so long? He'd been so focused on ensuring Galen was all right and then Nimue, that he'd simply found greater comfort in that than seeking his own volunteer. And there hadn't been much opportunity through the rest of the day. He figured he would have time when there was time to spare, but he'd left it dangerously close.

He only hoped he could maintain control of the symbols.

Ash had given him directions to a woman on the third floor, but as he exited the elevator, he caught a glimpse of Trellain and Juliet hurrying down the corridor. Something about the positioning of their bodies, the closeness of one to the other, the bend of their arms and the speed with which they ran, seemed strange.

Then Emrys noticed the drops of blood on the floor leaving a trail behind them. He ran after them and knocked on Juliet's door.

Trellain answered. Blood poured from a gash on his forehead, and his nose and cheeks were bruised. His hand clutched around the handle of a metal rod raised to strike. But when he saw Emrys, he lowered it and invited him in.

"What the hell happened to you?" Emrys came closer to examine the damage but fear streaked down his spine. If Trellain was answering the door… "Where's Juliet?"

"I'm here." She walked out of the bathroom holding a wet cloth. Her hair was disheveled, but she didn't look injured. Emrys turned to Trellain. "Who did this to you?"

Trellain sat on the chair, and Juliet wiped his face of dried and wet blood. "Owen." He hissed as she pressed the cloth to his wound.

"Sorry," she said.

Trellain grunted. "He jumped me when my back was turned, the coward."

"But why?"

"Stop moving," Juliet ordered. "We met Owen and his little pack of whiners at the elevator on the top level. I don't know how he manages to get these people to follow him around. Anyway, they were wound up about something. We tried to get through without a fuss, but he confronted us, saying we were complicit in the deaths of *thousands*—" she rolled her eyes as she said it— "and that we were supporting your plot to take over the ark in exchange for being made into Darisami. He's really lost it this time."

The confrontation must have happened just after the Darisami had left. "And he punched you for that?"

Trellain relaxed under Juliet's efforts. "He punched me because I called him a nothing and a nobody and said that if he wanted to blame anyone for Providence, he should look in the mirror."

"You also called him a cunt. That's when he jumped you."

Trellain's shoulders buckled and fell. "He didn't have me for long, though. He doesn't weigh much, and he was easy to flip. He was on his back before he knew what happened. Then I walked away calmly."

Juliet stopped dabbing at his forehead. "Excuse me? I *dragged* you away. You were about to kick him in the head."

"He would have deserved it too. Might have made an improvement to his stupid face."

"Yes, but then we both would have been torn apart

by his followers. Luckily, there were other Prosperous around to intervene. Next time, we might not be so fortunate."

"You should tell the council," Emrys said.

Juliet's look bordered on patronizing. "I don't think that's going to do any good. His support is growing, and I've seen him recruiting. A lot of people I don't know have been asking me how I feel about you four and whether I trust you."

"And what do you say?"

"I tell them to go away."

"But they keep coming back," Trellain said.

Juliet wiped the last of the blood off Trellain's face. He smiled up at her, and she smiled down at him. Emrys may as well have not been in the room. Gentle and pure infatuation exuded from them. Trellain hooked his arms around her knees. "Thank you."

"Shame I can't do anything about the bruise." She tilted his head a bit, the light catching on the shiner.

"You can kiss it better."

She laughed. "I don't think that'll help."

"I'll be the judge of that."

She smiled and kissed him with a depth of emotion Emrys could feel from across the room. He looked away until they parted, and she sat on Trellain's lap. "Sorry, Emrys, what were we talking about?"

He waved it away. "It's fine. I wanted to ask you something. I've been taught how to exchange and wonder if you'd like to undergo it?"

Juliet and Trellain shared a mixed look. Had they been curious about it? Had they already decided it wasn't for them?

"I promise you it is safe, and it'll speed up the healing process for that bruise. You'll also be stronger for a while."

"Great, so I can throw Owen even farther next time." Trellain beamed like a kid given a BB-gun for his birthday.

Emrys chuckled. "That's a definite benefit. You also get to enjoy a moment of euphoria."

"And what do you get out of it?" Juliet asked.

Her scrutiny made him feel like he was right back in Providence working under her supervision. Only this time he had no reason to obfuscate.

"You replenish my strength, and I get to live for another twenty days, but it's not about me. This is something I want to give to you as penance for what I've done to you and your lives. For what I've taken from you. It's time I gave you something back."

"You don't—"

"I do," he cut her off. "You don't have to deny it. I did you both wrong. This will in no way make up for all of it, but it's a start." That familiar tremor returned to his chest, an uncomfortable exposure to his past deeds and the wish for redemption.

"What do you think?" she asked Trellain.

"We can trust you, can't we, Emrys? We've heard about Boston. Even if only part of it is true, that's still a lot to worry about."

He placed his hand over his heart. It soothed some of the unease. "You have my word. But this is about you, not me. If you say no, that's the last of it." And he still had time to find the volunteer.

Trellain looked at Juliet. "I'm willing if you are."

She turned to Emrys. "All right. Let's do it."

He smiled. This felt right. The tremors stopped, flushed out with a cool excitement glittering with crystals. He asked them to lie down on the floor. There was only one single bed, so he grabbed the cushions and blankets and made it as comfortable as possible.

Trellain offered to go first. He lay down in Emrys's arms. He was a heavy guy, but Emrys easily held his weight. Juliet sat on Trellain's left and held his hand.

He remembered the words he'd heard Ash use. "Now, to be clear, I will take a piece of your soul and energy so I can live, and in exchange, you will experience euphoria and a short-lived increase in strength and vitality. Death is a rare possibility, but I wouldn't do this if I thought I was putting your lives at risk. Do you consent?"

He looked at Juliet and smiled. "I do."

"And you too, Juliet?"

"I'll reserve judgment, if that's okay." She took hold of Trellain's hand and kissed its back.

"It is." He looked back at Trellain. "Are you ready?"

"Ready as I'll ever be."

"Then let's begin."

He breathed deeply and centered himself. He fought to calm the trepidation that had disturbed the waters of his soul. He didn't want to show his reticence or his lack of experience. He needed to be in control and confident.

He held Trellain's free hand so he could maintain a tighter grip. In the solitude and darkness of his mind, he summoned the first symbol, held it steady, then connected it to the second, bringing the energy with him.

He tensed. It was impossible not to.

The first symbol resisted being connected to the second. It didn't like being thwarted from the harvest, especially this close to his end time, and it writhed within the energy of the second. He held firm. This was his mind. He controlled what happened.

He swept into the third, the puerile symbol for splitting, all that energy collecting where it didn't want to be, before connecting to the fourth unfamiliar symbol. His breath hitched a little. Fear, perhaps, the unknown, the terror at killing Trellain when it all went wrong, but he focused and dispelled all distractions, all emotions, all worries, and the fourth symbol blazed with all its might.

It was ready.

He was ready.

He let it go.

Trellain's back arched, and Emrys maintained a strong grip on his hand. He distantly heard Juliet ask if Trellain was all right, her voice shattering, but by the time he recognized it, he was gone, and he sank down as Trellain's soul swept into him, a torrent, a raging river that cascaded through his body on its rapid run, leaving behind mere whispers of the depths of Trellain's soul, catching bright his happiness at being with Juliet and his shame of following Emrys. It didn't linger and while the energy deposited in Emrys, the soul departed, snagging a piece of Emrys's own that it dragged into Trellain.

All tension left their bodies following a buildup of energy that had released and rushed through his mind. He connected deeply with Trellain. Not as deep as a full harvest, but deep enough to recognize him, to want to honor him and his life force, to feel joined in a way that no words could describe.

Trellain moved in his arms, breathed deep and cracked his spine, drawing Emrys back to the moment. His eyes drifted open. Juliet watched them both. Emrys regained enough control to slip Trellain out of his arms and push himself back to allow space for Juliet.

"Would you like to proceed?" In his dream state, Emrys's words had little sound.

She checked on Trellain, felt his pulse, watched him breathe.

"Trust me, Juliet. He's better than fine."

The wound on Trellain's forehead sealed, and the bruising on his nose and cheeks faded.

She gasped. "How…"

"Let me show you." He held out his hand.

She hesitated, a glance at Trellain, then accepted his invitation. She lay in his arms, beside Trellain, and he began.

This exchange required less effort, like he could do it in his sleep. It was faster too. Whether that was confidence, or experience, or the ease granted from being in bliss, knowing he could survive without killing.

Her soul rushed into him, and he found what he expected to find: her strength, her openness, her honesty. He knew Juliet because she lived without fear of hiding. He felt how he'd hurt her when he'd killed Jared. He felt the conflict that raged in her at the connection she had with Emrys, but she couldn't bring herself to hate him. And he felt her sadness over Brink's death but also the disappointment she felt in her herself, that she had wasted so much time on someone who couldn't love her.

But then came Trellain. A man she had never thought of twice, who had riled her when he was a Golden Goon but who she had grown to love over the hard weeks past. She had hope.

She left part of her soul in Emrys, and the rest returned to her body stronger than before. She relaxed and murmured, and the rush came through him, buffeted by the joy at knowing he had eased some of her suffering and made her stronger for the time ahead.

The high didn't last, and a nagging sensation grew within him. A disturbance, a pain that wasn't hard to bear but was persistent and expanding.

Growing pains.

Nimue was right. He screwed up his face. His shoulders

tensed as he tried to dispel the uncomfortable pain. He wanted to get away from it, but there was no escape. The best he could do was hope not to disturb Juliet and Trellain.

He shifted Juliet out of his arms and placed her next to Trellain. He whispered thanks to both of them. The pains worsened.

"Emrys?" Juliet said half-dazed.

"Yes?"

"Thank you for coming to us and showing us who you really are." Juliet smiled and curled up against Trellain. He hugged her tight, his mouth seeking hers, the energy in the room shifting.

Emrys had to leave. But though he could sense their burgeoning need for each other, he relished the warmth in Juliet's words. Yes, he was glad he'd come, and that Juliet had seen him for who he truly was.

$\maltese$ 15 $\maltese$

Every muscle, every bone, every cell stretched, strained, aged, maybe some even died, and unleashed a pain like tectonic plates grating against each other. They shifted through Emrys's body, buckling and snapping with no part of himself able to escape change. He ground his teeth, but the pressure exploded spikes into his jaw and brain. Each footstep sent shockwaves reverberating up his legs, setting off a perpetual chain reaction of earthquakes and avalanches. When he was able to pry his eyes open—and keep them open—he was surprised that parts of him hadn't broken off and fallen to the ground, discarded limbs and chunks of flesh that had shriveled up and dropped away.

His progress was glacial, fearful of moving forward yet even standing still afforded no respite.

He was Pangaea breaking apart.

He was the San Andreas Fault.

He was human.

And it hurt like a bitch.

He steadied himself against the wall and closed his

eyes, but the turmoil inside continued and without a point to focus on vertigo rose up and he tilted off-center.

"Emrys?" Galen's voice ricocheted inside his skull. His arms hefted him up. When had he sunk to the floor? Galen's touch, usually so welcome, set off a wave of nausea. "Are you all right?"

If he spoke, he'd be sick. Violently. It was hard enough to think straight while dying in slow motion.

"Let's get him to his room." Ash. In control. Slight sense of worry.

Or was Emrys projecting?

They carried him to his room and lay him on the bed. Or maybe it was the floor. Nothing gave any comfort, any ease. Nimue had survived it so he would survive it too. Unless this was something else. Unless he'd gotten the symbols wrong. Unless he'd been too late.

"What happened?" Galen's hand rested heavy on his shoulder. The weight of it reached all the way down to his stomach and continued its downward pressure like he was trying to grind him into the dirt. Resisting made it worse. "Was it the exchange? Ash, help him."

"I don't know how. I don't know what's wrong with him." Offense tinged his voice. Like he was to blame. Which he was.

If he and Magnus hadn't been experimenting, they wouldn't have found out how to do this and Emrys wouldn't be dying.

He forced himself onto his back. He could push through this. But moving took an age—took as long as the Paleolithic. He forced his eyes to stay open as every inch of muscle and skin contracted and locked. "It's not Ash's fault." The strain came through his voice. "I'm...getting older."

Galen frowned at him and then at Ash. "What do you mean?"

"Oh." A small smile spread across Ash's lips and grew into a big Schadenfreude grin. "Ohhh. Yeah, I remember now." He laughed. "Sorry. I forgot about that."

Emrys wanted to kill him and watch that smile disappear into dust.

"Forgot what?" Galen asked.

"He's growing. Exchanging allows us to age, but when you haven't done it for a while, your cells are a little out of practice."

"But he doesn't look any different."

"Not to us, but at a cellular level, his body is doing something it hasn't been allowed to do for five hundred years. You didn't notice it because you're new."

"How do we make it stop?" Galen's hand squeezed Emrys's. That should have been something to be thankful for, but the torment was consuming much of his mental energy and the pressure Galen applied was about as welcome as being body-slammed by an overweight walrus in metal armor.

"We can't. Not unless he goes back to harvesting, which isn't allowed. He'll get used to it in time." Ash leaned over Emrys. "Nimue went through this too, didn't she?"

Emrys nodded. It was the easiest thing out of two very difficult things to do.

Ash smiled. "She must be thrilled."

In a way she was. Emrys, however, could have done without it.

"Who did you exchange with?" Galen asked.

"Juliet. Tre—" He tried to force out the rest of the name, but his tongue felt like it had split down the middle.

"Trellain? Are they okay?"

He nodded.

"And Emrys is fine, too." Ash tutted. "Stop being such a baby."

Emrys narrowed his eyes at Ash. Or at least that was the intention. He ended up screwing up his face like an infant refusing to eat pureed lamb and turnips. If he'd had the strength, or even full control over his limbs, he would have taken a swing at Ash. But he stayed put and let the rubble crash through him and break him into particles to be rebuilt again.

"While you're so agreeable, you can listen to our new plans." Ash sat beside Emrys on the bed, dropping his weight carelessly so the mattress moved and Emrys shattered. "Galen and I are going to investigate how to get the crops to grow."

"You—" Emrys struggled to voice his objections.

Ash splayed his hand over his chest and feigned astonishment. "You've made a great decision? Why, thank you, Emrys. We think it's a good idea too."

He growled, but it came out more like a mew.

"Stop it, Ash," Galen said. "And don't worry, Emrys. We'll be as safe as we can, but the fact is the humans need those crops to grow, and if there's something we can do to help, then we should try."

"But what if you kill yourselves?" he said through gritted teeth.

"That's a risk we're willing to take. We won't be reckless, but we're hopeful we can find a way to get it to work."

"Yes, Emrys. You may not have thought much of Magnus's work, but he was methodical in his experiments and he didn't put himself in danger."

Wasn't that the truth? How many times had he let Ash be the guinea pig?

"I don't like it."

"That's fine, but this is what we're doing. You're not in

charge, no matter how many times we keep getting tricked into deferring to you."

"You're not helping," Galen said to Ash. "Emrys, I know you're worried, and I am too, but we have to try. If the dissenters get any louder, we're going to be in trouble. The showdown with Owen plays right into their hands, and we need to prove that we're more than parasites."

"He's right, Emrys. I've managed to keep a lid on hostilities the past decade, but the appearance of three more Darisami—three more mouths to feed, if you like— has put into sharp focus the fact that the humans still can't depend on the earth for their food. Their patience has run out, and the dissenters will fan those fires for their own designs."

"Fine." Emrys couldn't say much more, rhetorically or physically. He knew they spoke sense. He didn't like it though, but not because of what they might discover, but because of the precarious position they were putting themselves in.

That should have been Emrys's job.

Galen was too young. So was Ash. Emrys should have been at the forefront of the charge. Instead, they'd made this decision themselves. He could argue with them, say they could come up with the theory and he was going to put it into practice, but something about the way they had delivered their report told him that would be no use.

He'd been wrong enough times in the past to want to break the habit.

"You mean it?" Galen's face lit up.

"Yes. Let me know if I can help." Like his cells, he could only change a little at a time.

"We will. We should let you rest so we can get to work." Ash stood, but Galen lingered, his hand remaining where it rested on Emrys's side.

Was the pause meaningful? Was Ash's choice of words, the emphasis and repetition of 'we', deliberate? When Galen did start to stand, Emrys channeled all his strength into taking Galen's hand and holding him back, a silent plea for him to stay.

Galen sank back down and turned to Ash. "We can start tomorrow."

Emrys's lips cracked as he bent them into a smile, but the rejection on Ash's face turned it bittersweet.

Ash blinked. His lips tensed. "I guess it is late. See you tomorrow then."

"You can stay too," Emrys said.

Ash stopped.

Emrys's declaration unsettled Ash, but Emrys's body was rebelling enough that he didn't need nor want more unease. He wanted to rest within some comfort until the pain passed. However long that took.

"Are you staying?" Galen asked.

Ash hadn't moved but the crease in the middle of his forehead had deepened, carved with agony and desperation. "Not tonight. I'll let you rest together. Goodbye." And he was gone from the room before either Galen or Emrys could convince him otherwise.

At least Galen stayed. He pulled off Emrys's boots, then his own, and turned out the light. He lay in the space Emrys made with his body, and Emrys draped his hand over Galen's side, holding him close as much as his strength allowed.

But even as happy as he was to have Galen there, the look of loneliness on Ash's face made sleep hard to win. And when he did it was to dream of Ash and Galen.

❧ 16 ❧

E MRYS WOKE WITH HIS ARM AROUND G ALEN AND AN erection he could use to hammer nails. And if the way Galen was pressed up against him was anything to go by, he was willing to be the wall. The thought of following through set off a fantasy that burned a trail from his brain to his balls.

Emrys rolled onto his back and froze, waiting for agony to surge, but apart from a mild niggle in his limbs and a dryness in his mouth, he was free of torment. He sat up, slowly, in case his body was yet to wake and dump a tsunami of suffering on him, but he was untroubled.

"You're feeling better?" Galen rolled towards him.

"For now. How are you?"

"I'm good." Galen smiled up at him and it was one of his familiar smiles, one unguarded and unafraid. One of assurance and enticement.

"We've got to exchange with the foragers today." Galen tucked a hand behind his head, his bicep bulging. "Do you think you can handle it? The rest of us could manage."

"It's better I get used to it, right? I don't want anyone

thinking I'm shirking my responsibilities." And exchanging might ease the pain next time. "When are they due?"

"They're coming this morning, but first…" Galen's finger touched Emrys's hand and stroked a line across the back of it, sending a shiver racing up his spine. "We probably need to talk."

There were many things Emrys needed to do. Talking was way down the list.

"What about?"

"Ash," Galen said. "You invited him to stay last night, or don't you remember?"

Emrys lay down next to Galen and stared at the ceiling, stalling so he didn't have to stammer out his answer. "I remember."

"Well?" Galen shifted so he was looking down at Emrys. "Why did you ask him to stay?"

"He looked like he didn't want to leave."

Galen's smile glittered. "Is that the only reason?"

Emrys chewed on his bottom lip, uncomfortable beneath Galen's bright-eyed interrogation. "I thought it might be nice if he stayed. For you."

Nope, not quite ready to reveal everything.

Galen laughed. "For me, huh?" He lay back down and curled into Emrys's side.

"If you wanted it. I know this is going to sound strange coming from me, but Ash has a lot of love to give."

Emrys had known Ash back when he was young and more than comfortable with sharing his love with many people. Though he was committed to Magnus, the two of them had their own arrangement, one which Emrys had considered merely some ploy to entrap their victims.

But as Emrys had spent time with Ash, he learned that wasn't true. Ash's love was intoxicating, and Emrys had forced himself to deny it in case he had to kill him.

"And you think it's love that he wants?"

Emrys chuckled. "Well, not just love. But you only have to see how Ash is with the donors to see that he's not confined by notions of loving just one person."

Galen bit his lip. "And you? Are you confined by notions of loving just one person?"

The question suspended him in time. He hadn't thought about it before, not when life was hard enough and the scraps of love he'd subsisted on were all he thought he deserved. His instinct was to say he could only love one person, but that was an old condition, one he'd carried from an old time. When he looked back on his life, when he considered who he had loved, he found he was much happier when he didn't restrict himself. He loved Myfanwy, but he'd also loved Lysander as much as he'd cursed him. He'd loved Sian. He loved Galen. He loved Nimue.

And he'd loved Ash but had denied himself the truth of it when he knew what he was going to do to Magnus.

"I've been alive too long to believe that love is so finite and cruel that it must exist in isolation."

"So that's a no, is it?"

He laughed. "Fine, that's a no. What about you? You like Ash, don't you?"

"It's like you said. Everybody loves Ash." Those who weren't jealous of him. "I think you do as well. That's why you asked him to stay."

"Not quite. I felt sorry for him and—"

"Thought you could make it better?" Galen looked up at him. "You'll never change, will you?" But Galen said it with a smile, like he approved.

"I just don't want to fight anymore. So if that means you want to pursue Ash—"

"If *I* want to pursue him?"

He laughed, hoping it didn't sound as anemic as he

thought it did. "Look, I don't hold out much hope that Ash will ever warm to me, but I don't want to stand in your way."

"And what if I want both you and him? Would you be comfortable with that? Wouldn't you want both of us too?"

"I'm not sure that's an option."

"But if it were?"

Emrys felt naked and his instinct was to retreat behind old safe patterns. He knew the answer Galen wanted, and it was the same one he wanted too, but there was something dangerous about saying it aloud, about committing himself to it. There was too much damage between him and Ash to think it could be easy.

He didn't deserve it.

"We should get ready." Emrys turned away and started to climb off the bed, but Galen's hand grabbed him.

"Don't, Emrys."

"What?"

"Don't lock me out like this." The plea burned in Galen's eyes. "I've opened myself up to you by saying I'd like more from Ash while being with you. And I think you want that too."

Emrys's skin prickled with the closeness of Galen's observation.

"I think you wanted to love Ash back then and you wanted to be with him. When you told me about him, it was clear that you loved him. Otherwise, why would you spare him from death?"

Galen's words sliced a long slow line over the surface of his heart, the agony of exposure welling up within him. He wasn't sure he could handle it. "I don't——" He traced infinity on his thigh.

"Please, listen. I think Ash was a step too far. You saved Nimue and you could justify that. She became the daughter you lost. But Ash… He was something else." He took Emrys's hand in his and interlaced their fingers. "I think you thought Ash would come between you and Nimue. You thought you couldn't have both. That you didn't deserve both. So you scared him away. But now you can have everything. You can have us all. Is that what you want?"

Emerald eyes shone their green spotlight on him, brighter than the moon and far more welcomed. Galen saw him, but how deep did that acceptance go? He didn't know what to say, didn't think he could speak. He surged forward and pressed his lips to Galen's.

"I don't know what I want beyond this moment," he said when he pulled back. "And I don't know if I want anything with Ash, even if he wants it. But I won't stand in your way with him. I won't act the jealous lover. And I won't sabotage whatever you want to have with him. If Ash has taught me anything, it's that life is too precious to spend it embittered, and I wouldn't risk your resentment."

Galen kissed him again, thankful, forceful, and resolute. "Thank you. And don't worry, I'm not going to jump him straight away. We have to exchange with the foragers first, and even before then, there's something else I want to do." He laughed, and the dam inside Emrys's chest broke as he followed Galen into the shower.

"You're late."

Though Ash addressed the two of them, Emrys was the one who was treated to his full glare. Galen merely slipped in behind him.

"Sorry," Emrys said. "The foragers haven't been yet, have they?"

Ash and Nimue were the only other people in the room. Nimue fixed Emrys with an appraising look that made his collar itch.

"No, they're late too. They're never late." Ash sat on the edge of the bed, his foot bouncing up and down. He stood again and paced.

"Did you sleep well?" Nimue asked sweetly, and Emrys narrowed his eyes at her. She cackled and rocked in her seat. Galen blushed, and the color flooded from his neck up to his ears. Emrys wanted to lick them.

To distract Nimue from continuing on with that line of questioning, he told her about the growing pains he'd experienced, and they shared notes. She was also keen to see how a second exchange went, whether the pain would be as bad or whether it would show at all. Ash was vague on his recollections.

After about half an hour, a knock at the door had Ash rushing to open it. "Finally."

He opened it to reveal about twenty men and women, dressed in loose-fitting clothes. The ones at the front smiled and returned Ash's welcome as he invited them in, but the last few seemed less eager. They entered, but they kept to the walls.

"Where are the others?" Ash asked. "And what happened to you?" He tilted the head of one of the men, one of those who was reluctant to be in the room. Emrys had missed the gash on his cheek and the darkening skin around his nose.

"We're the only ones willing to be donors," a woman said. She had dark brown hair and a solid, strong build. She looked like she competed in decathlons.

"I'm still not decided," the one with the bruising said.

Ash frowned at him. "Why? Forager teams usually have thirty in them. Does that mean the others aren't going?"

"Oh, they're going," the woman said, "but they've been listening to the complaints put out by that refugee. What's his name?"

"Owen?" Galen asked stonily.

"Yeah, that's him," she said.

"What's he been saying?"

"That you three aren't to be trusted. We got into an argument. That's why we're late. Him and his morons intercepted us and said we were all brainwashed traitors who you'd end up killing."

"Thorn, you believe them?" Ash asked the guy with the bruises.

"No, but…it's worth considering. We don't know these other Darisami very well, and Owen comes from

Providence. He's got stories and they're not…comforting."

Emrys tried to keep his muscles loose, but every one of them contracted, from the soles of his feet, to his asshole, to his armpits and scalp. He should have killed Owen long ago. Now he'd never get the chance.

"Did Owen also tell you he was one of Emrys's most devoted followers and was quite happy to persecute anyone who didn't believe he was an angel?" Galen said.

"No." Thorn hung his head. "No, he didn't say that."

"Typical." Galen took charge like a captain settling restless troops. "Look, everyone, I know this is all new, but we mean you no harm. You are perfectly safe with us. No bad will befall any of you for being a donor, but we understand if you would prefer only to work with Ash until you get to know us more."

The small group against the wall looked relieved, but the woman who seemed in charge was having none of it.

"Bunch of wimps. Kaia and Samantha have been fine, and I saw Juliet and Trellain earlier. We don't have time to waste on this weakness." She stepped forward and offered her hand. "Emrys, my name is Nadja, and I'll be your donor if you'll have me."

She was forthright, forceful, determined, a real leader who cut out the bullshit. He liked her. "It would be my honor."

He shook her hand, and she gave a relaxed smile.

"Right," Ash said. "Let started."

Emrys and Nadja took up a position at the far end of the room. Nadja's declaration pushed the first donors to assign themselves to Nimue, Galen, or Ash while the others waited, almost as if they were forming a line at a barber's.

Even Emrys had an audience.

But he couldn't focus on them. Nadja deserved all his attention.

"Thank you for speaking up," he said.

"Thank you for giving me this gift. I can't stand people making judgments without gaining their own experience." She dropped her voice. "To tell you the truth, I want to get out of here. Being stuck underground makes me claustrophobic."

He knew the feeling. "Have you been on many expeditions?"

"Lots." Memories filled her smile. "They're hard work, but every time I come back, I can't wait to go again. I know what you give us is magical, but it's what I can do with the power that I crave. I guess I'm addicted to the adrenaline, but I also know I'm doing good. We bring back so much that we can use. I'm so grateful that Ash did what he did. It's allowed us to do so much, and I've seen more than most."

"I am honored to give this to you."

"Thanks. Now let's get on with it."

Having an audience scrutinizing him and Nadja for any adverse effects made the exchange slightly harder than the ones he'd been through the day before. But he managed, and Nadja's soul swept into him, giving him a taste of her life, of the ruined world she loved, the adventures on which she thrived.

He experienced her joy in travelling as far as it was possible to go and her desire to reach farther. She was an explorer like those of old, making discoveries that their people had never known. She was the start of a whole new age of pioneers, of humanity crawling out of its cocoons in search of something greater. What world would they discover?

The euphoria washed through him and replenished his

strength. He held her until he could be sure of his control, then laid her down to rest alone. He dreamily moved to a clear space, his head floating on his neck as it lifted to address the waiting foragers. "Who's next?"

He didn't take their hesitation to heart. They could accept what he was offering if they wanted it, but if they didn't, that was fine too. He was happy either way.

Blissfully happy.

Eventually, a man lay beside him. They repeated the ritual of consent, and the second exchange went easier than the first.

As did the third.

The growing pains stayed at a distance. Or if they came upon him, he was numb to them. Either way, he was thankful, suspended in the largesse suffusing him. He didn't have to worry about the exchange going wrong. The fourth symbol was stable, and the risk of harvesting minimal. He was more at risk of turning them into a Darisami than killing them, but even that worry was abstract, distant, unemotional. He exchanged. He felt joy. He connected. He moved on.

And finally, they had whittled down to the last forager —Thorn.

Nimue and Galen and Ash were done. Thorn could have his pick of any Darisami, but he'd waited for Emrys. Thorn swallowed hard, his glances furtive—or perhaps anxious—yet determined.

Emrys held out his hand. "Are you ready?"

He nodded quickly. If nothing else, Emrys would be able to heal his injuries. He sat in front of Emrys, but when Emrys encouraged him to lay beside him, he refused.

"Do you mind if…if I lie in your lap?"

Emrys blinked at him, and in his groggy state, it felt like it took an eternity for his eyes to open and shut.

"Whenever I've been with Ash, it's made it easier. Made me…calmer. To be held."

Emrys was about to ask why he didn't go with Ash, but Thorn had made his choice. "Of course. Whatever works best for you."

Thorn gave a shy smile. For such a strapping guy, he seemed incredibly gentle. No wonder Owen had picked on him. Thorn spun around and nestled in Emrys's lap. He opened his shirt to expose his chest, picked up Emrys's hand, and placed it on his bare skin, pressing it down on his sternum, on his heart, and closed his eyes. He kept his hand on Emrys's.

Emrys went through the questions to gain consent. Although Thorn answered with his eyes shut, his voice was steady.

The exchange began.

When Thorn's soul swept into him, he saw why Thorn had been so reticent. That was his nature, to be swayed by others, to doubt himself. Owen's words—though he knew them to be wrong—had been persuasive, and Thorn had questioned what he'd already experienced. He was open to other possibilities, but in the spur of the moment, he lacked the ability to discern what was fact and what was fiction.

Watching Emrys exchange with the others had reaffirmed his belief—his certainty—that what he underwent was a good thing, that the Darisami were good, that this was not only necessary but decent and pure.

That openness served him well on his explorations as a forager. While Nadja was all force, he was considerate and had saved her than once from a rash decision.

Behind those memories, into his childhood, were the loving parents who were meek and mild, who had befriended Ash many years before they learned he was anything but human. When his revelation came, they did not allow it to wipe away all they knew of him. They weighed his confession in quiet reflection while others had been quick to fear and judgment. Thorn missed them. Being held in Emrys's arms brought him some revival of that old joy.

When the exchange was complete, Emrys's eyes fluttered open. The wound on Thorn's forehead closed, the skin healed, and the only blemishes were the tears running out of his eyelids. Emrys bent down and kissed him on the forehead. "Thank you." He lay Thorn down to sleep.

He looked around the room. The Darisami were the only ones awake. Everyone else was on the floor, some entwined together, all floating in euphoria. Emrys's eyes landed on Nimue's. The strain on her face was evident. The growing pains had arrived.

"We should leave," she said to him.

Even if the donors could regain full consciousness, they didn't need to see him and Nimue in pain. They might worry. He got to his feet and took hold of Nimue's hand.

Galen rose up to meet him. "Do you want me to come too?"

Emrys smiled. Bless him. He could barely hold his head up. And while it would be sweeter to pass the pain with him, he didn't want to bring Galen down. He kissed him, a kiss that lasted for an unmeasured eon and would have lasted longer if Nimue hadn't tugged on his arm, causing an aching spasm.

"Thank you, but I'll be all right." He looked at Galen, at the clouds in his green eyes, at the stars twinkling behind them. "You stay. You stay with Ash."

And he meant it.

He left the room with Nimue, not yet feeling the full effects of the growing pains but knowing they were coming. She hurried him, the vice on his hand squeezing harder, and they burst into her room.

She dragged him to the bed, climbed on, and pulled him to her. She lay down and aligned him with his chest against her back, draped his arm over her, and snuggled in tight. She held onto him, and he held onto her. She was warm against his body and her warmth fired his heart.

She's Nimue. Not Sian.

But he was thankful all the same.

And even more thankful than when the pain rolled and churned and crushed him into oblivion.

❧ 18 ❧

Emrys and the Darisami attended the foragers' departure an hour after dawn broke. Many Prosperous were there as well, bathed in the gentle warm light amid the gray and brown and yellow. But the light also exposed divisions.

The thirty foragers had split along the lines of donors and Abstainers. That was the name Emrys had heard whispered in the early morning.

Abstainers.

But while the distribution was obvious, the difference in their abilities was stark. The donors had more energy, more pep. They looked invincible.

The Abstainers looked troubled.

"I know." Ash stood beside Emrys, frowning at the foragers. "I gave them the opportunity first thing this morning to exchange but they refused."

"What do you think will happen to them?"

Ash flicked his hair back behind his ear. "Hard to say. I can't remember the last time a full forager team went without exchanging. I hope their pride doesn't push them into doing anything rash. We don't want them trying to prove something."

Ash saw reasonable people. Emrys saw walking corpses.

The foragers' sleds and wagons were packed and ready to go. The councilors conducted a small ceremony, thanking the foragers for the work they were about to undertake for the good of everyone, and wished them a safe journey.

Nadja, Thorn, and a few donors thanked the Darisami for their gift. That simple act of thanks before commencing their mission lanced the fear in Emrys's heart. Not fear for themselves but fear of being blamed for their failing. He was a part of this. He had helped make this good thing happen. And no one had died in the process.

Perhaps not everything he touched had to die.

"Where are you going this time?" he asked Nadja.

"South."

Towards Providence.

"Why?"

"The north is getting too cold for us at this time of the year. There's little to bring back other than memories. From what you and the others have reported, there is a good amount between us and Providence that can be of use. We've neglected it of late."

"Stay away from Providence. Promise me." He said it fast, like he was swerving to avoid a car crash.

"We won't go that far. I've no desire to meet anyone who would turn you away." She clasped his forearm in farewell then called out for the foragers to start moving. They pulled their carts, the donors already edging into the lead. Emrys watched them depart.

"There go more fools you've brainwashed with your poison."

Owen's voice speared Emrys between his shoulder blades. He and the other Darisami turned around. Owen was flanked by a small group. Their mouths were harsh gashes, their eyes unrelenting spotlights, their presence hostile.

"If the Abstainers die because of your lies, I'm holding you accountable," Emrys said.

"More threats!" Owen raised his voice. "Did everyone hear this monster threaten my life?"

Shouts of assent from his gang followed, their raucous noise stopping other Prosperous on their return to the city.

"What's going on here?" Diwali stepped beside Emrys and forced herself into the conversation like a mother hen facing off against foxes.

"This thing threatened me." Owen pointed his finger at Emrys.

If he kept leveling his fingers at Emrys, he'd find them snapped off. Emrys tilted his head to the side, wanting to pop the bubble in his neck, but the joints crunched instead and he got no relief. "I can assure you, Councilor, I've done nothing of the sort."

"Liar." Owen hopped up and down on the spot, throwing his arms wide as if to distract people with his arms instead of the truth. "All you do is lie. These people heard it."

They shouted their agreement. His display was clearly working for some.

"Diwali, he's stirring trouble," Ash said. "Owen's lies are the reason why ten of the foragers left without an exchange. Of course, it's their choice, but they're going to find the journey harder than usual."

"I was wondering how that happened." Diwali pursed

her lips and addressed Owen and his gang. "Citizens, return to the city. If you have complaints, you can bring them to the council, but I won't have people thinking they can intimidate others simply because they're different."

The group booed and hissed, and the venom in their response forced Diwali to step back. Out of fear or surprise. Probably both. Such open dissent was clearly not the way of things in Prosperity. He flicked his gaze to Ash and worry prickled its way down Emrys's throat.

Lost for words, Diwali tried to ignore the mob and walk towards the city, but their jeers and taunts followed her.

"Monster-lover!"

"Traitor to her species!"

"Dead woman!"

Diwali kept walking until the mob lost interest and swung their attention back to the Darisami. Owen swaggered to the front. He'd changed since Providence…or perhaps he had always been this hate-filled and now it had burst free. Emrys had tolerated the sniveling worm in Providence and showed him mercy when what he should have done was take Owen's soul the moment he laid eyes on him.

Now he was stuck with him.

"We won't be silenced, demon. We will stop you from seizing power at every opportunity. We will not let you drag us into another reign of terror."

Emrys crossed his arms and let a smile lick his lips. "Unless you get to benefit from it, right?"

Hellfire blazed in Owen's eyes. "I never benefited from anything."

"Oh no? What about all that love and adoration and power? Looks to me like you're doing the same thing here."

Owen lifted his chin to look down his nose at Emrys. He raised his voice too. "Nothing's the same. I've woken up to how you blinded me in Providence, and it's my sacred duty to stop your evil from infecting another ark."

"Come on, Emrys," Galen said. "I'm sick of listening to him. He was nothing then, and he's nothing now."

Owen marched on Galen, getting close to his face, far closer than he dared to get to Emrys. Had he forgotten Galen was just as dangerous?

"What would you know of being nothing?" Owen said. "Son of a councilor, captain in Security, first priest, first favorite, first everything. And now you think you can be first in Prosperity too? You sicken me as much as he does." Owen stalked back to the mob and punched the air. "Down with the Darisami!"

They echoed his cry, chanting it as they returned to Prosperity. People got out of their way and stared after them, confusion and disgust rife on their faces. But how many times would the people hear it before they agreed?

Next time, it might not be Owen who walked away but the Darisami.

***

Emrys's natural instinct was to hide from the conflict that Owen was fomenting. Hearing 'monster' shouted through the halls brought back flashes of the night Sian had been killed when the villagers—when his community—were willing to commit bloody murder on him and his daughter. If he could shut himself in his room, he could avoid the name-calling and keep the chill of fear from freezing his spine.

But the Darisami agreed that they should be seen as much as possible. For too long, they'd been creatures of the shadows, hiding from the moon and hiding from humans. It was no wonder Owen and his group were so quick to hate.

Despite Prosperity being Ash's home since the Fall, he seemed the most disturbed by Owen's performance. As if his rhetoric had undermined Ash's self-confidence. He had his ardent followers, but even so, the vehement way Owen spoke against them was unsettling.

They scattered throughout Prosperity, inside and out, deciding it was best they spread themselves through the city and integrate into its population.

Better to look less like a gang.

Less like a pack.

Less like a threat.

Nimue and Ash remained inside the ark while Emrys and Galen headed for the surface. There was no construction needed, so they were put into the fields. They chose opposite ends even though Emrys wanted to be beside Galen while he experimented.

Galen said he'd be careful and discrete, but they were mere words. He had no marked territory to explore, no map, no inkling of the danger, no way of knowing if he was about to plunge into death's abyss. But Galen fixed him with a look that dared him to argue, so Emrys didn't.

Instead, he joined the humans and plowed fields at a steady pace, working in time with them, stopping when they stopped, talking when they talked. He'd been playing human long enough he had no problem falling into the charade. It was only when they rested after hours of toil and they looked like they'd run a marathon in fifteen minutes that he realized he wasn't puffed. He could have kept going. He could have done everything himself.

But that was the Emrys he was trying not to be. The one who assumed control because it was easier, because he thought he could, because he thought he *should*. He let himself relax into their company, and they welcomed him. They shared with him and smiled with him and became one with him.

Most of them had been donors before and those who hadn't didn't show any resentment or reticence. They merely hadn't yet taken the opportunity. They intended to, but there had always been a reason to delay. Nothing sinister. Nothing antagonistic. Nothing mistrustful.

"I'd be willing to exchange with you any time you wish. You only have to ask," he told them.

They thanked him and said they might would one day, but that wasn't what they needed. They thrived on pulling together, on working together, on being together. An exchange could enhance that feeling, but it wasn't essential. They were already connected.

If only the Darisami could have exchanged before the Fall. If only they could have connected more people to the mysteries of the soul, to feel that energy, that sense of oneness that he had taken for granted. The euphoria was a physical rush, but it was also metaphysical.

And now it didn't come with murder and guilt.

But whether these people ever came to him to be exchanged—those who'd done it previously, those who'd never done it—didn't matter. They were citizens together. And the more he worked with them, the more he shared with them, the greater their bond. Owen could try to break it, but it wouldn't be from a lack of Emrys putting in the work to bring them together.

The day ended, and they returned to the ark. Galen met him on the way back. "No success."

The peace that Emrys had experienced from a day of toil evaporated. "Did you spend the whole day experimenting?"

"Not all of it. There was work to do. I didn't want people to become suspicious. But I tried different things throughout the day."

"And?"

"Some recognition, but I can't push it past the point where the line cuts through the curve. You know the spot I mean?"

He nodded.

"It's taunting me, but no matter which way I turn, it shuts down." Galen massaged the back of his neck, his hand kneading at the knotted muscles, but if it bought him some ease, it didn't extend to his face. The skin around his eyes held onto his frustration like it was a life-raft.

Emrys smoothed his hand across the back of Galen's shoulders and dislodging his hand. Galen relaxed beneath his touch. "Don't worry. If it's meant to be, it will happen."

"I hope so." His voice lost some of its strain. "How was your day?"

Emrys told him about his aim to create more of a connection with the people, but he hadn't finished when Juliet and Trellain found him and interrupted. Their faces were rigid with tension.

"What's wrong?" They were already inside the entrance tunnel of the ark, but he could see farther down to a large gathering of people. They stood staring at the wall as workers washed it.

"One of the Abstainers painted the walls with the words 'Death to the Darisami.' He's been detained, and they're cleaning it off," Juliet said.

"Is it safe to keep going?"

People had already caught sight of them.

Trellain shrugged. "I guess but be warned that the way you threatened Owen this morning has made things worse."

"Threatened?" Galen said. "He did nothing of the sort."

"But that's how it's being presented, and he has a lot of friendly ears and friendly mouths who like what he's saying."

Galen swore. "Little toad. I can't believe people are listening to him."

"Why not? Owen has a good story to tell, and he's found a ready audience." Juliet bent back the middle finger on her left hand, pulsing it until the knuckle cracked. She then shook out both hands. "Look, I know what you do is safe, and it's got its benefits, but I'm wondering if you should all give it a rest for a while."

Shivers raced up his spine and spread out across Emrys's shoulders, gathering weight, gathering tension, gathering doubt. "Is that what people are saying?" He shifted from his left foot to his right foot, but the pressure on his shoulders didn't move.

"Some of them."

"Even people who support us?"

"No, but the ones in the middle think it's a good idea. They're saying if it's going to cause this amount of conflict, maybe you should be rationed."

The weight grew heavier and compressed his lungs. "Ridiculous. People must see we're not a threat and that can't happen if we starve ourselves. We have to feed eventually, and this is the safest way of doing it. But we need to be seen more. We need to connect with everyone better."

"But there's only four of you and a lot of Abstainers. How can you compete?"

"By convincing one person at a time." Emrys walked deeper into the tunnel and passed the half-wiped off graffiti, passed the people and their stares, and tried not to think of the one word that remained: death.

$$\text{\ae}\quad 19\quad \text{\ae}$$

Juliet was right. There weren't enough Darisami to counter the effects of Owen's Abstainers alone. For every person he spoke to, Owen's group infected fifty. Emrys enjoyed working in the fields and interacting with people, making and solidifying connection, but anti-Darisami sentiment was spreading like a contagious disease through an anti-vax enclave.

Fewer people wanted to talk or work with him. Some even put down their tools and reassigned themselves elsewhere, whether out of prejudice or out of fear that the Abstainers would target them.

Fights had erupted between those who were fiery about expelling the Darisami and those who saw nothing wrong with them. The Abstainers didn't like anyone abstaining from an opinion either.

Emrys kept working.

As did Galen, but his experiments yielded no results. And what was originally meant to be a project that Galen and Ash worked on together soon became one that all four of them were assigned to. Emrys tried to tell himself that it had nothing to do with feeling safer locked away together. He countered it as much as he could and forced himself out to talk to people well into the night, suffering the jeers and taunts of the Abstainers as they pursued him, catching the fear and apprehension in the eyes of those who wanted to avoid unpleasantness.

The one bright spark was that a rival group had galvanized in support of the Darisami. It was comprised of donors, Juliet and Trellain among them, as well as Kaia and Samantha and some of the exiles. It proved to Emrys that having a personal connection with people was going to be their greatest defense.

Yet his personal connection with Owen was at the root of the problem. That bond had twisted into something ugly. Whenever Emrys saw him, he was always in the midst of his followers. If Emrys went close, he started on his tirade, and Emrys had to leave.

He continued his mission throughout Prosperity, as did the others, until the city settled, and the Darisami came together to experiment. If they could unlock the souls stored within themselves and use them to replenish the earth, could anyone deny that they were doing good?

But the experiments came to nothing.

Galen had smuggled a plant inside for them to work on in private, and while it stayed alive, it also stayed silent and static. Emrys carried that disappointment with him through the cries and jeers the next day and the next, through glorious sun-soaked days while the earth baked but yielded nothing.

On the fourth day after the foragers' departure, Emrys walked back to the ark after the tilling was done—but the hard work continued. More people had to be convinced.

The Darisami supporters were growing in numbers, but protests were limited, and clashes were infrequent.

So far.

Only the diehards had abandoned their posts to protest. The council hadn't yet clamped down on either side, and from what he'd been told, they were unlikely to. The security forces were small and untested, and the council was divided on what should be done. Some claimed the suppression of one group should equal suppression of the other.

A smear of black oil remained on the wall inside the tunnel, a reminder that it had once said 'Death to the Darisami.' The long march down the tunnel felt like a procession to the guillotine, with expressions of guilt or pity lobbed his way. He kept his eyes forward. He'd get back to his room, shower, clean himself of the dust and dirt, then return to walk the ark's corridors to extol the virtues of a Darisami–human partnership. The good will Ash had developed over the decade was eroding, and Emrys took it as a personal failure.

"Emrys?" A woman tapped him on the arm, having come up behind him while he was lost in his thoughts. She smiled a wary smile.

He stopped and tried to put a name to her face. Brown hair, green eyes, tanned skin. *Anna.* They'd worked together in the fields a few times, shared a few conversations.

"Hi, Anna. How are you?"

"I'm fine." Her smile shuttered. "Actually, no, I'm not fine." She laughed nervously. "I don't know why I said that. I…uh…I have been feeling very tired lately. It's been ages since I've had an exchange, and I was wondering…I mean to say…" She swallowed the words and her indecision. "I'd like to volunteer for an exchange. Now, if you're free."

Emrys's heart lifted, and a smile stretched across his face, so big it started to hurt. "Of course. I'd be honored."

She let out a long breath and her shoulders relaxed. "Thank you." They started walking. "I've been meaning to see Ash—"

"Would you prefer Ash?"

"No, no, that's not what I meant. I was going to say I've been meaning to see Ash, but I didn't get around to it and I thought I could work through this…tiredness. Then you showed up and things have been a bit fractious, but with everything that's going on…if you have to stop exchanging, I'd like to get in before you do."

He halted. "What makes you think we'll stop?"

"That's what people have been saying. It's not true?"

"Not unless someone has made the decision without telling us. Who's been saying it?" As if he didn't know.

She shrugged. "It's something that's going around. They're saying you're going to start rationing the numbers as punishment for people speaking out against you and that we have to…offer…something extra to ensure we were chosen." She placed her hand on his shoulder and stroked his arm in jerking movements, like he was covered with bumps and jagged rocks.

Emrys frowned at her touch. He shouldn't have been surprised that Owen was so adept at spinning disinformation, but he was disappointed that people had been so ready to believe it.

"Oh, sorry. Should I have not said anything?" She snatched back her hand from his arm and fluttered it at the base of her throat, a rapid tap-tap-tap spelling regret and fear across her face. "I really do need to exchange."

Her distress was clear, torn between the fear of the unknowable Darisami and the bone-deep concern for her own health. Owen had caused this needless conflict.

If I ever get my hands on him again…

"Anna, whoever told you this is lying." His voice came out gruff and he hoped she took it for unyielding conviction and not his fury searching for a target. "I have no intention to stop exchanging, and you do not have to offer anything. This is of benefit to us both, but I'm not going to do anything without your consent. Do you wish to go through with it?"

She relaxed her shoulders, and her smile softened. "Yes, yes I do."

"Good." They walked together and made small talk, but Emrys's answers soon became monosyllabic. The lie had to have come from Owen and the Abstainers sowing more mistrust and false information about the Darisami and their deeds. His lies were destabilizing the ark, but Owen didn't seem to care.

Emrys couldn't even kill him because that would only prove what Owen had been saying was true.

That the Darisami killed everything they touched.

'Death to the Darisami' persisted in the background. The volume increased as he and Anna exited on the floor of his apartment. They rounded a corner, and the sight of chanting demonstrators hit him in the chest. At least fifty people blocked the corridor that led to the Darisami's quarters, all clamoring, all shouting, all working each other up into a fever pitch.

Anna stopped short. The color drained from her face, her pale skin taking on a deathly pallor.

"Come on. I won't let them hurt you."

He'd fight every last one of them if he had to.

He broadened his chest and walked with his head high. The Abstainers shrieked when they saw him. They didn't charge, but they made it difficult for him and Anna to pass. Their noise filled his skull. It was hard to discern one sound from another, to unpick the words from the mayhem. He caught some of them though, cries of 'Whore!', of 'Traitor!', of 'Unclean!'

He gripped Anna's hand, but they'd only reached halfway when she ripped it out of his grasp and disappeared back the way they'd come. He tried to follow, calling out to reassure her, but the crowd surged and cheered at the loss of his 'victim.'

He saw Owen's face among the crowd, his smug, vicious grin far enough away that Emrys couldn't get him without breaking the people apart. The harvest symbol flashed inside his mind, wanting to be freed, wanting to cut away this obstacle—*all* these obstacles—but he didn't release it. It was just as well the zealot was out of reach.

He forced his way through to the corridor that led to his apartment. The crowd didn't fully extend down it. At least there was that. At least they respected some privacy. But the Abstainers weren't there for the Darisami. They were there to ensure other humans weren't foolish enough to attempt an exchange. They had shoved a cork in their supply, and their throats were parched.

He knocked on Ash's door, and the Darisami let him in. Galen and Nimue were also present.

"Did they give you any trouble?" Ash asked.

"They scared off a donor." Emrys told them about Anna, including the rumor that they would deny citizens unless they received sexual favors.

"Gross." Galen wrinkled his nose.

Nimue's expression mirrored his. "Thankfully, none of my donors have suggested such a thing."

"I should hope not." Emrys paused. *Donors? Plural?* "Wait, you've been exchanging?"

"Yes. A lot. But it's getting harder to sneak them away from the crowd." She said it so matter of fact. Like she was talking about inviting people over for coffee, rather than what it felt like, which was more akin to breaking people out of a maximum-security prison.

"What do you mean 'a lot'?" Ash asked.

"I exchanged with about six yesterday."

They stared at her. *Six?* Had they heard correctly? Greed streaked down Emrys's gullet.

Ash frowned, and Emrys had never seen the lines so deep on his forehead. "You went searching for them?"

"No, they found me. Hunted me down in fact."

Ash looked like he didn't know what to make of this information. "Who…who are these people?"

Her shoulders bunched up to her ears, and she splayed her palms, moving them as if she balanced their souls in her hands. "I don't know. Women mostly, a few men, some children." Her patience was waning.

"But…but…why you?"

Poor Ash. He wasn't used to being second favorite.

"Why not me?" Nimue's eyes pinged wide. "It may have escaped your attention, but you three are, for all intents and purposes, men. And adult men at that. I am much less threatening."

Emrys snorted, and she cut him with a glare. Despite her ire, and his slight envy that he wasn't so similarly sought after, he was glad for her. He didn't know if the more she exchanged, the faster she'd age, but if it did, he wanted that for her. And he understand why citizens would think she's the less threatening out of the four of them.

He hoped they never had cause to discover the depths of her ruthlessness.

"Anyway," she said, "it's not going to matter how many people seek me out if the Abstainers scare them off. What are we going to do about them?"

"Right now, I'd gladly harvest Owen's soul," Galen said.

Ash scratched at his sternum. "Get in line, but we have to control ourselves. Anyone dies, and we'll be run out of Prosperity."

"About how many citizens would you say you've exchanged with, Ash?" Emrys asked.

"Probably half, if that."

That meant about six thousand citizens who didn't have any experience with Ash on which to base their hate. "Why so few?"

The muscles in Ash's cheeks tightened. "There's only one of me, Emrys. I don't need to exchange all the time, and not everyone has been willing."

Emrys caught the scent of Ash's defensiveness. There'd been hints of the real reason scattered throughout Prosperity, lingering in the expressions of the citizens, and now it was time to deal with it. "Do you have favorites?"

"What are you implying?" Ash flexed his fingers, ready to run.

Emrys was ready to chase, but not wound, not kill. "Nothing, but I'm trying to gauge the size of the opposition and what they have against you."

"If you're looking to assign blame, you should look at your own actions. Owen's problems stem from the way you treated him." Ash's voice tried to deflect, to circle around so Emrys would take a different track, but he was wise to the move. And he held onto the rightness of his pursuit.

Even so, he had to be firm, and his voice reflected that strength but also his concern. "I'm not disputing my role in all this, but Owen's found fertile ground in which to grow his complaints."

"There have always been people who don't agree with what I do. That doesn't mean I'm at fault."

"No, but perhaps you could have done more work to bring them over to your side."

"*More* work?" Ash's lips retracted to the verge of a snarl. "Have you any idea how hard it was to *not* get kicked out of this place once I came out? Pretty fucking difficult. And it was because of the relationships that I had invested in over the years prior that I was able to stay."

"I'm not attacking you, Ash." But he had wounded him in trying to get closer to the truth. "I'm trying to find out where the problems—"

"I am not a problem, Emrys. If anyone's the problem, it's you. *You* brought these people here. *You* created that zealot. Not me."

"Ash. I'm sorry." Emrys sighed and eased back. He'd chased Ash into a bolthole, but he couldn't be allowed to stay there. "I didn't mean it to sound like I was blaming you, but we have to face facts. A big contingent in Prosperity didn't like you before we got here, perhaps one larger than you realized. That discontent out there is not new."

"And that's my fault, is it?" Ash folded his arms across his chest.

"It doesn't matter whose fault it is. We need to find a way to fix it, or we're all going to starve. Can we agree on that, please?"

Ash huffed out a jagged breath. "Fine."

Emrys smiled, for Ash's relenting and for himself at having brought him out. "Thank you."

But now that Ash had accepted Emrys's assessment, it left him little to hide behind. He was exposed and he looked wretched because of it. "I didn't mean to have favorites. It just sort of happened."

He put his hand on Ash's shoulder and squeezed. "I know. And you're lucky there are so many people who want to be your favorite, and I get that it made it easier, but now we have to do the hard work."

"And it's good that there are four of us to share the load, right?" Galen gave an encouraging smile.

"Okay." Ash didn't seem all that convinced, but Emrys let him wallow. He'd probably never suffered the brunt of an angry mob before. Emrys envied him his inexperience.

"Right. Suggestions for what we can do?" Emrys said.

"We need to get the council back on board," Nimue said. "They need to take control of the situation. They've been missing in action."

"That's because there are councilors who want us to fail," Galen said. "They're playing a waiting game to see if the problem gets sorted for them."

"But how soon before someone gets the gold from the armory and opens fire?"

It was a miracle it hadn't already happened.

"I'll go and demand a meeting with the council," Ash said. "We have that right."

"I think we need to continue what we're doing by being seen by as many people as possible," Emrys said. "They need to know we're not a threat."

"What about exchanging in public?" Galen asked.

"Risky," Nimue said. "The Abstainers might try to stop people getting through or disrupt the ceremony."

"But if it's out in the open and protected by those who support us?"

"More preaching to the converted, though. We need to convince those who are on the fence."

"Though it wouldn't hurt to address the larger crowd and invite people to come forward. Anna can't be the only one. Others must need reassurance. They may want an exchange."

"Very well. I'll talk to Diwali," Ash said.

"And we'll start exchanging in public," Emrys said. "Who knows? It may be wildly successful." But even as he said it, his heart squeezed with the worries of all that could go wrong.

★ 20 ★

It took two days for the council to meet. The delay had Ash worried. The fact that when they did meet, more than half of the councilors stared at the Darisami with open hostility worried Emrys more. The way the meeting progressed did nothing to allay those concerns or quiet the turbulence in his stomach.

"The policy has not changed." Ash's voice belied his weariness at repeating for the tenth time in response to the tenth asking about rumors regarding sexual favors in exchange for souls. "Whoever wants to be a donor can be a donor. We do not ask—nor would we accept—anything beyond the exchange of souls."

"And yet we hear that sex is frequently part of your ritual." Finley occupied the central seat on the lower bench. The councilors had moved since the last time they'd convened. Diwali was in the back row, far to the left.

Ash splayed and stretched the fingers on both hands, straining them as he took a breath. "That is nothing but heresy and innuendo. Sex is not part of the ritual but merely an occasional byproduct with willing and consensual participants." He closed his hands into fists. The veins on the back of his hands popped. "And I am rarely one of the participants."

Galen intervened. "Councilor, everything we do during an exchange is done with consent."

Finley's eyebrows popped and he blinked three times in rapid succession. "Is it? You have been in Prosperity how long? Two weeks? And before that, you killed our kind without restraint. You may think our lives mean little, but the council has a responsibility to ensure that everyone is safe."

"And they are," Ash said. "The only thing that's putting them in danger is this dissent."

"Why? Because it upsets you? Because it angers you?"

Ash's hair had fallen in front of his face. He brushed it back, his fingers getting tangled in the ends. He gave a sharp tug but didn't register any pain. "You're twisting my words, Councilor. Citizens are being harassed because they want an exchange or voice support. Why has the council done nothing to control these dangerous elements in Prosperity? They are the real threat."

"A real threat to your diet. You've told us that you need our life force to survive, but how do we know that's true? And if it is true, why should we go on feeding you when it puts our lives at risk?"

Ash gaped at the councilor, his lips working to form an argument, but nothing emerged. Favor had turned on Ash, and he was not used to it. Emrys had much more experience with fickle and short-lived humans.

"Since when have any of you been at risk?" Emrys spoke with as much authority and strength as his voice could carry. Conciliation had its limits. The Darisami were fighting for their survival, and he'd be damned if he'd be a casualty after getting this far.

Finley considered him, his gray eyes still and assessing. He didn't answer. Joni, sitting to his left, tapped him on the forearm, and he ceded to her.

The small, feral councilor took up the fight, adopting an overbearing mother pose, faux concern brimming in her watery eyes. "People frequently tell me they feel strange and unwell after going through an exchange, and that those effects don't dissipate."

Emrys shifted his attention to her. "Which people? Who are they? Specifically."

"I'm hardly likely to divulge my sources, am I? Who knows what you might do to them? They also have concerns about the long-term effects."

"Such as?"

"Well, the effect on children born after an exchange." She scrunched up her face, her cheeks ballooning like she'd eaten rotten lemons, her words acid, her thoughts rank, her outrage calculated. "They appear different, and there is an increased incidence of deficiency among them."

Her words crawled up Emrys's spine, each one puncturing a hole in his flesh that made him twitch and tighten. "That is a lie, and you know it."

"Do I? Do *you*? Your abilities have never been fully studied, but your presence and power have far-reaching consequences. Look at the people who support you." She meant it figuratively, because no one had been allowed into this closed session of the council. "They are increasingly violent and quick to anger. Not to mention they are stronger than they would be if they hadn't been interfered with. Many of those who disagree with you have ended up in the hospital from being attacked when they were simply expressing their opinions."

Emrys's chest squeezed around his lungs, wringing them of air. What was happening? No matter what argument was put forward, there was always another crazier one to back it up.

"Councilors, can we please stick to the facts?" a young Black man on the council named Quinn said. "The only fights I have seen are those started by the Abstainers."

"Of course you would say that." A smile flickered across Finley's lips before it vanished, but Emrys had seen it. "You are well known to frequent Ash for exchanging, and one wonders what favors you have granted him in return for such a thing."

Quinn beat his fist on the bench. "Watch what you imply, Councilor."

"There is no need to raise your voice, Quinn. Unless it's a side effect of the exchange." Joni smirked, less concerned at hiding where her loyalties lay.

Diwali stood from her place on the sidelines. "Councilors, this squabbling demeans us all. I think we can agree —can we not?—that Ash has provided a great service to Prosperity over the years, and we would not have made such progress without him."

Finley leaned back in his chair, in control, and strummed his fingers on the bench. "Really? How can you be sure? Our people work in the fields, yet nothing of use grows, while he lolls about in bed taking our souls and fucking our people."

"He cannot make the earth fertile!" Diwali shouted.

"Then what good is he but to give us false hope? It is my opinion, and that of the people I represent, that the entire exchange program should be halted and undergo extensive investigation."

Ropes knotted themselves around Emrys's stomach and spleen, strangling any positive feeling for life in Prosperity and leaving him with an intense nausea. *Investigation?* From there it was only a short step to experimentation. If they survived that long.

"Councilors, we need this as much as you do," Ash said.

"Wrong." Finley leaned forward. "You need it far more than us. And if you can't accept scrutiny of what you do, then perhaps you should leave."

"I am a citizen as much as anyone else here." Ash's voice was loud, firm, steady, but if he was feeling anything like Emrys, his insides would be quaking. Could it all come undone so easily?

"Really? You aren't human. The arks were made for humans, not soul-eaters. We can survive without you, but you can't survive without us. That makes us different. And that makes us in charge."

"I am appalled by the language I am hearing," Diwali said.

"And I am appalled at the lack of oversight that the council has given to ensuring the safety of *human* citizens. It has gone on far too long, and it is time we voted."

Emrys licked his lips, his gaze flicking from one member to another. He had to speak, but he was worried that if he opened his mouth he'd retch. He shoved the bile back down his throat. "Councilors, you are no doubt aware we have undertaken many public exchanges over the past few days to large groups of people. They have witnessed the benefits that it provides humans as well as Darisami." Although he and Nimue had limited their demonstrations due to the growing pains. It wouldn't help their cause for people to see them writhing in agony. "The public gatherings have been successful—"

Joni burst from her chair. "This morning fights broke out!"

"Because the Abstainers attacked." Emrys crushed his

own hand to stop from shouting. "It's only through our supporters' reasonableness that no one was hurt. But the public gatherings have been successful. People have seen that no harm comes to them. Surely it stands to reason that they should continue."

"No, it does not," Finley said. "The long-term effects must be studied, and we can't do that if exchanging continues. I suggest we have a cooling off period of two months—"

"Councilor, we can't—" Ash blurted.

"*Two months* so the consequences of prior exchanges have worn off completely. We will then test all citizens and assess them for permanent damage."

Damage. Not effects.

"All those in favor?"

Emrys watched as hands went up, more hands than stayed down.

"The ayes have it. The soul-eaters are hereby forbidden from exchanging with any human for the next two months on pain of expulsion or execution. Meeting adjourned." Finley banged the gavel and rose from his seat.

Just like that, it was done. Runaway trains were easier to control. What was strange was how numb Emrys felt, not angry, not vengeful, not even disappointed. Just… numb. Like it was an event too momentous for his brain and heart to comprehend, like the end of the world.

The councilors stood. Those for the ban left the room, while those against it came forward to speak with Ash.

"After all I've done for this city—" Ash started.

Diwali scratched at her palm, over and over. Her eyes refused to settle on any one Darisami. "We understand, Ash. This is not what we want either, but things are tense right now."

Ash stared down the councilor. "I know they're tense, Diwali. Abstainers have camped outside our rooms, and no one has done anything to clear them. Now we're banned from doing what we must do to survive. You have signed our death warrants."

She patted the air with both hands as if that would be enough to make things better. "Easy, Ash. We'll fix this. Once everyone's calmed down a bit, we'll move for another vote. Let's take this opportunity to disperse the crowds, then we'll work with them."

Her ridiculous suggestion, her *politician's* suggestion, brought some of the feeling back to Emrys's body but his blood remained cold. "With all due respect, Councilors, they aren't interested in being worked with. They're zealots and cannot be swayed from their position."

"We must try regardless."

"And in the meantime, what happens if we starve?"

She didn't have an answer; none of the supportive— yet ineffective—councilors did. He sensed an invisible shrugging of their shoulders. That would be one way to remove the dissent—remove the Darisami. The councilors left, but Diwali lingered behind and lowered her voice. "They can ban exchanging, but we can't watch every citizen all the time." She exited the chamber.

"They know how often you have to feed, though, don't they?" Nimue asked.

Ash stared after the councilors. "Yep. Every twenty days."

"And they've given us sixty. We're fucked, aren't we?" Galen said.

"Only if we play by the rules," Nimue said, but she didn't look pleased about becoming a killer again. The ability to age suited her.

Ash roughly brushed back his hair. "They're well-armed with gold, and even if we were able to take control, we'd lose a lot of the city's support in doing so."

A slow-to-wake panic warmed Emrys's blood. "Then we'd better figure out how to make the earth green again," Emrys said. "Or else we're dust."

THE OFFICIAL ANNOUNCEMENT FORBIDDING EXCHANGES came through the public address system the next morning, but the Abstainers had been celebrating through the night. Soldiers were deployed in full kit, but Emrys and the Darisami didn't know whether their weapons contained gold bullets or the regular kind. Considering that an Abstainer beat up a donor right in front of a guard, it seemed safe to assume that they were not there to keep the peace.

The Darisami continued with their experiments, continued with their mission, continued to be visible, but the more they were seen, the easier it was for them to be targeted.

Even out in the fields, Emrys couldn't avoid the Abstainers. A group followed him everywhere, Owen always among them. From constant companion to constant accuser.

Sanctioned by the efforts of the council, Owen saw nothing wrong with standing in a field and calling for him to stop whatever evil he was doing, whatever poison he was putting into the earth. According to him, it was because of the Darisami that the earth didn't grow anything the humans could use. The Darisami, and Emrys in particular, must have worked their wicked magic to strip the earth of its fertility.

Funny. Salem's ruins lay five hundred miles away.

The soldiers did nothing, so Emrys was forced to ignore the complaints and condemnation. Some farmers remained close, those who believed the Darisami delivered more positives than negatives, but the Abstainers outnumbered them three to one.

Where were all the prior donors? Why didn't they come to the Darisami's defense? Why didn't they speak up?

They were out there. But when they got a fist to the face for not cursing the Darisami, why should they stick their neck out and risk injury or death when the soul-eaters could defend themselves?

Emrys understood. He didn't like it, but he understood.

He plowed field after field, staying beneath the blazing sun until it went to its bed and twilight came, and, when the moon emerged, he shone like a beacon. The diehard protestors stayed, but others faltered, forced to find food, to ease the straining in their throats, to replenish the fluids they had lost through sweat and spit. Maybe some of them got heatstroke. Maybe some of them would die.

Another thing he'd be blamed for without enjoying the relief of their souls.

Emrys kept working, shining away in the field, a target for their contempt. He ignored them as best he could, but he looked up when their cries took on renewed energy and noise. The crowd didn't part, but it shifted to accommodate the arrival of Trellain, Juliet, and a group of supporters.

He speared the hoe into the dirt and watched as they

jostled their way through the Abstainers, not stopping to fight. They kept their attention on Emrys.

"Are you going to stay out here all night?" Juliet asked.

He shrugged. "What else is there to do?"

At least out there, he wouldn't have people begging for an exchange. No one had done it yet, but there had been questions and longing looks. The other reason he remained was so the Darisami could continue their experiments with the symbols. They were due soon. The plant in their quarters was still alive, but the walls had been getting too close. And yet the crowd might make it impossible to work. He was likely to let his hand slip while the harvest symbol was live and accidentally-on-purpose take an Abstainer's soul.

"You can fight this decision. You know it's wrong."

The jeers continued in the background.

"I know it, but they don't." Emrys nodded at the Abstainers. "They've got what they wanted."

"That doesn't mean it can stay that way," she said.

"Look, I understand, but us fighting too hard will encourage them. We're working on it, but we need time."

Juliet crossed her arms. "Well, while you take time, there are people here who are fighting for you and getting hurt on your behalf. You know that right?"

Emrys grimaced. "How badly hurt?"

"What?"

"How hurt are they?"

"A few have ended up in the hospital. No one's been killed. Yet."

He told himself he was just concerned for their well-being and not stuck on the thought that a life could go to waste when his kind needed them. "I know it may look like we've given up, but trust me, we haven't. We just don't want people to fight our battles."

"You were fine with it in Providence."

He snatched the hoe out of the dirt and shoved it back deep. "No, I wasn't. I never wanted that. But whatever happened in Providence is behind us, and it's a lesson I've learned. We are doing our best to make this right."

"And in the meantime? They want to see you, Emrys. All of you."

He spread his arms so more light caught him. "We're here. We're always here. Working beside you. Pitching in. Doing our bit." Unlike the Abstainers who seemed to have been granted dispensation to avoid their chores.

"That's not what they want from you."

"It'll have to do for now. If we exchange, we're in trouble, and that's not going to help anyone long term."

"More plotting?" Owen walked up to them. Emrys hadn't noticed his approach beneath the noise of the crowd. He was bolder than before, coming into their midst, and his bravado encouraged the crowd to trample the earth and swell their support behind him. "This is why we can't let down our guard," he shouted to the people, and they shouted their agreement.

"Go away, Owen," Juliet said drily, like he was nothing more than a gnat pretending to be a wasp.

"I have as much right to stand here as you do, Juliet." He got into her face, but Trellain pushed him back. Owen didn't have the element of surprise this time and with Trellain being bigger, broader, and tougher, he backed down, but not by much.

"Still believing the lies, are you, Trellain?"

The former soldier didn't speak, and his imposing silent presence, a hard stare that didn't shift from Owen's, even unsettled Emrys. He had no doubt that with all Trellain had been through, all the shit he'd done and endured, he wasn't going to let Owen get to him again, or to Juliet.

Owen swallowed, unnerved. Most of his followers

couldn't see the bob in his throat, but Emrys did. And Emrys smiled.

"Get lost, Owen," Juliet said again. "We're talking, and you're not welcome, here or anywhere."

His eyes flared in the reflected light of Emrys's glow. "You think you can boss me around? Me?" His voice cracked then soared up in pitch. "Look at who I have behind me." He swept his arm over his gathering of misfits. "You have no one. No one."

Emrys sighed. "That's enough, Owen. Why don't you take your people inside? They need their rest. They can hassle me tomorrow."

He tried to sound concerned, but there was a dismissive edge to his voice that hit Owen hard, like he'd struck a match and Owen had caught alight. "You can't get rid of us that easily. We won't rest until you're out of Prosperity. You and all your brainwashed fools."

Emrys cracked his neck and ground his jaw together. As much as he wanted to stay outside, as much as he had work to do, Owen and his people wouldn't be deterred. The Darisami would have to stick to conducting their experiments indoors. In the distance he saw three shining lights. Now was as good a time as any to leave.

"Come on, Juliet. It's not worth it."

Emrys hefted the hoe and marched back towards the entrance, through the crowd, toward Darisami companionship. He'd gone maybe ten steps before a fight broke out behind him, as the two groups met each other and clashed. In among it all was Juliet and Trellain, but he could only make out part of the scene as faces and bodies writhed in shadow.

He crashed into the fray, hoping to separate the two rival groups. He roared for them to stop while he charged for the center. Nimue and Galen and Ash interceded behind him and broke up the scuffle, more shouts rising behind him, but he continued to the middle, to where Trellain and Juliet battled Owen. He arrived to catch the flash of light on a metal blade before it sank into Juliet's stomach.

Trellain caught Juliet as she fell, Owen's hand still on the handle of the knife, an ordinary knife, not made of gold, but still made to be lethal. Blood dripped black from its tip. He froze and stared at Juliet as she collapsed into Trellain's arms. The crowd continued to rage and the moment of shock on Owen's face morphed into one of wicked and opportunistic triumph.

Emrys grabbed Owen by his shirtfront, the shock of Emrys's speed shattering his elation. Juliet forgotten, his battle forgotten, everything forgotten except that Emrys was a Darisami and his touch was deadly. Owen was too terrified to struggle.

Good. Time to end this.

Emrys hoisted him into the air. The harvest symbol blazed in the front of his mind, fed by rage, fed by the immolation of his false cloak of impotence. Owen's soul was his to take.

Mine. Mine. Mine.

Owen's soul would taste of mercury and triumph. All he had to do was let the symbol go. It had been too long since he'd taken a soul and slaked his thirst.

"Emrys! Help her!" Trellain's voice shattered his fury.

What was he doing? He couldn't kill Owen. But neither could he drain his rage so quickly. He growled and, with a strong arm, threw Owen far from him and the damage he'd done. Where and how he landed, Emrys didn't care. He hoped he'd broken something. He rushed to Juliet's side.

The crowd's noise lessened. Perhaps some had run

away, but those who remained closed in, watched, pleaded for his help.

"You heal her, Emrys." Trellain was determined. "You heal her now."

"It's okay." Juliet gasped. "I'm going to be okay. Don't worry. Don't get in trouble for me." She grunted, hand pressed against her wound, blood weeping between her fingers.

Emrys's head snapped up. There was too much of an audience. He needed space to concentrate. He needed privacy. He'd only get one chance to do this. Decision made, he bound to his feet.

"Bring her."

Trellain hefted her into his arms and followed Emrys to the closest building. Emrys hurried them inside and ordered the others to not let anyone in.

Ash grabbed him. "If you exchange with her, you'll be arrested."

"Let them try." He slammed the door and the first symbol blazed into existence.

❧ 22 ❧

Spectators packed the council chamber. He stood
alone before the councilors, but he didn't feel alone.
Owen's Abstainers occupied seats behind his left shoulder,
but the Darisami supporters packed the rows on his right.
When the summons came early that morning, the two
camps set up on the Darisami's floor picked up their
protest and moved it to the meeting.

It was so early, in fact, that not all of the councilors
were present, but try as Finley might to start proceedings,
Emrys refused to speak until all eleven had taken their
seats. The supporters made enough noise that it was
impossible to continue. Even the presence of the guards
and the threat that they would be used wasn't enough to
quell their protests.

Owen's Abstainers raised their voices in protest for the
meeting to begin which added to the chaos. It should have
made Emrys jittery, but seeing the Abstainers so evenly
matched with the supporters pleased him.

As did the corner Owen had backed himself into.

The four councilors who supported the Darisami

showed up fifteen minutes after Finley had declared the meeting open. They glared at their fellows on the bench.

"Now that the other councilors have deigned to join us," Finley shouted above the din.

The crowd quietened a little, enough for Diwali to speak.

"And if the honorable councilor had informed us more than five minutes before this meeting was called, we would have been here sooner. The councilor is on notice for his lack of respect for this office."

Finley sucked his teeth. "If I may proceed, we have a report that Emrys the Soul-eater exchanged last night in direct contravention of the council's orders. Therefore, he and the other soul-eaters should be banished."

Cheers erupted from the Abstainers. Boos from the supporters.

"Who am I accused of exchanging with?" Emrys had spent centuries devouring the souls of councilors and criminals, priests and pretenders, lawyers and liars. He could argue with Finley and the rest of the Eleven.

"Juliet, one of the exiles."

"And what proof do you have? Has she made this claim?"

"Multiple witnesses saw you take her into a building on the surface while she was unwell. When she emerged, she was whole again."

Emrys frowned deeply and scratched his head. He enjoyed a little theatrics every now and then. "Unwell? What do you mean unwell?"

The councilor stilled.

Diwali leaned forward in her seat on the back bench. "Yes, Finley, what do you mean by unwell?"

He flicked his hand, but Emrys's words were made of

spider web. "It doesn't matter what I mean. Did you exchange with her?"

"Why would I exchange with anyone? It has been banned. As for your so-called witnesses, what would they know of it? What have they said? Were they inside with us when this alleged exchange was meant to take place?"

"They claim she was injured, and you healed her injuries."

He inclined his head, deepened his frown. "So she was injured? Not unwell?" The more obtuse he was, the more Finley's face reddened.

The councilor laced his hands together, keeping his index fingers extended. He pointed them at Emrys. "Don't play coy with me. You know exactly what you did."

"I do. I also know what I didn't do, and I didn't exchange with Juliet. Is there any proof?"

He glowered then pointed at Juliet. "You. Stand up."

She did, smiled sweetly.

"Lift your tunic."

"Excuse me, Councilor. Why would I do that?"

"Because it's an order."

Authority cut a dangerous line through Finley's voice, but Juliet was not so easily bullied.

"Am I under arrest?"

"No, but you are assisting this inquiry, and your refusal to comply shows contempt for us and our ways."

"Which part of me am I supposed to be showing the people gathered here? My navel? My breasts?" She pointed to them, sparking titters among the spectators.

Finley's scowl deepened. "You are being deliberately evasive. You know which part I mean."

"I do not, Councilor. Emrys didn't exchange with me, and I have not been injured."

"She's lying!" Owen bound to his feet. "You know she's lying." His screech almost brought a smile to Emrys's lips.

"Show us the left side of your stomach," Finley said slowly and darkly.

"I think this is highly uncalled for," Quinn said.

"Be quiet. This is an investigation."

"More like a witch hunt," Quinn added.

"Silence!" Finley bellowed. "Juliet, lift up your tunic, or I will have the guards rip it from you."

This had a predictable effect on her supporters, and Finley blinked rapidly, perturbed, frustrated.

Good. He'd make more mistakes that way.

Juliet held up her hands for quiet. "Very well, Councilor." She lifted the edge of her tunic to reveal unblemished and unmarked skin. She turned, showing it to everyone in the court.

"You see?" Finley said. "Not a mark on her. You exchanged last night."

Juliet lowered her tunic. "So because I have no mark on me, no injury, that means I have exchanged?"

"Yes."

Juliet smiled and frowned at the same time.

Something about the playful nature of it tickled Emrys. "Tell me, Councilor, if I am meant to have exchanged with Juliet and healed her of her injuries, how did she get that injury?"

"I understand there was a fight."

"Was there?"

"Yes, and you know it. There were plenty of witnesses."

"I saw a disagreement that was started and perpetrated by the Abstainers while I was working in the fields. I was harassed and stopped from doing the tasks that Prosperity demands by people who should also have been working.

Now, that oversight aside, I don't know why Juliet would get an injury that would require me to exchange with her."

"Yes, Finley. Explain yourself. How do you know of this alleged injury?" Diwali asked.

Finley's gaze shifted left and right. "I…I heard it from some of the citizens." His voice wasn't nearly as certain as it had been.

"What did you hear from them? Exactly." Diwali's words cut away the chaff.

"That…that Juliet was stabbed."

"Stabbed?" Diwali's voice peaked. "That is extremely serious. By whom was she stabbed?"

"It doesn't matter."

"It very much does matter. Because while you seem fixated on Emrys exchanging with a citizen—seemingly to save her life, I might add—you should be more concerned that there is someone in Prosperity going around sticking knives in people. Who stabbed Juliet?" Diwali beat her hand on the bench in time with each word of her question, a drumbeat that would not stop for this weak man.

The rod in Finley's spine melted like it was made of gallium, easily molded under low heat. He sank lower in his chair. "I don't know. It was a rumor."

"So I am to be tried on rumor alone, am I?" Emrys scoffed.

"But Juliet—"

"Which is it, Councilor?" Diwali said. "Either she was stabbed and exchanged, or not stabbed and therefore did not exchange?"

Finley remained silent.

"Anyone else wish to speak?" Diwali leveled her gaze at Owen. "How about you? You always seem to have plenty to say."

Owen jumped up. He wasn't about to let common

sense or self-preservation dictate when he should or shouldn't speak. "You know they're dangerous. You're covering up for them." He pitched his body forward over the barrier that separated the co-accused from the gallery.

"What exactly am I covering up?" Diwali kept very still. Emrys admired her quiet power.

"You know!" Owen shrieked. "You all know. Everybody knows!"

"All I know is that this has been a waste of time when we should be pulling together to settle the unrest that has lately hit Prosperity. Now, unless any other councilor has anything to add—perhaps some actual evidence—I think we can call it a day." She waited but no one responded to the call. "No? This meeting is adjourned." She rapped her knuckles on the bench and the meeting was over.

She rose from her seat, but instead of a conspiratorial grin for Emrys, he received only frustrated anger that they should have been brought back there so soon. This time, they'd gotten lucky.

Next time, it might not go their way.

***

The Darisami waited for the knocking on the door to stop.

"You've got to admire their persistence." Nimue lounged on her back on a collection of cushions and stared at the ceiling. Her fingers interlaced over her chest.

Emrys stood leaning against the wall beside the door, thankful for a moment's quiet.

Since the council meeting three days before, would-be donors had regularly showed up to ask for an exchange. Diwali may have intimated that they should continue to conduct their dealings in private, but anyone knocking on their door had to go past the Abstainers camped in the corridor. They'd know if anyone had been exchanged or even suspected of it. That would be the Darisami done for. It was easier to leave the door unanswered.

But Owen was not content with merely stopping their supply. The Abstainers continued to follow Emrys and the others wherever they went, but their tactics changed. Instead of shouting all the time, they watched in silent disapproval, keeping the same distance at all times and hanging around like shades.

It was annoying.

And creepy.

It wore the Darisami down, and after three days of it, they decided to stay indoors, away from judgmental eyes and the pressure of being both demon and savior.

Added to that was the frustration of not getting the plant to respond to the symbols.

It was still alive, sitting in its pot on a small table in the center of Ash's donor chamber. Taunting them with its secrets. Emrys tried not to hate the thing—for its disregard, its neutrality, its impossibility.

"Maybe the symbols don't work on plants." Ash sat staring at it with his chin resting on his steepled hands. "Perhaps there's nothing to learn."

Galen sat opposite Ash, his stare no less intense. "But we felt something."

"And we know the release of souls has an effect on the environment," Nimue said. "There must be a way of tapping into it."

"Why? Perhaps it only happens when a Darisami dies." Ash leaned back and rested on his hands.

Nimue rolled onto her side. "I refuse to accept that."

"As do I."

Emrys walked over to the plant, sat between Ash and

Galen, and stared at the plant. They'd been through so many combinations, tried so many twists and turns, that it seemed impossible they had anything left to try. But they all felt it, that something on the edge of their grasp.

"Do the symbols mean anything?" Galen asked. "Like are they letters in another language? I remember some bit of pre-Fall history about characters corresponding with whole words."

Emrys shook his head. "Not that I'm aware of. Nimue?"

"No." She rolled over and took up the remaining place in the circle. "I looked into it a long time ago, thinking there might be some correlation. The word Darisami derives from *Darisam*, a Sumerian word meaning forever, but the symbols don't correspond to any Sumerian letters. If they are connected to any language, it's lost to us now."

"So if the symbols don't mean anything, what about what they look like?" Galen asked. "To me, it's like the harvest symbol is an incision across the soul, separating one from the other."

"Yes, but when we get to that point on a plant, it fades. Why?" Nimue stared at the plant as if willing it to reveal its secrets.

"We've had more success with the half-turn back," Ash said.

"But then it collapses," Emrys said.

They looked at the plant a while, a hum, a tension, a buzz in the air, agitated by their frustration, knowing they were on the cusp of something.

Or perhaps that was hope.

Hope is a dangerous thing.

Galen sat up straight like his spine had turned to lead.

"What is it?" Emrys asked.

"What's the difference between a plant and a human? Deep down."

Nimue splayed a hand as she half-shrugged. "The cells are different. Plant cells contain chloroplasts, vacuoles, and cell walls, which the animal cells don't. But what does that matter?"

"Perhaps nothing, but perhaps the added…I don't know…protection in the plant cells means we have to treat them in a different way. The harvest symbol makes a cut, but that's not enough for plants. They need something that actually punches through the wall, to break it completely to allow the power to flow." Galen scooted closer to the plant and touched one of the leaves, rubbed it between his fingers. His focus intensified. "What if it's not the symbol that needs to change but the physical?"

Ash sat up. "Such as?"

"I mean we keep getting to this point, and the plant expects us to do something, but then it doesn't happen. We keep thinking the symbol has to be different, but instead, we need to break something physically to get to the energy we need." Galen bit his lip.

Emrys sensed the symbol forming in Galen's mind. "Be careful."

Galen didn't acknowledge his warning but remained focused on the plant, the symbol ready, then tore the leaf. The symbol released, and they watched as the plant withered and died. Galen groaned. He let go of the plant as if he'd been scalded, and rolled on to the floor, clutching at his stomach.

Emrys's heart launched into his throat and he dashed to Galen's side. "Galen, talk to me!"

Galen grabbed hold of him and took Emrys with him as he doubled over in pain. Ash and Nimue crowded them while Galen gasped and bore down. Was he dying?

No, he can't die.

Ash ran to the door and vanished.

Emrys watched helpless as Galen fought through the pain, every passing precious second pounding in his neck, his temples, his skull. "Galen, what's wrong?"

But the only response he got was Galen's iron-like grip like he was the rope and Galen the shipwrecked survivor.

Ash returned with Trellain and Juliet.

"What's wrong with him?" Juliet dropped beside him. Trellain too.

"We don't know," Emrys said.

"Galen, look at me." Trellain took hold of Galen's head. "I'm here. Exchange with me."

He shook his head, small, sharp movements. "No. Can't. Don't. Need. To."

If he wouldn't exchange or harvest, what could he do to save himself?

"Don't be a hero," Ash said. "Exchange if you need to, before it's too late."

But Galen held on, and unless he was going to do it himself, they could do nothing but wait.

Juliet took his other hand. "We're here if you need us."

But he didn't take from them and Emrys's heart continued to thrash, its beating increasing until it became nothing but a marker of time counting down until the end.

The end of what? Galen? Me?

Emrys didn't know how long they waited. It could have been hours. His head felt like it had been pummeled for hours. It might have been minutes. But when Galen's grip eased, and his breathing returned to normal, relief washed through Emrys with the strength and sting of hydrochloric acid. Galen relaxed and stopped moaning. His weight sank into Emrys.

"How do you feel?" Emrys asked.

"Like shit. But alive." He looked at Juliet's hand still in his grasp then at Juliet. "Thank you." He looked at Trellain. "Both of you. It means a lot that you were willing to offer yourselves."

"Don't mention it." She smiled, squeezed his hand, and pulled back to Trellain. He pecked her cheek.

"What happened?" Nimue asked, insistent as if Galen's pain was nothing but an irritating side event.

"We don't need to change the symbol, but we have to break the plant's cells for it to be completed. After that, it's pretty damn fast and pretty damn unpleasant. It's like there's a defense mechanism. It sprang this booby trap on me. It felt like it dumped all these sharp rocks through my body over and over."

"Like an avalanche," Nimue said.

Galen frowned. "I guess." What would he know of avalanches? "It just kept going through me until the plant's soul, life force, energy, whatever, was finished."

"And how do you feel now?" Emrys stroked the side of his neck. What if he'd truly died?

"No different than before. I don't think it's a life force we can use to sustain ourselves."

"And if the pain you went through to get it is any indication, we wouldn't want to," Nimue said.

"Wait," Juliet said. "Are you trying to get souls from plants?"

The Darisami looked at each other. What did they have to lose by telling the truth? Success wasn't a possibility.

"Sort of. We're trying to find a way to make plants grow."

She and Trellain looked at the withered remains. "But you've killed it."

"Yes."

Her eyes widened, her skin paled.

"Please don't mention this to anyone," Emrys said. "Because if they see we've killed a plant, as well as being able to kill people, that's us finished."

"We really are trying to help," Galen said.

She didn't look reassured.

Nimue rolled her eyes. "Anyway, this doesn't make any sense. Ragnar and Wyatt didn't snap twigs before they died. They exploded."

Emrys considered it. Out of everyone there, he had witnessed the deaths of more Darisami than any. "What if that rush, that explosion, is enough to damage the cells? Perhaps it only requires a subtle change, not something as dramatic as breaking it?"

They looked at each other. It was a theory. Not a particularly sound one but a theory nonetheless.

"But how are we going to get to that stage? How fast was the intake, Galen?" Nimue studied the plant.

"Fast enough, but I didn't add in the rest of the symbol that connected the first to the second or the others."

"We should try that." Ash looked to Emrys.

"But how? The test subject is dead, and we can't go do this outside, can we? They see us withering crops, they'll burn us at the stake." Fear tripped through his voice.

"I think the bigger issue is going to be how we can make plants grow on a broader scale. We can't break every plant, every seed. It's not feasible." Galen sat up carefully but reclined against Emrys. That connection gave Emrys strength. And it gave him an idea.

"What if it's not about the individual but a shared life force? What if once we break one, it connects us to all the others?"

Nimue looked at him, then at Ash and Galen. "We won't know until we test it."

"But how are we going to do that? The Abstainers follow us everywhere. They'd love to catch us killing crops."

"Can we help?" Trellain asked. "We could collect what you need and bring it to you."

"Or to our rooms?" Juliet said. "Somewhere private they can't follow."

Emrys looked to Nimue and back to Juliet. "That could work."

"How many do you need?"

"I guess five should be enough."

"At least," Galen said. "But be careful. We don't want to raise anyone's suspicions."

"Or hopes."

"We'll be cautious. We can start tonight. At least we won't glow." She and Trellain stood to leave.

"Juliet?" Galen got up after her. "Thank you for what you were about to do. I know things haven't always been easy between us, but I am grateful."

"I figure you would have done the same for me." She brushed her hair out of her eyes and behind her ears, not a self-conscious, small move but one of confidence, of presence, of certainty.

Galen nodded, much like he would have nodded to another soldier. "I would."

"Then that's good enough for me." She opened the door to see Owen standing in front of a wall of Abstainers.

"What's going on in here? More exchanging?" He stepped into the doorway, half-crossing the threshold. His head strained on the end of his neck.

Emrys blocked the plant from view, while Nimue, Galen, and Ash formed a barricade between him and the entrance.

"Excuse me, I'd like to get through." Juliet tried to push her way past.

Owen grabbed her shoulder, but Trellain's hand clamped down on Owen's wrist hard and fast. Owen winced and was forced to let her go. "Exchanging is illegal." He rubbed at his wrist.

"We know," Galen said.

"Then what were you doing in here if not exchanging? Plotting another coup?"

"We'll invite you next time," Juliet said. "Now get out of the way."

Owen shifted enough to let her and Trellain through. She found her people at the back of the crowd and was gone. Owen turned his attention back to the Darisami. "We know you're up to something, and we're not going anywhere until we find out what it is."

"Well, you're in for a rather dull night then." Nimue pushed her way forward and out through the crowd. Owen ordered some of his people to follow her. She would take them on an endless chase through Prosperity and eventually lose them. She'd done it before. She thought it funny.

"Good night, everyone. Sleep well." Ash closed and locked the door on Owen's impotent rage. Silence blanketed the room, and the three of them looked at the plant.

It was well and truly dead, shriveling to a fraction of its former size, its yellow parts turned to a murky moldy brown. Whatever it had to give, it had given to Galen and then some.

"I'll get rid of the evidence." Ash carried the plant into the bathroom and soon after, they heard the sound of the toilet flushing. Ash returned to the room with an empty pot. "Are you sure you're okay, Galen?"

"Yeah, I'm fine. The pain's passed. Like the euphoria but not like the euphoria. It's a shame we can't use it."

"We used to experiment on animals too," Ash said. "It didn't work. Nothing worked. It surprises me, considering what we've discovered. We thought maybe the life forces were incompatible. Anyway, it's not like there are many animals left out there now."

"Harder to find than the plants," Emrys said.

Galen screwed up his eyes and pressed the heel of his palm against his forehead.

"Are you okay?" Emrys asked.

"Some residual effects. I think I need to lie down for a while."

"It's late anyway," Ash said. "And there's been a lot going on. We could probably do with the rest."

"Amen to that," Emrys said.

"You two can take the bed if you don't want to go out into that crowd."

"We can all share the bed, Ash. It's big enough," Emrys said.

"No, I'd prefer to be over here." He sat on a pile of cushions about as far from the bed as he could get. "I just want to sleep the rest of this night away." He turned from them, faced the wall. Discussion closed.

Galen shrugged and pulled Emrys over to the bed. Emrys didn't feel like sleeping, but he wanted to be beside Galen. There was more to think about and discuss, his mind catching on the implications of their discovery and the trials they had yet to face. But beside Galen was where he knew he had to be. No matter what he said about the pain being bearable, a tension remained around his eyes, like he had a migraine and the lights were too bright.

He settled on the bed behind Galen, draping his arm over him, happy to have his body pressed up against him and the familiar curve of his ass and spine nestled where it was meant to be.

But though he felt at home, when the lights went out, his mind drifted to Ash, alone on the floor, and the hurt that had been splashed over his face. Galen slept, but Emrys didn't.

And though he listened out for Ash's deep and heavy breathing, it didn't come.

23

Three days had passed since Galen had harvested the plant. Three days in which Trellain and Juliet had been busy collecting new test subjects. Three days in which Emrys had put his strength into turning soil, planting a new crop the Prosperous put their hopes into, and ignoring the presence of the Abstainers.

Ash, Nimue, and Galen were outside too, dotted elsewhere around the valley, being seen and being followed, but the time had arrived to continue with their experiment.

When the end of the day came and the Prosperous put down their tools, he joined them, pressed in among the middle of a throng of donors, sandwiched in where it was harder for the Abstainers to follow. He felt supported, safe, secure. And more than a little self-satisfied that the Abstainers were having a hard time tracking him.

He continued down the tunnel, then someone tapped him on the back. He ducked and surged forward to appear in the midst of another group of supporters as the first splintered off and turned to the left. He continued to the right.

He didn't look around to check whether the Abstainers followed. They could be anywhere and anyone. He had to keep going. They paused at the elevator and waited for it to return, then he entered amid donors who filled the car. They descended three levels and the doors opened onto another group of supporters.

The group inside the elevator moved out, him with them, but he merged with those waiting, and they marched down the corridor. When they passed another group, he slipped through them, walked with them a way, then deviated down an empty corridor, making his way alone to a designated apartment that Emrys had never been to before. He knocked.

Nimue opened the door.

He blinked at her, perturbed, uncertain, but she grabbed him and pulled him inside, sealing the door behind them. "How did you get here so fast?"

Juliet and Trellain were already there, but Nimue should have still been out in the fields.

"I ran, and they weren't fast enough to follow me."

He frowned. "Risky."

She rolled her eyes. "Oh, please. Like it matters."

The apartment was like the others, with its sitting room set out with chairs and tables and sofas and a screen. But the bedroom was arranged differently. The bed had been pushed against the wall, giving space for two long tables set up side by side to make a large square. And on it were not just five plants, not ten, but…

"Twenty plants altogether," Juliet said. "We thought you might need backups, and taking one was as easy as taking two, though a few have died in the past couple of days."

He staggered towards them. "This is amazing."

A knock landed on the door, and Trellain went to answer it. Galen and Ash had arrived. They stared at the plants too.

"You've done a great job," Galen said. "And the level of coordination to get us here was perfect."

"A lot of people support you. Don't forget that."

"They don't know what we're doing in here, do they?"

"No, and they don't know exactly which room you've gone to either."

"But it wouldn't be hard to track you with their security systems so perhaps you should start," Trellain said.

They'd spent time over the past three days learning from Galen what he'd done, so they were ready to go. And they'd agreed, after much heated discussion, that Emrys would go first.

He stepped up to the first plant. His nerves tingled, making his fingers itch and shiver. They had no way of knowing if the plants would respond to anything beyond the first symbol, or even if they could get to it without being sick or killing the plant in the process, but that's why they'd chosen to use only one plant first.

Galen had said that they needed to be quick with the connector symbol because the plant responded fast to the harvesting. They may only have a fraction of a second to get it right and…

Emrys pulled his hand back. "Wait, something's not right."

"What do you mean?"

"I mean, the symbols are all in our head before we release them to exchange. We shouldn't break the plant during the first symbol, we should break it during the fourth. We've been trying to kill the plant, not exchange with it."

His heart jolted. That's what had been bothering him. He took the leaf in his hands, between his fingers as if he were about to harvest, and concentrated on forming the symbols, the first through to the second through to the third and to the fourth, the familiar strain as he bent them to do something unexpected.

And when it was ready, he tore the leaf and let the symbol go. He held his breath.

Nothing happened.

The plant didn't respond in any noticeable way.

"Did you do the symbols right?" Ash asked.

"I think so."

"When did you let it go?"

"At the end."

Galen smiled. "No, no, no, the fourth symbol has a slice too. Like the first. See?" He traced it in the air. "*That's* when you have to release it, to allow it through. Here, I'll do it."

Galen took up the plant and before Emrys could stop him, he'd already formed the symbols. The strain rose on his face, his skin turned red, the veins and tendons bulged, then he released the symbol and ripped the leaf a fraction later.

A shockwave of energy unleashed from Galen's body and rippled through them all. They stumbled backwards, but Galen flew across the room and slammed into the wall. Emrys's heart went with him, dragging him behind a few seconds later to collapse next to Galen. The lights flickered and buzzed. He gathered Galen into his arms, shouting his name, while his eyes refused to focus, his neck lacking the strength to support his head.

"Galen!" What if the plants had taken everything from him? What if they were a Darisami's doom and not their salvation? He was meant to go first. Always.

The lights stopped flickering, and he could see Galen clearly, a dreamy expression on his face, his body limp in his arms. "Galen?"

"Emrys…" Juliet said. "You should…"

Nimue's hand rattled his shoulder until he ripped his attention away from Galen and focused on the plants. The sight froze his breath in his throat.

It wasn't possible.

The plant Galen had torn grew taller and wider before his eyes. Leaves erupted from its thickening stem at a rate that verged on the horrific, like some alien lifeform multiplying to spread out and conquer the Earth. And the effect wasn't restricted to one plant, but to the ones next to it, and the ones next to them, and not just the plants but whatever seeds had lain dormant in the soil too, erupting in a mixture of greens and yellows and flowers, oh God, flowers.

How he'd missed flowers.

Galen squeezed him. "I want to see."

He helped Galen stand, and they watched as the twenty plants grew strong, bloomed, and turned the air fresh and earthy and alive.

"You did it." Juliet was awestruck. Breath sparkling in her words. "You actually did it."

Tears welled and stung Emrys's eyes, a held breath released, a dam wall broken to flood a drought-blighted land. They could do good, more good than anything they could have hoped for.

The plants continued growing, forcing the Darisami and humans to stand back from the explosion of life. Galen, Trellain, and Juliet stared in wonder at the miracle. Those post-Fall beings had never seen anything like it, but for Emrys, Ash, and Nimue, it was like coming home. He remembered the world as it had once been, the beauty that had gradually eroded, as it became scarce and the marvels that he had once taken for granted were stripped out of the earth and obliterated.

They were back.

And it was thanks to the Darisami.

Nimue went up to the nearest plant and touched it as if she wasn't sure it was real. She looked at Galen. "How do you feel?"

"I feel fine." He paused. He touched his chest, prodded, probed. "No, I feel amazing."

"No side effects? No weaknesses?"

"Nothing."

"We should watch you."

"I tell you, I feel fine."

"You say that, but what if the plants have taken your reserves? What if tomorrow you're nothing but dust?"

"I'll watch him, Nimue," Emrys said.

"The other question is, can Galen do this again?" Ash asked.

"I don't see why not. He's had a major effect on twenty plants, and he's only taken about two souls."

Nimue looked at Emrys. "Do you think it's exponential, or will we all have the same effect no matter how many souls we've taken?"

"Ragnar and Wyatt only affected a small area, and they'd been harvesting a long time."

"Yes, but their life force wasn't directed when it was expelled. Perhaps. Emrys, what if we can turn the whole valley green?" Nimue *vibrated* with the possibility.

Excitement bubbled in his chest. He wanted to control it so he didn't get disappointed, but his heart cartwheeled away from any attempt at smothering this joy. "There's only one way to find out. Tomorrow. We need to gather everyone tomorrow and try this out."

"Do you think it'll be enough to convince them that we're on their side? Enough to allow us to exchange again?" Galen said.

"We could hold them to ransom," Nimue said. "Demonstrate our power, but say we require a treaty."

Emrys paused. "No. We can't hold this back. Not for ourselves. We need to be selfless in this."

"I agree," Ash said. "They need to know that we're all in this together, and we can't do that by pitting ourselves against them. What we do, we do for everyone."

"Tomorrow then," Emrys said.

They made a quick plan, speaking to the council early that they wanted a meeting outside Prosperity the next day. Juliet and Trellain would also spread word through their supporters. They would meet in the afternoon and give a small demonstration before directing them to plant as much as they could. That should give everyone enough time to join them and bear witness.

Nimue left the room. Juliet and Trellain said they'd stay behind in case anyone tried to enter. It also gave them an excuse to stare at the plants, the pull too much for them to leave. He understood that feeling well. It was even hard for him to go, but Galen's tugging—and the stroke of his strong fingers up and down his spine—was enough to rip him away.

Ash hung back, hesitant, the only one who seemed not to have somewhere to go or someone to celebrate with.

Emrys passed a look to Galen, raising his eyebrows and shrugging his shoulders. Galen's smile shone and he nodded like an excited puppy. He gave Emrys a nudge. Were they really going to do this? A growing urge to get Galen alone twinned with his desire for Ash. Maybe the third time would be the charm.

"Ash, why don't you come with us?"

Ash's head shot up, and he looked at Emrys.

"If you'd like to." Emrys held out his hand.

24

Emrys and Galen left the room together, while Ash said he'd follow behind at a discrete distance. They encountered no Abstainers until they reached the same level as their quarters. When they spotted Emrys and Galen, their aggressors hurled their insults.

They walked through together and ignored them all, especially Owen, as they were pelted with questions about where they'd been and what they'd been doing. What had they done to ensure Prosperity's downfall? Whose souls had they corrupted? Whose lives had they destroyed?

But their high-pitched interrogation, the hate on their snarling faces, the curling of their fingers into claws, wasn't enough to dampen the excitement bubbling in Emrys's stomach. They were going to do good. They were going to save the world. He walked with his head held high past the Abstainers, through the cloud of their spite-filled utterances, and down the corridor into Galen's room.

"Are you sure you want to do this?" Galen asked.

"Absolutely. I can't wait to see the look on Owen's face."

Galen frowned at him. "Owen?"

"Yeah, when the valley turns green."

Galen laughed.

The realization of what he'd actually been referring to sank in. "Oh." Emrys laughed. "Sorry, I thought you meant something else."

"Thank God you did, because I don't really want Owen here for this."

"That would be a mood killer."

A silence stretched between them, a tension that pulled from Emrys's gut. "So…"

"So…" Galen echoed. "Were you serious about inviting Ash in?"

He was already on his way, but it's not like they'd had a proper chance to talk about it. And not away from the excitement of making the plants grow.

His stomach was a jumble of emotions, of excitement and trepidation and insecurity and lust. They popped and pinged, making it hard to think straight. He forced himself to breathe and that calmed him somewhat. "I was. If it's what you want."

"I want it, but only if you want it too. I know we spoke about it before, but it never really seemed a possibility. Not the three of us together anyway."

"If you're having second thoughts—"

"No," Galen said quickly, and the forcefulness of his response stirred something in Emrys's balls. "No, it's just… I want it. I want both of you. I want to see what happens and if it can work, but not if it jeopardizes us."

Emrys rubbed Galen's arm. "I would rather you be happy than force you into anything that you don't want."

"What do you mean?"

"I mean, if you want Ash separate from wanting me, I don't want to stand in the way."

"But you want Ash too, don't you?"

A knock at the door saved Emrys from answering. He opened it. Ash was there. He'd come. But he didn't look relaxed. He looked wary. Emrys stood aside to let him in and closed the door behind him.

"Well…I'm here. Are you guys sure you're ready to do this?"

"Emrys?" Galen asked.

He felt trapped under Galen's question, a quivering in his soul as if it wanted to escape. Did he want this? Did he want Ash? He looked at the Darisami, taking in the whole free-love spirit of him. The hair he wanted to knot in his hands. The lithe body he wanted to pin beneath him. The lips he wanted to crush with his own.

And the past he wanted to make right.

"Ash, I—"

He held up his hand. "Stop, Emrys. This doesn't have to mean anything more than sex. I know you look at me and see Magnus."

He flinched. "That's not true. I see you and what I did to you."

"Then stop. I'm not here to go over our history. I'm for now. I'm here for Galen and for you, but most of all, I'm here for me. I don't expect you to do anything you don't want to, but for this moment, on the cusp of tomorrow and what it's going to mean for the future of the world, I want you both, and I want you now, and I want you for me and me alone. That's what I want. What do you want?"

He wanted the past to have never happened. He wanted to not be hated or feared. He wanted to be loved and to not worry that love would destroy him. His eyes glanced Galen's encouraging smile and Ash's open yet defiant expression.

He knew what he wanted.

He closed the distance between him and Ash, slipped his hand up the back of Ash's head, his fingers sliding through his hair, and pressed his lips to Ash's mouth. All resistance melted. Ash welcomed him, let him in, their tongues meeting, and their breath speeding up and igniting desire.

It was like the kiss they'd shared a hundred and fifty years ago, when Emrys had lied to Ash about what he was in San Francisco to do. Ash had been nothing but open then—and he was nothing but open now. It was Emrys who'd changed, a piece of him cracking that allowed the innermost part of himself to break free.

When Ash pulled back, Emrys was left breathless. All the possibilities that could have been, all the hate that had kept them apart had been swept aside and given them a fresh change.

Ash turned to Galen and extended his hand. Galen pulled his tunic over his head, revealing that hardened chest built of muscle. Galen approached and met Ash's lips, the two of them moving against each other while Ash's hand squeezed Emrys's shoulder.

Emrys expected to feel jealous watching Galen kiss Ash. He expected some nascent envy to rear and poison his blood. But it didn't stir. There was no place left for it. He had been jealous before when he thought he'd lost Galen, but the past few weeks had shown him he hadn't lost anything but had gained much. Ash was never going to be the one to take Galen from him.

If Emrys was going to lose him, it was from his own doing.

And there was no denying that watching Ash and Galen together made him harder than diamond.

Galen's free hand reached out and tugged the bottom of Emrys's tunic, trying to lift it off his body. Emrys did it for him and kissed Galen's neck, sucking at the muscle and vein to raise the blood to the surface of his skin and moans to his throat. His fingers grabbed desperately at Emrys's body as he and Ash devoured Galen. He sucked hard at Galen's neck while his hand slid down Galen's chest, his abs and beneath his waistband to wrap around Galen's hard cock. He pumped him as Galen succumbed to his own pleasure, a plaything between Ash and Emrys.

Mid-moan, Galen wrenched himself away from their attention and adoration. "Not so fast, guys."

He dragged them by the hand over to the bed and sat on the edge. He tugged at Ash's trousers, forcing down the zip, while Emrys went for Ash's tunic and lifted it over his head, his pale slender body with its dark nipples, not as young as he once was but still a picture of perfection. Emrys placed his hand on Ash's chest and ran it down his smooth body, and Ash shivered. Galen took Ash in his mouth, his cut, erect cock long and thin and sliding effortlessly down Galen's throat.

Ash closed his eyes, arched his back, and tilted his face to the ceiling. Desire shot through Emrys at seeing Galen work his mouth over Ash, at seeing Ash so pliant, his body stretching, aching for every sensation. Emrys kissed his collar bone, kissed his neck, kissed his earlobe, kissed his mouth, Ash responding to him as much as he responded to Galen.

In the next breath, Galen had Emrys's trousers down and his cock down his throat, and Emrys was swearing into Ash's open mouth. Pleasure ricocheted up Emrys's body, and he held on tight to Ash, held on tighter to Galen's hair as his lover pushed him to fuck his face.

Desire overwhelmed decorum like metal left too long in a furnace, and the air in the room charged until he thought chromium would melt. Emrys pulled out of Galen's mouth, his body lurching forward as he sought to reclaim what he'd been denied. In one deft swoop, he picked Galen up and threw him on the bed. He ripped his trousers from him, and with a free hand, grabbed Ash and climbed onto the bed.

Emrys and Ash could have so easily focused on Galen, pitting him in between them so they could avoid confronting their issues, but that was not what Emrys wanted—and not what they wanted either.

They shifted positions, hands explored, mouths followed, lust raged. Emrys knew the rough touch of Galen's hand, the smooth touch of Ash's. Galen's kisses were hungrier, his mouth bigger, lips softer, whereas Ash was almost fleeting but not afraid to use his teeth to bite, a sensation that made Emrys quiver.

Galen leaned back and turned his head to Emrys. "I want you to fuck me."

Emrys's cock throbbed—from the demand as much as the idea. Galen retrieved lube from the drawer beside his bed and handed it to Emrys. He lathered it on his cock and wiped it over Galen's hole, his finger teasing and toying.

Galen pushed back on all fours, eager, and when Emrys placed the head of his cock on Galen's opening, he was eager again, the pressure and resistance building before relaxing. Emrys slipped inside, the warm, secure feeling of Galen taking hold. Emrys pressed his forehead against the base of Galen's neck, holding on as pleasure rippled up into his stomach, and he tensed to keep himself from coming.

"Yes, yes, Emrys." Galen's moans swallowed coherent words.

Ash watched them, and Emrys watched Ash, the still, calculating ache in his eyes, the angled smile, the taunting way he bit his bottom lip and jerked himself while sitting back on his heels. Emrys rode Galen harder, and Galen's hand shot forward and latched onto Ash's wrist and squeezed as he turned his head and groaned into the sheets.

Emrys couldn't take his eyes off Ash. Curiosity colored his eyes, but there was a decision forming within them, a need, a desire, a demand. He wanted something.

"Do you want to fuck Galen?" Emrys asked, and the simple question had Galen writhing beneath him. Emrys wanted to see it, wanted to see how Galen responded to Ash's cock, his own way of making love.

But Ash shook his head, wistful, willful, wicked. He crawled forward until his face was an inch away from Emrys's. His ice-blue eyes crystalized with lust and filled Emrys's vision. "I want you to keep fucking him." He kissed Emrys then snapped back and grabbed him by his hair. "While I fuck you."

The assertiveness, the want, and the downright dirtiness of the way Ash said it brought a whimper to Emrys's throat. He couldn't look away. He wanted that. He wanted that so badly. But he couldn't bring the words out to say yes, not with Galen bucking his hips and grinding on him, not with the mental picture of Ash fucking him. All he could do was nod his head.

Ash smiled and kissed him roughly. He directed Emrys and Galen, putting Galen on his back and with Emrys between his legs, chest to chest. He was out of Galen's ass for less than a minute but even that was too long given the strength of his need. He plowed him, loving the velvet-coated vice of Galen's ass engulfing his cock and the reddening of his neck and ears as he writhed in the redolent pleasure-pain.

But he was also anticipating Ash—and Ash took his time. He stroked his hand down Emrys's spine, raising a chill, raising his desire so Emrys drove harder into Galen. The sound of his moans and Ash's touch creating a feedback loop of ecstasy.

Ash teased Emrys's hole with a lubed finger, keeping just outside and around the edges, a hard thing to do as Emrys continued to fuck Galen, his attention split between wanting more of the pleasure he was getting to wanting the pleasure he expected Ash to provide. Ash was teasing him. He knew it. And he didn't want to give him the satisfaction…but without succumbing, he wasn't going to get satisfaction either.

He focused on Galen, on the intensity of his gaze, on the dance of sensations across his face, while Ash's finger circled and teased Emrys's hole. He stilled as Ash entered him, pushing past the ring of muscle with two fingers, hard and delicious. He buckled and crashed onto Galen's body, as Ash forced his way in. It was exactly what Emrys wanted. His cock stiffened, and he arched forward and went deeper into Galen.

Ash wasn't gentle. Ash wasn't slow. He kept going, smoothly, determined, deeply, and Emrys was fully in his control. Ash hit his prostate with his long fingers, and Emrys spasmed, gasped. He managed to prop himself up, but Ash hit him again, and he shook. Galen grinned up at him, and Emrys kissed that grin off his face and moaned into his mouth as Ash moved in and out, finger-fucking him.

He regained some composure, some strength, but he was subservient to Ash's probing touch. With the feel of Galen wrapped around his cock, the dual pleasure was enough to send him careening to the edge.

But he didn't want it to end.

"I swear to God, Ash, if you don't fuck me now, I'll—"

"You'll what? We both know you want me inside you,

and you'll wait until I'm good and ready." Ash's breath was hot against his ear.

Was this his revenge? This torture? This torment? This teasing? Having him writhe like he'd been skewered on a stake?

Ash grabbed Emrys's hair and sharply pulled back his head. His neck strained, but he submitted to Ash's control, desperate to be at his mercy. Ash pulled out his fingers and gave him almost as much pleasure going out as going in.

"Are you ready for me, Emrys?"

"Yes." He forced out the word in a hurried breath. "Yes, Ash."

"What do you want me to do?"

He moaned and panted.

Ash tugged his hair harder, rougher. "Tell me."

Lust emanated from the tight knot in his balls out to the very tips of his nerve-endings. He knew what he wanted in every fiber of his being. "I want you to fuck me." He grunted the words between clenched teeth, tingling with the pleasure of surrender.

He sensed Ash smile without knowing if he did. He couldn't see him. And apart from his hand holding onto his hair, he couldn't feel him. Galen was the only body there was, and it was enough, yet he wanted more.

"Ash?"

Ash answered with his cock, pressed against Emrys's hole and harshly given. He was relaxed enough for him, but he still gave some resistance, and Ash, who Emrys had always thought of as being gentle, took him as if his comfort and pleasure didn't matter.

And that in itself made Emrys wild. Ash's long, slender cock slipped inside him and kept going, supercharging those pleasure centers as he moved in and out from behind, while Emrys buried himself in Galen.

The dual ecstasies worked with each other, not against. There was something about being in between these two men, about being the object that they extracted their gratification from, that separated him from all thought, from all awareness other than the hot, tingling sparks that erupted and shot through his body like thunder and lightning during a monsoon.

He couldn't focus on either man but was hyperaware of everything, of the pressure and width and depth that Ash fucked him, of the strength of Galen and the way he raised his hips and stretched himself for Emrys to get even deeper, and the rapture in his body as he chased from one joy to another.

Between these two men.

With these two men.

For these two men.

Somewhere among it all, no matter how hard he tried, not matter how much he wanted the moment to last forever, his body could not withstand the need for release, the exponential rise in his pleasure. The desire raised like lava in a volcano, building pressure, building speed, building until he could withstand it no more, and he came with a force that wiped his mind and obliterated him from the universe.

25

The sound of the door opening roused Emrys from his sleep, and he lifted his head in time to see Ash sneak away. Galen continued to slumber. His arm was draped over Emrys from behind, his gentle warm breath on the back of Emrys's neck. That feeling of home settled over him, but not everyone was where they should be, safe and secure.

Why had Ash left when there was no need?

At least none that Emrys knew.

He could have let him be. Ash may have wanted to shower, or to sleep in his own bed, or simply be alone, but something nagged at him. Something about the way Ash had looked at him last night, something about what he'd said about his denial of the past that Emrys couldn't dismiss.

He slipped out of bed, pulled on a pair of trousers and a tunic, and with bare feet, crept from the room. The Abstainers had gone. It must have still been early. He knocked on Ash's door, trying to limit the amount of noise he made in case someone kept vigil around the corner.

Ash opened the door, bare-chested but wearing trousers. He frowned. "What is it?"

He didn't look pleased. Maybe coming here was a mistake. Maybe coming last night was a mistake too.

"Can I come in?"

Ash stepped aside and closed the door behind them. "I was about to take a shower. Is something wrong? Is Galen okay?"

Emrys stood in the center of the room, the distance between him and Ash an uncomfortable block with dull edges considering what they had shared during the night. "He's fine. Still asleep. I wanted to check you were all right."

Ash folded his arms across his chest. "You didn't have to." His expression was on the hard side of neutral.

Did Ash want him to leave? Was their threesome nothing more to him than an encounter, once finished never to be repeated? That wasn't what Emrys wanted.

"I know, but I wanted to."

"Look, last night…it doesn't have to mean anything." Ash shrugged, half-opened and extended his hand as if he was untangling himself. "It's just a thing that happened."

"Do you regret it?"

"No. Do you?"

His chest prickled like grass seeds caught in his clothes. If Ash wanted to be alone, he'd go, but not without telling him how he felt. "Not at all. But just because you say it doesn't *have* to mean anything doesn't mean I don't want it to."

Ash's smile was small but powerful, containing within it endless meanings that Emrys could only begin to unpick and refashion into something right. "I think you and I are a bit far down the road for that, aren't we?"

"But we can try. All of us." Emrys took a step forward, just one.

"I don't know. I don't know if I want that. I…"

He forced himself to take another step even as the muscles in his chest pulled like the reins on a bridle. He took another step. "I hurt you. Not last night. Centuries ago. And I'm sorry. I truly am. I was wrong to take Magnus from you."

Ash hung his head even as the sorrow flashed down his face. "Stop, Emrys."

He'd do anything to take away that sorrow. "Why?"

"It's not about what you did to me or to Magnus. I knew what Magnus was doing was wrong, yet I convinced myself it was right." He lifted his head and uncrossed his arms but not before his right hand kneaded his sternum. He licked his lips and looked away, at some other point in the room. He swallowed and he breathed out. Then he looked at Emrys. "I'm glad you killed him, because he needed to be stopped."

"But…you said—"

"I know what I said." His voice raised a little in volume and speed, like he had to get the words out. "I was angry at you, but I was angrier at myself. I didn't want to admit that he was wicked, and that I condoned it. Fuck, I even helped him." Ash stalked across the room, keeping his distance from Emrys, before stopping at the foot of his bed. He kept his back to Emrys.

Emrys wanted to touch him.

"Part of me wanted you to save me. I didn't know any other Darisami, just Magnus. Then you came, and I thought…I thought I could escape." He faced Emrys. His eyes shimmered. "I thought I could turn my back on everything Magnus was doing and that would make it all right. That it would save me."

"You knew I was going to kill him?"

"No, that possibility didn't even cross my mind, but I did become suspicious with how you treated me." He huffed out a laugh, part bitter, part sweet. "You were so noble, so gentlemanly. You were the better part of Magnus, and you kept me at arm's length like I was some virgin you had to protect. It was strange and old fashioned, but irresistible. And I thought if I kept you around long enough, you'd take me away." A shiver rippled through Ash's body, and he hugged himself tight. A second shiver followed the first.

"I'm sorry, Ash. I didn't know."

"I know you didn't. I couldn't let you know because then I'd have to admit to myself that I was as much to blame as Magnus. Then when I introduced you two, you seemed so enamored with him, so engaged with what he —" He closed his eyes for a brief moment. "With what *we* were doing that I thought it'd never happen, that I was foolish to even consider you could want me."

"Why didn't you leave?"

"He was my maker and…and I was afraid of being alone."

"You'd never be alone, Ash. Too many people love you for that."

He scrunched his nose and his shoulders like the words had crawled over him and he wanted to shake them loose. "Too many mortals and no Darisami. Anyone I got close to would not be able to understand what I was, or I'd end up killing them."

"I know what you mean."

Ash smiled. "Of course you do. Because we're the wicked Darisami. Soul-eaters. But with Magnus I could believe, at least for a little while, that I wasn't this unclean thing. Then you came along, and I was forced to confront that reality—and the reality that you were going to kill me too."

"I wasn't—"

He put up his hand. "Please, Emrys, you don't have to lie. You killed Magnus and you were going to kill me. I saw it in your eyes. I saw all the hate and disgust that you had for Magnus, and you had it for me too. Admit it."

The itch returned to the middle of his chest but crept up his throat. He rubbed at his neck, heat bursting beneath his abrasive touch. How could they have a future if they didn't resolve their past? He forced himself to speak the truth.

"Yes, I admit it. I intended to kill you too. At first." He spoke softly, his guilt dampening his voice. No matter how much he thought he'd confessed to, there was always more. "I thought I'd get close to you, and you'd lead me to Magnus, then I could kill him and kill you too. Then everything you two had done would have been wiped out and destroyed…but I changed my mind."

He stretched his lips over his teeth, uncertain of how much to tell, of how much he wanted to divulge, even to himself. "I made a distinction between Magnus's evil and yours. Just as you made concessions for him, I made concessions for you. And believe me, if I'd wanted you dead after I'd killed Magnus, you would have died then."

He closed the distance between them and extended his hand to touch Ash—on the arm, on his chest, on his shoulder, anywhere—but he froze mid-reach, closed his hand into a fist, and pulled it back. "You wouldn't have had time to see the look in my eyes because I would have killed Magnus in secret then come for you. I wanted you to see me kill Magnus. I wanted you to have that warning. I wanted you to know so then if you attacked me, I'd know where your heart truly lay."

"There were better ways to find out."

He nodded. "But I knew you wouldn't want me after you saw me kill Magnus, and I wasn't sure I could want you too, knowing what you'd done as his companion. I couldn't have you and continue to fight my crusade." He rubbed his fist with his other hand and stepped back—but the sting in his heart remained, expanded, worsened. "I chose wrong."

Ash grabbed him. "No, you didn't. You did the right thing. I was so ashamed about what I did, but I couldn't deal with it, so I hated you. I never confronted my own guilt. I never admitted to the role I played in those people's torture." He squeezed on Emrys's forearm. "I took some small comfort in thinking that I had, at least subconsciously, brought Magnus to his end by introducing you into our lives." He relaxed his grip, and his hand slid off Emrys's skin as he turned around and sighed.

"What is it?" He wanted the intimacy back.

Ash folded his arms and scratched his bicep. He looked back at Emrys from behind fallen locks of blond hair. "I lied to you about the symbols. It wasn't Magnus who discovered the exchange symbol. It was me."

Emrys chuckled with good nature, hoping it would ease Ash's pain. "I know. Galen told me."

Ash pinched the bridge of his nose and screwed his eyes shut. "But I didn't tell him everything. I didn't discover the fourth symbol until long after Magnus was dead. I turned my back on all his experiments, not that that should have been hard. I lost myself in harvesting. I wanted the euphoria." He brought his fingers to his lips, bunching them as if collecting the words that emerged but they slipped out. "I loved it as much as I loved my self-pity. It drowned out my longing for you. I didn't want to do the hard work because I thought that it might lead to more suffering. There's a perfection to harvesting. It's quick. It's merciful as well as merciless. It's beautiful."

"But you changed. You found a reason to try again."

"I fell in love with the people I surrounded myself with, and I wanted to share the euphoria with them without having to turn them into killers." He slipped his hair behind his ears. "And I wanted to make amends for what I'd done. I threw myself into experimentation, taking the best of Magnus's work and leaving the worst behind. But it wasn't until the Fall, when I ended up in here, that I really made the discovery. I was already on the cusp, I knew it, but after I got locked in here, I fell in love with a man named River." He smiled on his past. "I discovered how to exchange because of him. I couldn't risk killing him. I couldn't risk being discovered. And I couldn't kill hundreds of survivors. They reminded me too much of those people we had trapped in our dungeon."

Ash unfolded his arms, wiped his hands down his thighs. He looked more confident, more like the Ash Emrys had once thought him to be, comfortable with his place in the world.

"I perfected the symbols and told him what I was, and we exchanged our souls. We grew old together. That woman I exchanged with to prove the symbols worked, Kaia, she was his niece. She was part of our family. That's why I was so protective of her. I'd already lost River; I didn't want to lose her too, even after all this time."

Ash's sorrow struck Emrys's chest like a meat cleaver. "And you couldn't make him into a Darisami?"

"I wanted to. I offered, but he refused. Thankfully, that didn't stop us loving each other. When he died about ten years ago, I was forced to accept that I couldn't keep myself isolated and survive. I submitted myself to the humans' mercy and revealed to them what I was. And it felt good." He punctuated the word with his fist. "It felt right." And again. "And it felt like that I had something to offer them that could make up for the pain Magnus and I had caused."

"And you did." His voice floated on the awe he felt for Ash's courage.

"Yeah…but then you showed up." Ash bit his bottom lip, his mouth tilting to the side. "I'm sorry for trying to get you killed."

It was a simple apology, but it was enough. The emotion of it resonated in Emrys's heart long after the words faded. "I deserved it. And worse."

"No more than me." Ash sat on the edge of the bed, and Emrys followed beside him. They let silence fall like the dust of the past.

Emrys had always felt that his crusade to kill the Darisami had been justified, and Magnus was one of forty-nine who he'd vanquished. But he'd always felt bad about what he'd done to Ash and had dealt with it by ignoring it. At best, he thought Ash had perished around the time of the Fall like so many humans, like so many Darisami.

"What about now? Still want to kill me?" Emrys nudged him.

Ash smiled and shook his head. "No, quite the opposite." He released the full power of his ice-blue stare. "But I don't know if there should be anything between us."

"You didn't enjoy yourself?" Emrys couldn't look away. And it had nothing to do his pride being at stake.

"Don't get me wrong, fucking you was one of my life's highlights. I know you think I'm this free love kind of guy, but a piece of me always goes with whatever sex I have. And with you two, if I let myself, I'm worried I'll lose all of me."

"But why can't we lose ourselves in each other?" Emrys

rested his forehead against Ash's, reveling in the closeness, in the openness. "I can't force you into anything, but you should know that from what you've taught us about exchanging, I know there's no end to love and no need to be frightened of giving it away." He took Ash's hand and laced their fingers together. "You and I are old now, and I've spent too much of my life guarding my heart when I wanted it to be vulnerable. You showed me that when we reveal to the world what we are we are better for it. I want you, Ash. I've always wanted you. And I want Galen too, and I want us to be together. And Galen wants it as well."

He looked at him, shy, like the ice in his eyes was thin and about to shatter and Emrys would plunge into their depths. "Do you think it can work?"

"We can try. We've got all the time in the world."

Ash answered with his lips, pressing them against Emrys's with a desperate, grateful force, and he climbed onto Emrys's lap and wrapped himself in Emrys's arms. His willowy frame secure in his grip, endless possibilities burst in Emrys's heart.

Lysander's jealousy had marked the start of Emrys's immortal life. Galen and Ash's love could last him until the end of it.

Ash's kiss eased, and he relaxed into Emrys's lap.

"Now, how about we go back to bed? We've got a big day tomorrow," Emrys said.

And knowing he was about to change the world with Ash, Galen, and Nimue by his side and in his heart, he couldn't wait for the new day to dawn.

❦   2 6   ❦

"*Citizens of Prosperity…*"

The voice coming through the speakers rattled Emrys out of his sleep. Galen and Ash roused, shaking off contentment for confusion.

"*Remain calm.*"

"Whose voice is that?" Galen asked.

"It sounds like Finley."

A chill trickled through Emrys's body. "Get dressed."

"*Stay in your quarters.*"

They hurried out of bed and pulled on their clothes and boots.

"*The doors have been deactivated for your own safety.*"

"Are they coming for us?" Galen asked.

"I don't know, but we need to get out of here," Emrys said. "They could show up at any minute with gold bullets."

"*All access to the surface has been suspended. Prosperity is under siege.*"

Emrys's stomach froze so fast that fractures spidered across its surface. Prosperity under siege?

Galen caught and held his eye. "Providence."

It couldn't be.

"Providence is here?" Ash said. "But why?"

"They've come for us," Galen said.

Emrys tried the door, but as Finley had said, it was locked. "How many soldiers does Prosperity have?"

"Not many. A couple of hundred."

Providence had that many at least five times over. How many had they sent?

"Do not panic. You are safe inside Prosperity."

"We need to get out of this room." Emrys pushed the door, sensing for some give to it, but it didn't budge. "Help me break it down."

The three Darisami pressed their shoulders against the steel, then threw their weight against it. "Keep going." Emrys strained. The door bent, then buckled. "Keep going!"

They leveraged more force, and the door gave way with a shriek. They pitched forward, crunching it out of its frame until they created enough room to squeeze through.

Nimue stood in the hallway, picking at her nails with one hand and looking at them like they were late for a strategy meeting. "I've been waiting."

Emrys frowned. "How did you get out so fast?"

"Unlike some people, I haven't been to bed. What are we going to do?"

"My concern is Prosperity might offer us to Providence in exchange for a truce," Emrys said. "We need to make it hard for them to do that." Noises down the corridor turned their heads. "Right now, they think we're locked away, but we need to be visible, and we need to make sure they don't make a decision that affects us without our knowledge."

"Let's go to the top, to the tunnel," Galen said. "If

they're preparing for a siege, we can offer them help. Come on."

They headed for the backstairs, avoiding the elevators that would either be deactivated or filled with troops. They raced to the top floor and into a throng of soldiers, but while it was hard to discern the shape of one black-clad soldier from another, the mass itself was too small to counter even a fifth of Providence's forces.

And Providence would not have attempted this journey without a sizeable force.

"I hope there are more soldiers back in the armory," Galen said.

"Nope, this looks like all of them," Ash said.

Emrys swore.

The Darisami emerged from the stairwell and crossed behind the soldiers, but one turned and called for them to halt. Thirty guns armed and locked on them.

They stopped and raised their hands.

"We're here to help," Ash said.

But the soldiers didn't lower their guns.

Finley and Joni hurried through. Diwali took longer as she forced her way through soldiers.

"What are you doing here?" Finley kept out of the Darisami's reach. "You're meant to be in your rooms."

"We came to help," Galen said.

"We don't need *you*." Joni sneered. "Prosperity is under attack *because* of you."

Emrys ignored her and spoke to Diwali, who had the courage to come close enough so he didn't have to shout. "What's happened?"

"Providence showed up in the middle of the night on the outskirts of the fields."

"How many soldiers?" Galen asked.

"I'd say five hundred. Maybe more. We can't see them all."

"Is that more than we have here?"

"Much," Diwali said. "We could arm every citizen with a weapon, but they're not trained. We're farmers, not fighters."

"Have they sent any demands?"

Diwali looked uneasy. "They sent us a forager."

"A forager?"

"Yes. The teams were ambushed, and they're being held hostage."

They should never have gone south.

"Who did they send? What do they want?" Ash asked.

"They sent Slate." Diwali sagged under the weight of her worries. "They say…they say they're here to liberate us from…from…"

"From you freaks!" Finley shouted. "We're all going to die because of you."

Diwali pursed her lips. The uncertainty vanished beneath her ire. She looked the most adult out of any human there. And she knew it. "As much as I don't agree with the way Finley said it, the gist is correct. Providence promised they'd leave us alone if we send you, Nimue, and Galen out."

Not Ash. At least he can stay.

"And if you don't?" Emrys asked.

"They'll destroy everything we've built on the surface then attack the ark."

The surface could be rebuilt, but without the ark keeping them safe, the humans wouldn't survive. Nor would the Darisami.

"You forgot to say they'll execute the hostages if we don't comply." Joni's sneer was permanent. "Or do you not consider their lives as worthy as the soul-eaters', you sycophant?"

Diwali ignored her fellow councilor's hysterics.

"I want to talk to the forager," Galen said.

"He's busy," Finley shot back.

"I don't care. I need to know who's out there. How long have they given you to make a decision?" The commanding tone in Galen's voice reminded Emrys that he'd been a captain long before he'd been a Darisami. Finley's resolve quavered, and he kept quiet.

"Until noon," Diwali said.

"Four hours away. We'd better hurry."

They followed Diwali. Meanwhile, Emrys kept his awareness on the soldiers and the way they watched the Darisami. They'd heard their conversation. They knew what was at stake. Would one of them take the initiative and shoot to save Prosperity?

They'd get the glory. They'd probably be heroes.

If they survived.

Diwali led them to a room around the corner from the tunnel entrance. A wiry man with matted, dark brown hair and sun-blemished tanned skin sat at a table surrounded by councilors who startled at the Darisami's entrance.

"What are they doing here?" a councilor said.

"They're here to help." Diwali refused to engage with the older gray-haired councilor even as he spluttered his disagreement. She turned to Slate. "Tell them everything they want to know."

Slate folded his arms and leaned back in his chair.

Galen stood opposite Slate and pressed his fists into the tabletop. "Who's out there?"

Slate avoided Galen's gaze. "I've already told the council everything I know. I don't see why I should tell this invader anything else."

"Tell him, Slate. That's an order."

He tutted. "Five hundred soldiers or thereabouts."

"Who's leading them?"

Something flickered in his eyes. "I don't know."

Galen furrowed his brow and leaned closer. "Yes, you do. Tell me."

"I don't know anything other than what they told me to tell you." Slate jabbed his chin in Galen's direction, feigning an attack, feigning his toughness. "If we give you to them, they'll leave."

"What about the other foragers? How are they?"

"They're fine." But the words limped from his mouth.

He was hiding something. "You're one of the Abstainers, aren't you?" Emrys asked.

Slate shifted his weight in his chair. "If you mean I didn't exchange before going foraging, then yes."

Galen grinned at Emrys then turned back to Slate. "Why did they choose you?"

He shrugged. "I gave them the least amount of trouble."

"You mean you collaborated."

He bared his teeth. "I am not a traitor."

"Of course not. Because you're trying to save Prosperity, aren't you?"

"I wasn't trying to do anything except stay alive."

Emrys edged around the table, coming closer to Slate. The forager shifted so he could keep an eye on Emrys.

Galen continued his questioning in a softer tone. "Your ordeal must have been a hard one."

He answered, half-distracted, sitting up straight in his chair and putting space between him and Emrys, while remaining seated. "I'm strong."

"I can see that. But you didn't exchange. You must be tired."

Emrys was behind him.

"I'm fine. I don't need anything. Just rest."

"But we don't have time to rest." By now, Galen was sitting on the table, closer to Slate than the forager liked. "Providence is here. Everyone must work together. You should be healed. So you can help defend Prosperity."

Emrys put his hands on Slate's shoulders.

"Don't touch me!" He jumped up from his chair and backed away, but he ran into Ash and Nimue.

"Darisami, you are not to harm him," Diwali warned.

Galen turned to her. "Councilor, it is my belief that he is hiding something, and though I don't want to do anything without his consent, the fate of Prosperity hangs in the balance. He should undergo an exchange so we can find the truth."

"No!" Slate shouted. "Stay away from me."

Diwali looked from the Darisami to Slate. "Then answer Galen's question. Who is out there?"

"I don't know. I don't know any of their names." But he was too defiant, too evasive for it to be anything but a lie.

Emrys grabbed Slate by the throat and slammed him against the wall. Councilors and soldiers sprang into action, some arguing for, some arguing against, but it didn't matter as the Darisami formed a barrier, and as much as Slate squirmed and kicked and fought, he couldn't break Emrys's grip.

While the shouts erupted around him, Emrys shut them out and summoned the symbols. He strained against them as Slate strained against him, and when they were all ready, he let them fly. Slate's soul swept into him, but Emrys controlled himself and slowed the process. He only needed the most recent events, and if he wasn't careful, he'd go too far too fast. He pulled back.

Slate stumbled up to Prosperity's gate, more disheveled than he actually was.

Emrys went deeper in time.

The councilor from Providence stood in front of him. Isaiah. Emrys almost lost his grip. He doubled down. *"You know what to do," Isaiah said. "Convince them to open the gates, then we'll deal with the monsters."*

"You won't hurt any of our people, will you?" The foragers who'd exchanged had all been subdued and bound, despite their increased strength. The foragers who'd abstained had chosen wisely, listening to that exile from Providence. What good had exchanging done them against Providence's large force?

"That depends on Prosperity." The woman from Providence came out of the shadows. Kira. "If they try to protect the Darisami, then they are traitors to their species." Something about her chilled Slate to the core. She hadn't flinched when the foragers were taken and beaten. Isaiah was bad, but she was worse. Cold, calculating, cruel.

"What if they won't open the gates?"

"Then Prosperity is forfeit. We come in peace, but if they don't understand the threat the Darisami pose to the remnants of humanity, then the whole of the city must be stopped. You've seen our firepower. You know we can do it. But we don't want to kill anyone, so it's up to you to convince them to relinquish the Darisami. They have until noon before we start shooting hostages. Now, go."

Emrys had seen and heard enough. He completed the exchange, gave Slate his power, and retreated. The euphoria swept through him, but he shoved it aside—hard to do, but not impossible, not with the adrenaline coursing through him.

"What did you see?" Galen asked.

He dumped Slate back in the chair. His head lolled, unable to resist the ecstasy showering him.

"Isaiah and Kira," Emrys said. "Slate was ordered to

come here and tell you to give us up, or else they'll destroy the city."

"Did he collaborate with them?" Diwali asked.

"No, he merely took the opportunity to survive."

"You see?" Slate slurred. "I wouldn't hurt our people, but you…you would. You're going to kill us all. That's what they said."

Emrys should have stayed longer inside Slate's soul and found out why he was so easy to convert to the Abstainers' cause, but there wasn't time. And what did it matter? Isaiah and Kira, two of the five ruling councilors of Providence, were outside. They'd stopped at very little to get what they wanted—and Emrys was certain it wasn't to liberate Prosperity.

They wanted the Darisami's power.

"We have no desire to kill anyone," Galen said. "We need you. However, there's nothing stopping Providence from taking over and slaughtering whoever they want."

"If we hand you over to them, they'll leave us alone," Joni said.

"Do you really think so?"

Diwali tapped her chin, an uncomfortable silence spreading throughout the room. "How ruthless are they? Would they really destroy Prosperity to kill you?"

Emrys looked to Galen then back to Diwali. "They don't want to kill us. They want our power."

"Isaiah would stop at nothing to get as much power as he can," Galen said. "And Kira is ambitious enough to ally herself with a man she hates so she can get it."

Diwali shivered. "I'm glad we cut ties with them a decade ago."

Finley huffed. "If we hadn't, they might have been able to help rid us of Ash."

Ash rounded on Finley and forced him to stumble back

until he was backed against the wall. Ash, however, kept going until he was nose to nose with the councilor. "And why would you want to do that? Prosperity has only lived up to its name because of what *I've* given it, because of how *I've* thrown myself on your mercy and done something very few Darisami have ever done. I could have killed all of you and been done with it, and you show your gratitude through this weakness? You're not fit to lead anyone."

As much as Emrys enjoyed Ash's free-love persona, he had to stop himself from cheering at this rare display of force against young humans.

Finley tried to inflate himself, but he looked like he had holes in him that allowed the air to seep out. "Well, at least I'm human. And I belong here."

"Ash belongs here too." Diwali turned from Finley to Galen. "What do you suggest we do?"

The Darisami looked at each other. Something hung in the air between them that needed to be said but couldn't be heard by all ears.

"Can we have a minute?" Emrys asked. "We need to confer among ourselves first."

"All right, but don't take long."

Diwali herded everyone out, overruling Finley's objections that it was the humans who should decide what to do, not some freaks of nature. When they were alone, Emrys collapsed into the chair Slate had vacated, mild growing pains rising through him. He bore down, pressed on. He had to keep fighting.

"We could kill them all," Nimue said. "Go out there, slay Providence's soldiers. That would solve the problem. More than one problem, in fact."

"Wouldn't Providence send more?" Ash asked.

"Unlikely." Galen leaned against the table. "If Kira and Isaiah are out there, either Laurence and Elaina are in charge—in which case, they wouldn't follow—or else Providence is under lockdown awaiting their return. Either way, the forces they have now are likely to be all they're going to have."

"I don't think I can kill five hundred people," Ash said.

"Not without getting shot," Emrys said. "And those bullets hurt. Not to mention all the gold they've got, or said they've got." He remembered the night he'd been forced to leave Providence. The Five said there was enough gold in their guns to put him down. He had no reason to doubt them. "We wouldn't get far before they opened fire. Bullets —ordinary bullets—will slow us down. Then they'd finish us off with the gold when they realized we weren't going to give Isaiah and Kira what they wanted."

Nimue climbed onto Emrys's lap and leaned into his chest. He felt more keenly the shrapnel peppering his blood, the sharp sting of panic and fear at the idea of losing his friends and lovers. He wrapped his arms around her. "They can't honestly think we're going to turn them into Darisami? What's to stop us from killing them when we try?"

"They'll take one or all of us hostage," Emrys said. "If we take their lives, they'll take yours. And no doubt, I'll be the one forced to do it while you three will have guns to your head."

"And if we refuse to go, they'll kill the foragers, then destroy Prosperity," Galen said. "We could leave one at a time."

"And die one at a time." Emrys held Nimue closer and kissed her hair. He didn't want to watch her die. He didn't want to watch anyone die.

"Do they have enough firepower to destroy the ark?" Ash asked.

Galen nodded. "Providence was very good at developing ordinance. They'd wreak havoc and bring the city to its knees, if not cripple it beyond repair."

Ash sighed. "Looks like we were wasting our time trying to create a peaceful society, while Providence was to our south amassing weapons of mass destruction."

Galen rocked on the edge of the table. "If we stay inside, Prosperity falls. If we go, they'll want our power, but we won't give it, so we'll die. And if we leave, we'll eventually starve."

"We can't abandon everyone," Emrys said. "Like it or not, we're the reason Providence is here. We can't run away."

Nimue sat up. "In that case, I've got an idea."

27

"You want us to abandon Prosperity?" Finley's eyes bulged, and his neck strained as he stood in his place in the small room.

All eleven councilors were present.

"We're not abandoning it," Nimue said.

Finley scoffed. "It sounds like it. You want all of the citizens to go onto the surface where they can be massacred."

"That won't happen," Galen said.

Finley wheeled around. "Oh, and you should know, should you? I guess you're just like these tyrants. You were one of them, weren't you? Head of their Security. A councilor. And this Isaiah is your father? Tell me, did you come here to sabotage us from the inside?"

"Councilor, we don't have time for conspiracy theories." Emrys tried to sound calm. "We are in as much danger as you are."

"And yet you want us all to go where we can be slaughtered? Do you want our blood to grow the crops now?"

"Providence won't attack unarmed people," Galen said.

"Why? They've attacked foragers."

"They won't attack when they see twelve thousand of us. For all of Providence's military might, they have not had to do battle against an external foe before, and those five hundred soldiers will not be willing to mow down twelve thousand innocent people, no matter what orders they're given."

Finley rolled his eyes, giving Diwali enough space to speak up in a measured tone. "You're asking us to risk the lives of many citizens. Wouldn't it be better to stay here?"

"If you stay here, they will kill you. They'll collapse the entrance to the ark—and they won't have to look into your eyes to do it. Believe me, the spectacle of twelve thousand unarmed people will stay their hand."

Finley threw himself back into the center of the discussion. "And what then? We give over control of the city? Why don't we hand them you and be done with it?" He flailed his arms.

"Because we deserve to live as much as you do. We're citizens of Prosperity, no matter what some of you think, and we have a right to call this place our home." Galen stared down the councilor.

Finley backed off.

"If you're right and they don't open fire, you're not going to leave with them, so what will encourage them to go?" Diwali said.

"We want to talk to them."

Joni laughed. "And that's meant to solve everything?"

"We're going to convince them we do more good than harm," Emrys said.

"And how are you going to do that? Exchange with

them, I suppose. From what it sounds like, they don't want you anywhere near them."

"We can't go into specifics, because if it doesn't work, we don't want to disappoint you," Nimue said.

"If what doesn't work?" Curiosity slinked across Diwali's forehead.

"We cannot say right now, but if we're unsuccessful, we promise to leave Prosperity for good."

She frowned. "And if they attack us anyway?"

"Then we will fight on your behalf and take down as many of them as we can before we're killed. We'll defend you with our lives."

"Why do you need all of us out there then? Why can't you go by yourselves?"

"Because what we're going to do, everyone needs to see."

"You're not giving us anything specific," Joni said. "You could be leading us out there to our deaths."

"Do you really believe that of me?" Ash said. "I have been a citizen of Prosperity since the Fall. I worked hard and supported you and the city before I revealed myself to be a Darisami. And after that, I did everything I could to ensure peace within the ark, to give as much of myself as I could so you would not consider me a threat, because this is my home, and you are my people."

"But you have your own people now. Why would you need us?" Joni tried to look defiant, but her hands tremored. As much as she might hate the Darisami, she was terrified of doing battle without them.

"Because we need each other." Might shot through the core of Ash's words. He turned to include everyone. "Darisami cannot survive without humans, and if what we're about to do works the way we hope it will, you will know that humanity cannot continue without the Darisami." Ash placed his hand over his heart. "I swear on my life that we are only working on behalf of our combined best interests. Will you follow us to the surface? Will you trust us to keep you safe?"

28

THE SOLDIERS CHANGED OUT OF THEIR UNIFORMS AND returned to the tunnel before the Prosperous were allowed out of their rooms. Emrys paced while Ash and Galen leaned against the tunnel wall. Nimue sat on the floor, biting at her thumbnail. Apart from the two hundred or so soldiers, they had yet to see any other Prosperous.

The council had agreed to their plan but convincing the rest of the population to put themselves in danger was a hard sell. A hard sell they'd left to Ash, Diwali, and Finley. They'd appeared on camera and explained to the citizens what was happening and what they wanted them to do.

Attendance was voluntary. If anyone felt unsafe, they could remain behind. The message had been transmitted. The Darisami waited.

All of a sudden, Galen's head turned in the direction of the elevators and stairwells. Emrys followed as a hubbub of noise emerged. Nimue stood. Emrys's heart shot into his throat. Just because they came to the tunnel didn't mean they were willing to go further.

But their appearance broke the chains that weighed down his hope. Freed of dread, his head lifted, his mouth bowed into a smile, his chest inflated with the fresh air of impending triumph.

Juliet, Trellain, Leya, Samantha, Kaia and many more donors and supporters emerged, striding forward as if they were marching into battle, armed with nothing but their pride and duty. Emrys's mouth stretched wide. Their numbers were small, but it was a start.

Juliet approached him. "Are you sure about this, Emrys?"

"As sure as we can be."

"Do you think Isaiah and Kira did this themselves, or have Elaina and Laurence assented to it?"

"I don't know."

She tapped her finger on her sternum, and she didn't quite look at him. "I can't believe it of Laurence."

He put his hand over hers to quiet her distress. "Don't think about it. We'll get to the truth, but right now, we need to focus on keeping Prosperity safe."

"But why would Isaiah risk losing Providence just for revenge?" Her hand tightened into a fist, and she looked him in the eye, the tightening of her tendons like the tightening of strings that held together her determination.

"It's not revenge, it's power. And he thinks he's going to get it."

"Is it going to work?" Trellain asked. "Isaiah's always been a shoot-first-ask-questions-never kind of guy."

"Not if there are enough of us."

Juliet looked around. The crowd was growing but was it large enough? They were nearing the deadline. If they didn't hurry, hostages would start dying.

A commotion at the back drew their attention. The radio of the plain-clothed soldier beside him squawked.

The thoroughfares and routes to the top were jammed. People were fighting. He caught a mention of Abstainers.

"We should get moving," he said. Relocating twelve thousand people was going to take time. He gave a signal for the doors to be opened.

"Stop!" One raised voice pierced the noise. "Stop!" The screeching grew louder.

Emrys told them to move while he faced the next hurdle. The crowd shoved and coalesced, and Owen forced his way through with a band of Abstainers at the back, his tunic torn, his hair disheveled, his eyes wild and streaked with panic.

"You can't do this!" Owen stumbled out and stopped in front of Emrys. "It's suicide. You're leading us all to suicide."

"You don't have to come." Juliet sneered.

"None of us should go. It's all a trick designed to kill us. Providence isn't here. They haven't come for us." He pivoted side to side, pleading with people as they pushed past him on their way out of Prosperity. The terror dashed across his face, leaving deep, painful lines.

Emrys understood. Owen's sense of equilibrium had been destabilized, thanks to what Emrys had done to him. He'd shown Owen things that shouldn't be real then lied to him about them. Now he'd been given the truth, why would he trust it? Why should anything be real? As much as Emrys wanted to dismiss him, he couldn't walk away from this responsibility.

But he also couldn't carry it forever.

"Owen, the threat to Prosperity is real." He spoke with calm.

Owen's attention snapped to Emrys like a missile locking onto its target. "Of course you'd say that. You want us all to be outside so you can take Prosperity for yourself."

"We wouldn't need it if were empty. Listen, I know I wronged you. I know I broke your trust. But I also saved your life, multiple times. And you can blame me for all the bad things you did in my name, but it's not going to hurt me. It's not going to make any of it right. Instead, come with us. I promise you it's going to be worth it. I know you want something to believe in, and that's what I'm going to give you. I'm going to give you a future you can believe in, but you have to be with us when it happens. I'm asking you once more to be a witness, only this time for something true."

Owen looked at the people streaming past him, and Emrys saw the longing in his expression. He wanted to believe so much, but last time he believed in something he'd been exiled from his home. He wouldn't willingly walk away from the safety of an ark again, no matter how much Emrys wanted him to.

Owen shuffled back, his chest caving in slightly, his shoulders coming forward to protect himself. "I trusted you before, and it was all lies."

Emrys didn't reach forward; he didn't move. He didn't have to. "Not all of it. Our power is real, but what I made you believe wasn't. We're not angels, we're not demons, but we're not human either. What we are is part of the Prosperous. What we are is survivors, like you. Please, come with us, and let me heal the wrong I've done you."

Owen folded his arms. "I'm never following you anywhere again."

"The choice is yours, and so are the consequences." Like they always were. Emrys turned away.

The Abstainers hurled their insults, but Emrys kept walking, and soon their calls were lost far behind them until they could no longer be heard above the sound of thousands of bootsteps.

29

THEY REACHED THE END OF THE TUNNEL, AND THE DOORS opened to the day. Providence had taken up a position on the outer rim of the structures on the far side of the valley, but Emrys couldn't see them from where he stood. They were too distant, and they might not all have remained in one place. The buildings dotting the landscape could hide snipers, and the Darisami had to bank on the fact that Isaiah and Kira wanted them alive, not dead.

Yet.

It was with some trepidation that Emrys stepped out of the protection of the tunnel, but once he'd taken the first step, his stride lengthened, assured and ready. He had to show confidence. Even so, he took Galen's hand then Ash's. They were doing this together.

They left the safety of the tunnel. Rather than continue down the central road, which would take them to the awaiting army, they took the right pathway to one of the fields. Prosperity's soldiers dispersed throughout the crowd, discretely holding weapons in case they needed to defend themselves against Providence's army. They had ample weapons in the armory, but they wanted to show a pacifist force. Anything else would lead to trouble. And weapons in the hands of untrained civilians would lead to unnecessary death.

Frenetic energy kept Emrys going. He tried to convince himself he wasn't nervous, just excited. As long as he kept moving, he could fool himself. He climbed onto the roof of one of the houses and looked in the direction of Providence's army. Dust swirled in the midday light. They were marching to intercept Prosperity's people.

Good. They were coming to meet them rather than trying to take the city for themselves.

Emrys clambered down the roof and headed to the front of the column. The people formed a wall along two sides of the fields, leaving two sides open for Providence's army to come forth and witness. Isaiah and Kira would sense a trap, but what choice did they have but to go where the people were?

The one part of their plan they had to worry about were the hostages. Isaiah wouldn't give them up, and he could use them to make any demands he wished. But only if he was within shouting distance. An emissary had been dispatched to invite them to parley, but Isaiah hadn't yet responded.

The Darisami congregated with the councilors and watched as the army approached. However this went, they had made a good go of it.

"Thank you, Ash," Emrys said.

"What for?"

"For believing there could be a different way for the Darisami to live. If it wasn't for you, we wouldn't be here."

He laughed. "Are you sure that's good thing?"

"Well, maybe not exactly right here, but the potential —you gave us that."

"I'll take some of the credit, but the rest is because of you three. I was content with my small life, but you've shown me there was a whole world out there that I couldn't ignore. I'm glad I'm here with you. I'm glad we're going to change the world." Ash hugged him, and Emrys put all of himself into hugging him back.

This was worth having. This was worth fighting for.

Nimue cleared her throat. "Now all the kumbayas are out of your system, perhaps we could focus on the job at hand?"

A hush descended over the crowd the closer Providence came towards them. The Prosperous continued to spread far across the valley. With any luck, what the Darisami were about to do would be seen from a great distance.

If it worked.

Emrys's breath juddered in his throat, forcing it closed, expanding painfully as if his whole body were stretching like an overinflated balloon filling with his anxiety. They still had to make it work. What if the effects weren't as great as they thought they would be? What if they got the symbols wrong? What if Isaiah killed them before they had the chance to work their magic?

Providence was close.

The time was now.

Emrys and the Darisami marched forward, all Prosperous eyes on them, all hope on them. Static buzzed in his chest, like caffeine, like terror sparking and making his legs shake. He forced down his apprehension, but it kept bobbing back up, bubbling like metal yet to be molded.

Galen stood to his left, Ash to his right. Nimue stood in front of them.

Together.

They calmed him.

They strengthened him.

Whatever happened, they were doing this together.

Even if they died together.

They filtered through the crops, the yellow plants no more than calf-height, many snapping easily beneath their steps. Others had already fallen from being trampled by the Prosperous, but they'd soon be healed.

They walked into the center of the field and faced the army. The enemy slowed. Its soldiers were easier to see now, garbed in helmets and armor and armed with machine guns. They crouched and formed a wall. They swept their weapons across the silent sentinels of the unarmed Prosperous.

Emrys's heart rode high in his chest. The foragers were brought forward and forced to kneel in the dirt. The emissary was there too—with a gun pointed to his temple.

Emrys recognized Isaiah and Kira's shapes, donned in their armor and helmets, protected not just from bullets but the Darisami's touch.

Isaiah raised a megaphone and lifted his visor. "People of Prosperity, we have come to liberate you from the evil Darisami. Send them forth, and no one will get hurt."

The Prosperous kept silent. The Darisami didn't move.

"You do not have time to waste." Isaiah's voice strained. "Emrys, Galen, and Nimue, you are ordered to come here now and accept the punishment you should have had in Providence."

"He actually thinks we're going to go over there," Galen muttered to Emrys.

"Let's get this over with," Nimue said. "I think enough people are here."

Emrys nodded. "Ready? We'll form the symbols. Nimue, you break the leaf."

"Got it."

"Let's do this."

She crouched down, and Emrys put his hands on the back of her exposed neck. Galen and Ash placed a hand each on Emrys's arm and held on tight. Emrys closed his eyes, summoned the first symbol and forced it into the second.

"Stop!" Isaiah's command broke through his concentration.

He regained it, summoning the symbol again, forcing it into the second and the third.

"Stop, or we'll shoot."

From the third into the fourth.

"Everyone ready?" Nimue said.

Three gunshots went off, Emrys's heart lurched, his eyes shot open, and the symbols disintegrated. He looked at Ash, at Galen, at Nimue. None of them were wounded, but pandemonium broke out as he saw the bodies of three foragers lying in the dirt. The Prosperous broke their calm and charged. Emrys's gut chased after them.

Nononononononono!

Prosperous soldiers pulled out their weapons and opened fire, while Providence retaliated and mowed people down. Providence was outnumbered, but Prosperity was outgunned, and people flooded past the Darisami. Gunfire pierced the air, punctuated by screaming. This was not what was meant to happen. They'd lost control of the crowd, but they had to continue.

Emrys grabbed Ash and Galen's hands, and brought the four Darisami together, protecting a small crop of plants. Their bodies closed in together so they were harder to displace.

"Hurry," he shouted about the tumult, heart beating rapidly. "We need to be quick."

Nimue grabbed the leaf. They closed around her, Ash's

hand on the back of her neck, Galen's on her bared shoulder.

"First symbol!" Emrys roared. He closed his eyes, buried himself in as much calm and peace as he could manage among the bedlam. It was hard fought, but he got there, the harvest symbol calm and reassuring, the essence of Darisami.

"Second symbol!"

For transfiguration, for creating another such as them.

"Third symbol!"

For the vile act of splitting and bonding.

"Fourth symbol!"

For exchanging, new and unfamiliar but a salvation for him.

For the Darisami.

For the world.

"Hold it! Hold it!"

They balanced on the cusp of the fourth symbol, channeling as much energy they he could into the moment, building up a reserve before they sliced into the rest.

"Now!" Emrys screamed.

$ 30 $

THE ENERGY EXPLODED OUT OF EMRYS'S BODY, AND HE WAS thrown clear of the crops. His eyes shot open as he and the other Darisami flew from each other. He was pitched into the crowd and knocked people to the ground. They scrambled from underneath him and got to their feet, running towards Providence's army, but he lost all control of his body and sank into the dirt.

The plants dragged out every harvested soul he'd ever known, every one of an endless stream of thousands and thousands and thousands of lives he'd taken over centuries. They uncovered and stole every speck and spark of energy. Plundering from the farthest reaches of his existence, they ripped the souls out of his insignificant body and plunged them deep, deep, deep into the earth.

He could do nothing but lie back and let it happen.

A crowd circled him and offered help. They asked him what was wrong, but he could only just hear them over the earth's squalling. His pillaged souls returned with a sense of great power, of earth and element, of a world awakening. It tickled him gently at first, but then it hardened, its probing fingers digging into him, and he laughed as a different kind of euphoria welled up inside him.

It wasn't just the connection with one human soul, or even the connection of many human souls, but the connection with an earth that had witnessed more life than he could ever fathom. It was brutal, but it was beautiful, and it cared not for him or for anyone else. It gave and took and gave as it needed, and it took everything from him that it could harvest.

The earth beneath him rumbled and shifted and raised him up, and the people fell back from him, fell back from the earth. The sounds changed as the bullets became fewer and far between. He felt the prickly, lush feeling of grass beneath him, then the strong and determined shoots of plants and shrubs.

The euphoria and the connection waned enough for him to sit up and witness the greening of the earth, the creation of a new Eden, that had come from the Darisami and the humans. It surged inside him, raising tears to clog his throat and make it bulge as the earth gave up all that had lain dormant.

He saw Galen and Ash and Nimue and they shared the same smiles, all shared the same happiness and joy. They had done it. They had brought life back to the earth. They had done good.

And every human stopped their fighting and stared in wonder and awe at what they had done. The shouting died, but no more people died, distracted for that moment by something that very few had ever have seen in their lives.

The plants kept growing. Emrys stood and watched how it rippled out, as crops and shrubs and... Trees! Actual trees! He recognized wheat and barley and maize and berries and fruit. They spread out across the valley, and the people cheered and cried and praised them with desperate and happy tears in their eyes.

But though he wanted to stay and watch it, at any moment, Providence may resume its campaign. He signaled to the Darisami, and they sprinted through the dumbstruck crowd and out of the living and into a field of dead Prosperous. They kept running, running as fast as they could. They couldn't hope to stop all the soldiers, but they could stop their commanders.

They set their sights on Isaiah.

They reached the jagged border where Prosperity clashed with Providence. Standing a few lines behind the barricade were Isaiah and Kira. But though they had to go through soldiers to get them, most had lost interest in the fight, instead taking off their helmets and their gloves and lowering their weapons to reach down and touch the new life that had erupted beneath their boots.

And Isaiah and Kira were not immune to the wonders of the earth either. They clearly couldn't believe what they saw.

"How did you do that?" Kira said breathlessly.

"It's complicated but know this: you will never be able to do it thanks to what you've done here today."

Kira broke in half, pitching forward at the waist as if Emrys had punched her.

"We still have an army," Isaiah said. It was never about the discovery for him.

"Are you sure?" He looked at the soldiers, many now looking uneasy about defending Isaiah and Kira. "After what we've shown we can do, do you think they're going to kill us? You on the other hand…you have killed people for your own greed." He raised Isaiah's megaphone to his mouth. "Soldiers of Providence, you have invaded a peaceful people on the orders of these treacherous councilors. You have murdered innocent people by following their orders. Throw down your weapons now, and you will be shown mercy. Continue your fight, and you will die beside these wicked people."

Weapons hit the dirt in a wave stretching from the front line to the back.

"Traitors! Fools!" Isaiah shouted. "He's a liar!"

"That would be you, Father," Galen said.

Isaiah stared at his son as groups of soldiers manhandled Isaiah and Kira, forcing them to the dirt in front of Emrys. Isaiah fought but a few whacks to the back of his knees with a truncheon brought him down. Kira trembled.

Prosperity's councilors arrived.

"Diwali," Emrys said, "this is Isaiah and Kira of Providence. Their army has surrendered, but the choice of what to do to these two invaders is yours and the council's. We can give them a peaceful death, if that is your wish."

Kira winced before she could stop herself. Isaiah tried to wrestle his way free but was forced back to the dirt. Galen's face remained hard and determined. If he wanted Isaiah spared, Emrys couldn't read it in his expression.

"For the terror and death you have brought to our gates, we should execute you. But Prosperity took an oath long ago to value life, to hold it sacred, even when there are those who would wish to destroy it. We would be hypocrites if we did not maintain our values. However, we recognize that while your actions have been against us, they have also been against the Darisami, so we defer to them as to the punishment they wish to exact." She turned to Emrys. "If you believe that your lives will be in danger if they live, then you must act accordingly." Diwali bowed and retreated.

Isaiah and Kira should die. If allowed to live, they would only keep trying to steal the Darisami's power. But

Emrys's taste for death had dissipated. Enough people had died already. He had no desire to take more lives, no matter how well deserved.

He looked to Galen and Nimue and Ash, feeling self-conscious as this conference went on with such a big audience, but they had to make a decision. "I think we should let them go."

Ash frowned. "Are you sure?"

"Yes. We should let them return to Providence…and we should go with them."

"You can't be serious," Nimue said.

"Very much so."

Galen smiled. "I get it. So they can tell Providence what we did."

"Exactly. The world needs to be healed, and we can't do that by staining the earth with more blood. Do you agree?"

Nimue shrugged, callous as ever. Galen and Ash nodded.

Emrys threw the megaphone onto the dirt in front of Isaiah and Kira. "We're showing you mercy, though you would not show us the same. We will return with you to Providence and show the citizens there what we can do, and we will help your city as Galen and I tried to before."

Isaiah spat in the dirt. "We don't want your charity or your pity."

"You might not, but I do." Kira dismissed Isaiah and raced her chin as if pledging allegiance to Emrys. "I agree to return to Providence." She'd always been quick to change loyalties when convenient.

"Isaiah?" Emrys said.

"Come on, Father," Galen said. "It's more than you deserve. Or are you afraid of what awaits you in Providence?"

Kira shuddered. What atrocities had they committed to go on their crusade?

"I am afraid of nothing. Not even death," Isaiah said.

"Well, luckily for you, you won't have to meet your end yet. Let them up. They can go into a cell until we leave." Emrys turned his back on Kira and Isaiah. He approached the Eleven. "Do you agree with what I've proposed?"

Diwali smiled. "I think that is more than fitting for a citizen of Prosperity."

Elation rose in Emrys's chest, knowing he had a home, knowing he didn't have to hide, knowing that the world hadn't really ended. It had fallen but could rise again. He only had to look at the color around him, at the lushness, at the *life* in the people and the plants and the planet to know that they had a future.

"Emrys! Look out!" Galen shouted.

His heart rate spiked. He spun and met Isaiah's snarling face as he charged, his hand clutching Emrys's golden knife, but he was too slow to react, too slow to fathom it, too slow to save himself. Isaiah barreled into him and fought hard, and the knife slid into his stomach.

His belly turned molten, the gold blazing through him. Without thinking, the harvest symbol erupted in his mind, shot down his arm, into his hand, searching for a soul to snatch.

The Darisami pulled Isaiah off him, and with his retreat, Emrys's hand brushed Isaiah's bare skin. Emrys fell backwards, the knife sliding out of his stomach, the soul sliding out of Isaiah, and Emrys collapsed into Galen's arms.

The warring forces of deadly gold and salvaging soul pitched Emrys into unconsciousness and saved him from having to see all that Isaiah had been, all that he was, and all that he wanted to be.

＊ 3 I ＊

EMRYS WOKE, AND THE PAIN THAT HAD CHASED HIM
through his dream like a tiger through a jungle emerged
with him. He was in bed. In his room. In agony. The lights
were on, and he hissed as he tried to sit up.

"At least you're alive." Nimue crawled up the bed to sit
beside him. "How bad is it?"

He screwed his eyes shut, tried to dispel what was
imaginary, to cope with what was real. His fingers probed
where Isaiah had stabbed him. The wound had closed but
the skin remained puckered. Beneath that raised scar, and
throughout his body, he was subjected to mild stabbing
pains. In his right shoulder then his thigh, his neck then his
left eye. Their appearance was random, the length of time
between one and the next impossible to predict.

But he was alive.

And Isaiah was dead.

"Some residual aches, but it's bearable. Whether it's
fatal, we'll have to wait and see." He hadn't been
stabbed in the brain or the heart, two locations that
would have spelled his end, but like the poisoning in

Providence, he couldn't be certain that there wasn't some lasting effect, that flecks of gold might not cause later damage. Chronic and constant pain may be the legacy he'd have to bear for taking Isaiah's life and saving the world.

"You look like shit, but I think you'll live."

"How long have I been out?"

"About seven hours."

"Where is Galen?"

"He's helping coordinate Providence's soldiers. They seem to feel comforted having him around."

"And Ash?"

"Exchanging to heal the wounded."

Emrys sat up. "We should get out there."

She pushed him down with a lot less effort than he expected. "You're in no fit state."

"Then you should go. I'm all right."

"They're managing fine without me. I wanted to be here to take care of you. And protect you in case anyone got any silly ideas about finishing Isaiah's work." She reached to the side table and picked up his golden knife. "I thought you might want this back."

Emrys took it from her and turned it in his hand. It was definitely his. The same pinkish hue to the gold, the same heft, the same nicks and chips. "I thought they'd melted it into bullets." He felt some peace at holding it again. Though what was he going to do with it now he wasn't the Darisami's executioner?

"Never underestimate the power of gold." She giggled. "I bet Isaiah couldn't resist the poetic nature of killing you with it."

His hand tightened around the hilt. "Is Galen upset with me?"

"If he is, he hasn't shown it. But you'll have to talk to

him. I doubt he can really be surprised that you took Isaiah's soul to save your life."

"And Prosperity? Are they disappointed? Afraid?"

"No, they're all still too impressed with what we did."

A knock at the door.

"Do you want me to let them in, or do you need to rest?"

"Show them in. Just be prepared to defend my honor."

She rolled her eyes. "What's left of it."

While she climbed off the bed to answer the door, Emrys slipped the golden knife beneath the covers.

"What do you want?" Nimue said.

Emrys looked up. Nimue blocked the doorway as much as she could but she was too short to be effective.

Owen.

But not alone.

Behind him stood two armed guards dressed in black. Owen's hands were clasped in front of him, handcuffs chaining them together. But the defiance and anger were gone from his face, and instead, remorse glimmered in his eyes. If he'd had a cap, he'd be wringing it in his hands. "Can I speak to Emrys?"

"Why?"

"I've come to apologize."

Nimue turned to him and raised an eyebrow.

What did he have to lose? Nimue could protect him if necessary.

"Come in, Owen."

Nimue accompanied him. She slipped her hand into Owen's palm and squeezed. His body went rigid. "A precaution," she said sweetly.

The guards entered too.

"Why the armed escort?"

"I've…" He closed his eyes and breathed then opened

his eyes again. "I've been arrested for disturbing the peace."

"About time," Nimue said.

Owen nodded, which surprised Emrys. "I'm to stand trial, and I will accept whatever punishment they give me, but I begged them to let me come speak to you before I'm taken to a cell."

Nimue increased the strength of her grip, and Owen winced and sucked in his breath. "What ploy is this?" She looked at the guards warily, but they didn't move.

Emrys sat up straighter in his bed and summoned the harvest symbol, expecting a double-cross.

Owen gritted his teeth. "No ploy. I came to apologize for making your life difficult in Prosperity. I saw what you did out on the surface—"

"I thought you had stayed inside," Emrys said.

"With the other cowards," Nimue added.

Owen caved in on himself. "I had to see what you were doing. The problem is, I still believe in what you're able to do, but I couldn't reconcile it. I know I've been a menace since Providence. I know I've tried to ruin your lives. I was hurt, and I was jealous, but what you said to me before you went to defend the city made me realize that the only one I was truly hurting was myself."

"Except when our time ran out, and we couldn't exchange. Then it would have been us, too," Nimue said.

"Yes." Owen's voice came out small, ashamed.

"So what now? You want my forgiveness? You want me to speak on your behalf in front of the Council?" Emrys doubted he was capable of such magnanimity in his present pain-filled state.

"No, that's not what I'm here for. Forgiveness has to be earned. I'm here to be a donor."

Nimue tutted. "Don't want to miss out, huh?"

"Partly, but I heard you'd been injured. I thought if there's anything I can do to make it up to you, it's to give you my soul, whatever the cost."

"Do you mean exchanging or harvesting?"

Owen swallowed. "Whichever you think is right. The council have said that my life is yours to do with as you wish. The guards can confirm it. Whatever you decide to do. I know I need to make amends, and I can start by healing you. If you choose to let me live, then when I'm out of prison, I'll help with healing Prosperity. But that choice is up to you."

* * *

THE MOON DID NOT SHINE, AND NEITHER DID EMRYS Stone.

A new moon, a new chance, a new beginning.

For him. For the Darisami. For the world.

He walked beneath a night sky blazing with stars. Many of the Prosperous had remained outside, music blessing the air, fires lit to flicker, and laughter and joy palpable. He traversed the fields and forests, grass beneath his bare feet, the scent of earth and flower and life wafting into his nose. He could not walk more than a few yards without being stopped by one person or another, a crowd forming that he had to keep moving.

And once he made it past the merrymakers, he met the mourners. Around fifty dead in all, fifty he could not save, but fifty who had died defending the city and its people.

He took his time meeting them one on one, sometimes speaking, sometimes sitting in silence, letting the weight of their sorrow press down on him so he could ease a small portion of their burden.

It was impossible to have the happy without the sad.

He moved on from the mourners and continued farther to the camp where Providence's soldiers had been detained. Galen walked among them. He had organized the troops, and they mourned their dead too. It was hard to read the expression on the soldiers' faces. Who still resented him? Who still wanted him dead?

Prosperity's soldiers were given no trouble as they patrolled the borders. All the soldiers' weapons had been stripped and taken into Prosperity's stores. And if any wanted to sneak away, they were welcome to, but they wouldn't survive long in the wild alone. The journey they had already undertaken should have been enough to convince them of the foolishness of such an act.

They didn't want to leave anyway. They just sat and felt the grass and the plants and wondered at what might have been if they'd allowed Emrys to stay in Providence. Only he knew that none of this would have been possible if he hadn't been exiled.

Galen ran towards him and dove into his arms. He caught him, pressed his body to him and spun him around, reveling in the reassuring crush of this man against him. Emrys kissed him, and everything he wanted to say vanished in the wave of his relief. He devoured Galen's mouth, desperate for his tongue, his kisses, and his love. He could have kissed for an eternity, but in the end, it was Galen who broke for air and hugged him tight around his neck.

"You're okay." His voice was breathy and overcome.

"I am. I exchanged." He reluctantly set Galen down, but he took hold of his hand. And his worry broke through the rush of seeing him. "I was worried you'd be upset with me."

"Because of Isaiah?"

"Yeah."

Galen winced and tightened his grip. "I wish it had been different, I really do, but he made his choice, and if it came down to you or him, I'd choose you. Always." Galen kissed him again, and the last bit of tension vanished from Emrys's body.

They walked in silence back towards Prosperity, Emrys's gratitude resonating in his chest. Ash called out to them as he rushed from the cover of the shelters towards. Emrys's heart thudded at the sight of him.

Ash flew into his embrace. "I'm glad you're okay," he said hot and hard against Emrys's ear.

Emrys felt the love within Ash meld with his own. How lucky he was to have these two men and this whole world of great abundance. He'd believed he'd had everything before the Fall as long as he had souls to harvest, but when restrictions came, he realized how little he had, how precarious life was, all because he was scared of who he was and what was inside him.

"We really did it, didn't we?" Galen said.

Ash let Emrys go, and the three of them looked around at what they'd brought back to life.

"Do you think we can do it again?" Galen said.

"I don't see why not," Ash said. "I felt replenished after exchanging with the earth. I don't feel like it took anything from me permanently."

"I felt connected," Emrys said.

"Me too."

"So now we just have to do it again," Emrys said.

"But first, I think I'd like it if we got to spend some time alone together, connecting." Ash raised a seductive eyebrow and completed the look of pure sex and desire blooming on his face. "Don't you?"

Emrys laughed or else he'd moan and kissed Ash, then Galen. "I think we've earned it."

EPILOGUE

Dawn broke over Prosperity's verdant valley. A lot still had to grow. And a lot had to survive past the first week. The earth was still not yet healed, but in their little corner of the world, they had life, and from that, they could expand.

Emrys stood at the ark's exit with the Darisami and the Eleven. Juliet and Trellain had come to say farewell too, along with an assortment of other Prosperous.

Kira stood beside them, still with a wide-eyed expression on her face after Ash's exchange with her the night before. It had been a calculated risk. They wanted her to survive the journey, but they also wanted her to see that there was nothing detrimental from going through the procedure. That would help when they returned to Providence. Emrys repeated his vow that she would never be made a Darisami. She was forlorn, but he didn't doubt she continued to hope—and scheme—to take his power.

Foragers and soldiers waited on the outskirts of the field to begin their journey. Along the way, the Darisami would replenish the earth, exchanging with soldiers and foragers as required. They wanted to create a green carpet connecting Prosperity to Providence.

"Are you sure you want to go back there?" Juliet said. "You made a lot of enemies."

"I have to try," Emrys said. "Besides, Providence's soldiers want to return home." They were excited about the prospect of spreading the word of what Emrys and the Darisami had done. They had hope for the world again.

Juliet hugged him. "Be safe."

He hugged her longer than was necessary, but even then it wasn't long enough. She was a friend in the purest sense of the word and leaving her behind was a hard thing. He had offered to make her a Darisami—the world needed more now—but with no people on the verge of death, she wouldn't countenance taking a life to make hers longer. She just made him promise to return.

"I guess we'd better get moving."

The council gave their thanks, the dissenters having changed their loyalties and the Abstainers disbanded. No doubt pockets of resistance remained, but they were hard to find, and they would find it harder to attract an audience.

It was time to say goodbye to Nimue.

The four of them had decided that a Darisami needed to stay, but when it came time to deciding who that would be, Nimue had made the choice easy for them. The people had sought her out in ever greater numbers since they'd made the earth grow, and after spending centuries in a half-existence, not child, not adult, in Prosperity, she could be completely Darisami.

Galen and Ash said goodbye, and then it was Emrys's turn.

He and Nimue stood staring at each other before Nimue rolled her eyes and launched into his arms, hugging him tight. "Promise me you'll come back." She said it hurried and rough into his chest.

His love for her vibrated in his chest like a Tibetan gong in a mountain monastery. He felt it everywhere. "I promise." Tears squeezed out of his closed eyes and he kissed her hair. "Thank you, Nimue. For everything."

She was not Sian. She never had been. She had been someone entirely different. And the centuries had only been bearable because of her.

They slipped apart, fingers the last to touch, then it was done. They were ready. It would take at least three weeks to reach Providence, but they didn't know how long it would take to restore the damage done. Kira and Isaiah had destroyed much in order to chase after them.

But once it was done…

They had choices to make. As far as they knew, Clara was still alive in Endurance, presiding over a population of trapped and scared humans. But Clara could yet do some good, even if it came with her death.

Then there was the rest of the world to explore, more Darisami to find and to teach how to exchange and heal.

But no matter what happened, Emrys and Galen and Ash had a home to return to, and they had one another to keep them going.

Until the end of the world and beyond.

ABOUT THE AUTHOR

Daniel de Lorne writes about men, monsters and magic.

In love with writing since he wrote a story about a talking tree at age six, his first novel, the romantic horror *Beckoning Blood*, was published in 2014. At the heart of every book is a romance between two men, whether they're irresistible vampires, historical hotties, or professional paramours.

In his other life, Daniel is a professional writer and researcher in Perth, Australia, with a love of history and nature. All of which makes for great story fodder.

And when he's not working, he and his husband explore as much of this amazing world as they can, from the ruins of Welsh abbeys to trekking famous routes and swimming with whales.

Connect with Daniel and get a FREE short story. Be the first to know about new releases, cover reveals, giveaways and more.
www.danieldelorne.com

ACKNOWLEDGMENTS

Soul Survivor started out as an idea way back in 2010, but at the time I had no real idea that it would grow into a series and a whole world with far more to discover than one book could contain. I'm so glad it did.

When I wrote *Soul Survivor* I only had the vaguest idea of how it would end. In fact, what I've ended up with is not something I considered even possible back then. But now that *Soul Surrender* is done, I'm thrilled with how it worked out.

I hope you are too.

Thanks of course must go to my usual support tribe, including friends TJ Nichols and Nikki Logan for their early feedback, to Charlie Knight for their thorough editing and being a great sounding board, and to my husband Glen for him supporting my attempts at being a successful writer.

Finally, thanks to you, the reader, for joining me on this journey. I hope I haven't let you down.